THE FINAL OFFER...

Frank was inside. Hunched over the steering wheel, his face was completely hidden. Molly rapped timidly on the window, afraid of startling Frank awake. She was close enough to see the dandruff flakes clinging to the few thin strands spread over his pasty scalp. Molly began to sweat. Why didn't Frank move? Was he drunk? Had he passed out from the heat? She knocked again, harder this time.

"Frank," she called, wiping the sweat off her brow. Then, she noticed his hands.

Clutching the base of the steering wheel, Frank's hands were bloated to twice their normal size. Their color was completely alien in appearance. No traces of pink skin or thin rivers of blue veins created contrast on those colorless canvases. They were stark, pale white, like two large hunks of Havarti cheese.

The heat surged through Molly's clothes and robbed her lungs of air. She sagged against the side of Frank's car, then turned back to his hands, unable to take her eyes away from them, unable to digest their grotesque shape and color.

A Fatal Appraisal

J. B. STANLEY

BERKLEY PRIME CRIME, NEW YORK

THE BERKLEY PUBLISHING GROUP
Published by the Penguin Group
Penguin Group (USA) Inc.
375 Hudson Street, New York, New York 10014, USA
Penguin Group (Canada), 90 Eglinton Avenue East, Suite 700, Toronto, Ontario M4P 2Y3, Canada
(a division of Pearson Penguin Canada Inc.)
Penguin Books Ltd., 80 Strand, London WC2R 0RL, England
Penguin Group Ireland, 25 St. Stephen's Green, Dublin 2, Ireland (a division of Penguin Books Ltd.)
Penguin Group (Australia), 250 Camberwell Road, Camberwell, Victoria 3124, Australia
(a division of Pearson Australia Group Pty. Ltd.)
Penguin Books India Pvt. Ltd., 11 Community Centre, Panchsheel Park, New Delhi—110 017, India
Penguin Group (NZ), Cnr. Airborne and Rosedale Roads, Albany, Auckland 1310, New Zealand
(a division of Pearson New Zealand Ltd.)
Penguin Books (South Africa) (Pty.) Ltd., 24 Sturdee Avenue, Rosebank, Johannesburg 2196, South Africa

Penguin Books Ltd., Registered Offices: 80 Strand, London WC2R 0RL, England

A FATAL APPRAISAL

A Berkley Prime Crime Book / published by arrangement with the author

PRINTING HISTORY
Berkley Prime Crime mass-market edition / October 2006

Copyright © 2006 by Jennifer Stanley.
Cover art by Mary Ann Lasher.
Cover design by Jade Polanco.
Interior text design by Kristin del Rosario.
Photos on p. 212–13 by Jennifer Stanley and family.

ISBN: 0-425-21264-5

BERKLEY® PRIME CRIME
Berkley Prime Crime Books are published by The Berkley Publishing Group,
a division of Penguin Group (USA) Inc.,
375 Hudson Street, New York, New York 10014.
The name BERKLEY PRIME CRIME and the BERKLEY PRIME CRIME design are trademarks belonging to Penguin Group (USA) Inc.

PRINTED IN THE UNITED STATES OF AMERICA

10 9 8 7 6 5 4 3 2 1

For My Grandfather, Louis C. Winters

It's been over twenty years since I sat on your lap and we wrote a story together on that old type-writer, but I still feel your hands beneath mine each time I reach for the keys.

Acknowledgments

I would like to thank Pamala Briggs, Anne Briggs, and Holly Hudson for their feedback on early drafts; Jessica Faust of Book Ends; Samantha Mandor and Carolyn Morrisroe of Berkley Prime Crime; my brother Mead for helping me with the coin research; my son, Owen, for being such a good napper and thus allowing me some writing time; my husband, Tim, for cheering me on; and my family and friends for their continuous love and support.

I would also like to thank you, the reader, for taking the time to get to know Molly and the rest of the cast. I deeply appreciate the positive emails and letters I have received since the publication of *A Killer Collection*. Keep 'em coming, folks!

Indeed there *can* be no more important branch of art than that which regulates the forms of the furniture among which our children grow up, for such forms, according to their good or bad taste, their harmonious or their crude lines, their satisfying or their poor proportions, their skillful or their careless craftsmanship, must inevitably leave their impress on the minds of the young people who develop under their silent, but nonetheless eloquent, influence.

—Arthur De Bles, *Genuine Antique Furniture*

WILLIAMSBURG, VIRGINIA 1776

Thomas Fleming was bent over, robustly sanding a long yellow pine board with a piece of sharkskin until his forearms were flecked with wood dust. The boards were neatly joined using animal glue and thin wooden dowels until they had formed a perfect rectangle. This box would become the bottom case of Captain Tarling's new slant-front desk. Thomas ran his hands over the smooth wood. He loved the large knots and the shadows of dark grain within the yellow pine. It was a wonderful material to build with, subtle and malleable, unlike the inflexible and short-tempered man who had commissioned the desk. As if summoned by Thomas's thoughts, the silhouette of Captain Edward Tarling suddenly filled the doorway of Samuel Chauncey's cabinetmakers shop.

"Mr. Chauncey?" Captain Tarling called in his abrasive voice as he swept a white-gloved hand in an arc as if leading a parade. "How is my cupboard coming?"

Samuel put down the plane he was using to even out a thick plank of mahogany and turned to greet his client.

"Coming along very well, sir," Samuel answered amiably. "I've placed it first above all my other orders. The carcass is done and I am working on the doors myself."

Captain Tarling seemed mollified by this explanation. Samuel was the most sought after cabinetmaker in Williamsburg, and only colonists desiring fine furniture made in the latest styles placed their orders with Samuel Chauncey.

"That is well indeed, but I need my desk completed now—even before the cupboard," the captain announced with authority. "My wife and her china can wait. My business requires the desk most urgently."

"Yes, sir. I will see that it is finished by the week's end." Samuel offered a slight bow and the captain responded with a grunt, after which he swept from the workshop and climbed ungracefully into his open carriage, pausing long enough for the carpenters to note the run in his fine silk stockings. A stunning pair of gray mares with braided manes and tails pulled the carriage forward in a cloud of dust, but not before a young lady with honey hair turned her fair face toward the workshop and smiled demurely.

"His wig was crooked," Samuel mused to himself as he tugged on his gray beard. Then he turned to Thomas, who was rooted to the ground gazing after the captain's carriage. "Lad, never you mind that pretty face. Miss Tarling is well out of your reach. Now, as we have discussed, your apprenticeship has come to its end. I have nothing more to teach you, but before I let you go, I shall have you complete Captain Tarling's desk. This is a rare opportunity, my boy, to illustrate your talents. You see, the captain has requested certain . . . ah . . . novelties be added to this desk."

"Novelties?" Thomas asked, uncomprehending.

"He wants three secret compartments built large enough to hide—now what did he say?—ah yes, big enough to hide a handkerchief within."

Thomas raised his brows. "Three secret compartments

to hold handkerchiefs? How odd. I doubt that dandy of a man is only concerned with the cut of his coat. How can a man who grows rich trading in molasses instead of picking up a musket against the redcoats have any secrets worth hiding?"

Samuel took up his plane and resumed his work on the mahogany. "People fight in different ways against the Crown, Thomas. Keep in mind how much we depend on our sea trade for life's little luxuries. The captain has gotten ships through more than one blockade and provided our town with much-needed supplies."

"If I didn't have this crippled leg," Thomas muttered angrily for the hundredth time, "I'd do more than run some blockade! The captain could be attacking the British with his ships, not running to the West Indies for sugar cane and indigo. And it strikes me as odd that his are the only ships that return unharmed."

Samuel's weatherworn face wrinkled sternly. "Mind what you say about Captain Tarling. His hat may be worth more than my entire shop, but his finery conceals a sharp mind and a long memory for those who insult him. And he's a patriot, else he'd have run back to England with the rest of the cursed Loyalists."

"Not all of them went back," Thomas muttered under his breath and returned to his sanding. He worked long after the others had gone home, as he was a bachelor whose only love was for the wood he crafted. The weak light of two candles set in shallow bowls allowed him to work in blissful solitude.

"You're the last piece I shall make beneath another man's sign," Thomas whispered to the desk case. He retied his loose ponytail of ginger-red hair with a leather string and began to place the dadoes inside the case. Using a backsaw, chisel, and molding plane, Thomas spent several peaceful hours attaching the bearer rails and drawer runners. He tightly clamped the pieces of glued wood and then straightened up, examining his work. Today's labors had created the frame for the four graduated drawers which Thomas would fashion tomorrow out of black walnut.

Flipping through the book containing Mr. Chippendale's most popular designs, Thomas decided to replace the desk's typical ball and claw foot with a simpler style. Captain Tarling had asked for an unadorned, functional desk and, despite his dislike of the wealthy patron, Thomas approved of the captain's willingness to allow the beauty of the wood to speak for itself without gaudy carving.

As Thomas sketched the plain curve of what he thought the foot should look like, he found his eye wandering to Chippendale's drawings of pigeonholes. The possibilities for adding hiding places among the pigeonholes were numerous. What did Captain Tarling have to hide? And from whose eyes?

Thomas shrugged aside such aimless musings and prepared to leave for the night. First he would head home to the boardinghouse for supper and then perhaps grab a pint in the tavern afterwards. After all, there was cause for celebration. In a fortnight, he would be the proprietor of his own shop in Fredericksburg and men the likes of Captain Tarling would become an insignificant memory.

Chapter 1

It wasn't everyday that Molly Appleby found herself driving behind a dilapidated brown pickup with a
bumper sticker reading EAT MY GRITS. A minefield of rust
patches on the truck's body gave it a diseased look as it rattled noisily forward. The rear window of the old Chevy
was covered with the washed-out design of a Confederate
flag. Molly had spent the last two hours on Interstate 85
heading north for Richmond while staring straight through
the faded film of red and blue at the back of the heads of
two men in baseball caps. In between them perched a large
dog with long, floppy ears who occasionally stepped over
the man in the passenger seat so that he could stick a furry
head out the window, his pink tongue wagging ecstatically
in the wind.

Molly glanced down at her speedometer. She was doing
eighty, fifteen miles over the speed limit. Apprehensively,
she slowed down to seventy-five, craning her neck to see if
the gap in the trees would reveal a state trooper, waiting to

pounce upon unsuspecting speeders. The highway stretching from the North Carolina border to Petersburg, Virginia,
was a notorious speed trap. The niche in the trees was for-
tuitously empty, so Molly picked up speed again, unable to
resist getting closer to her canine friend in the pickup.

Molly turned up the radio and sang along to "Son of a
Preacher Man." Unlike most thirty-year-olds, she loved
oldies and knew the lyrics to almost every song that came
on her favorite station. As Molly bobbed her head in time
to the music, she wondered what her trip to Richmond
would be like. She was driving the two and a half hours
north of her home base in Durham, North Carolina, in order to spend a week documenting the hit TV show, *Hidden
Treasures*.

As a staff writer for *Collector's Weekly*, Molly regularly
covered the auction beat, visited tag and estate sales with
high-quality items, and interviewed collectors mostly living in Virginia and North Carolina, but she sometimes
traveled to Tennessee or South Carolina as well. Her region
covered a triangular area. Nashville was the western point,
Alexandria, Virginia, marked the northern border, and
Charleston, South Carolina, created the southern point.

Molly felt as though she had spent the last month in her
car. First, she had driven to Charlottesville for a well-
established show featuring country furniture. The exhibit
on loan at this year's show had been called, "Southern
Quilts and Their Stories." Molly had interviewed booth
dealers, customers, and the show promoter before paying a
visit to an elderly woman named Nancy Coleridge who
had loaned a portion of her quilt collection to the show. In
addition to her generous loan of fifty quilts, Mrs. Coleridge still had over two hundred vintage southern quilts
as well as numerous coverlets displayed in her mansion on
the outskirts of the city.

Molly had spent a pleasant afternoon sipping powerfully
strong mint juleps on Mrs. Coleridge's veranda as the older
woman told tales of the different places she had purchased

her quilts. From garage sales to some of the most distinctive auction houses throughout the country, Nancy Coleridge's hunting ground reached far and wide. After filling up the last line in her small notebook with the woman's stories, Molly finally excused herself and wobbled back to her hotel room, where she collapsed in a heap on the creaky bed. The two articles she had planned to begin that evening, one on the show followed by a second article about Mrs. Coleridge's breathtaking collection, remained unwritten.

She had only been home in Durham for a few days before her boss, a cantankerous, overweight man named Carl Swanson, called her into the office to send her packing to cover an auction in Charleston, South Carolina.

"Can't anyone else cover it?" Molly had pleaded. "I still have to write up the two Charlottesville pieces. I'm only halfway through the southern quilts article."

Swanson, irascible as ever, chewed frantically on his nicotine gum and howled, "No! *You're* going and you're going *now*!"

Molly beat a hasty retreat, grateful to get away from Swanson's fetid breath and crimson face. Ever since her boss had decided to quit smoking, he was more intolerable than ever, yelling at anyone who crossed his path and snacking feverishly on Krispy Kreme donuts, cheese crackers, or beef jerky followed by several pieces of nicotine gum. His temper was intimidating, but the odor of his sweat-stained clothes and foul breath was almost deadly.

After her escape, Molly barely had time to pop her head into Marketing Director Mark Harrison's office and explain that she was leaving town again. Mark had just returned from a marketing conference and they had plans to spend the weekend together. Since June, their schedules had only allowed for three dates, two of which were wonderful, romantic dinners and the third, a quick lunch before Molly hit the road again. Now, autumn was upon them and Molly felt that despite her efforts to call Mark nightly from the road, their relationship wasn't developing the intimacy that either of them sought.

Entering his office, Molly closed the door. Though some of the *Collector's Weekly* staff knew about the romantic nature of her relationship with Mark, Molly preferred to be discreet. She'd rather not have Carl Swanson making cynical remarks about her love life. Molly seated herself in one of the two chairs facing Mark's desk, nervously smoothed her long wrinkled skirt, and quietly told him that she was leaving for Charleston and would have to cancel their plans for dinner and a movie.

"We can't seem to get a break," Mark had sighed, running his long fingers through his sandy brown hair. His light blue eyes showed only a moment's disappointment before his customary shy, hesitant smile returned. "Don't worry," he stood and enveloped Molly in a quick but tender hug, "I'll be here when you get back."

Molly gazed up at him as he tucked a strand of her shoulder-length, dark brown hair behind her ear. She felt a sense of desperation welling up inside of her. How long could they put their relationship on hold? But instead of clinging to Mark and professing how much she longed to stay with him, Molly smiled weakly and fumbled for something to say.

Mark searched Molly's slate gray eyes framed with a sweep of long, dark lashes for a sign of what was going on in her mind. He longed to kiss her full, pouting lips, but they were at work, so he unwillingly released her. At five foot eight, Molly still only reached the level of Mark's wide shoulders. She let a hand rest on his arm, sensing his desire to kiss her.

"Okay, then," Molly had finally blurted, her heart thudding like a drum in her chest. "I'd better get going. Um . . . I'll call you."

Conscious of Mark's eyes on her body as she walked out of his office, Molly wished for the millionth time that she was a slim size six instead of a full-figured size fourteen. Her cheeks grew warm and she felt as though every single staff member was staring at her curvy hips, full breasts, and thick legs as she hastened around the cubicles and out to the lobby.

During the weekend in Charleston, where the muggy weather had necessitated three changes of clothes per day, Molly sat under a stifling tent taking notes through two days of lot after lot of Chinese export porcelain and heavily ornamented oak furniture until she thought she would swoon.

Molly left Charleston as soon as the hammer fell on the final lot. Driving well over the speed limit on the way back to Durham, Molly had called Mark at home, hoping to make a last minute Sunday night dinner date. His answering machine picked up with his soft, mellifluous voice and Molly left an awkward message saying that she had missed him and to call her soon.

The next day, his office remained empty. Molly was reluctant to ask Swanson to explain Mark's absence, so she approached the only person who catalogued every detail about each employee's life, both personal and professional, and wouldn't hesitate to share. Clayton, the self-titled "Queen of Classifieds," was the staff's most flamboyant dresser and was even cattier than a sorority girl. Molly adored him.

"Darling," Clayton cooed, smoothing a wave of his carefully styled salt and pepper hair as he sat down opposite Molly in the break room. He flung the tail of a pink and white checked scarf around his neck and reached for her hand, "Where have you been?"

"Miss me?" Molly asked, her flawless complexion lighting up with pleasure. "I've been everywhere but where I want to be," she moaned, letting her head sink down onto the white laminate surface of the table.

"You mean, you'd rather be in the arms of that dashing man down the hall?" Clayton gestured in the direction of Mark's office.

"Kind of hard to date a guy when you never see each other. He hasn't even shown up for work today. Do you know where he is, Clayton?" Molly asked.

Clayton examined his neat nails and pretended not to hear her question. "Do you think clear nail polish is too gay?" he asked.

"No. And you *are* gay," Molly snapped, narrowing her gray eyes at her friend. "Are you hiding something from me?"

"Well, I'm *certainly* out of the closet so, no, I'm not hiding anything," Clayton said mischievously and avoided looking at Molly. He liked to take his time whenever he had a juicy tidbit of gossip to share. Finally, he shrugged and sighed. "Fine, you win. No suspense for Miss Molly. Mark had to fly to Ohio. Something to do with his brother."

"Is he all right?" Molly was alarmed.

"The brother? I heard something about a car accident. Even though I had my ear pressed to your man's office door, I couldn't get *all* the details."

Molly nodded, brows creased with worry. "I have no way of reaching Mark in Ohio. I don't even know what town his brother lives in. I hope he calls me before I leave for Richmond in a few hours."

"Richmond?" Clayton grimaced. "Ugh. Not a good place to be gay. Too, too conservative. Still, they have some *fabulous* restaurants there. Better than the barbeque and chicken-fried steak crapola we have to eat around here. You'll just *love* eating in Carytown."

"Sure, but *who* am I going to eat with?" Molly felt depressed. "See you in a week." She sighed, scooping up her pottery coffee mug.

Now here she was in Virginia, twenty miles south of Petersburg following a sputtering pickup and singing the bittersweet lyrics of Simon and Garfunkel's "Scarborough Fair." She hadn't heard from Mark before leaving town and was beginning to feel that obstacles were going to continue popping up to prevent them from becoming a real couple.

Suddenly, flashing blue lights appeared in the rearview mirror of her seven-year-old silver Jeep. The lights belonged to a state trooper.

"Damn it!" Molly yelled as she pulled over to the shoulder. The pickup sped merrily onwards as Molly turned off her radio and rolled down her window, preparing for the worst. Even though she was paid a respectable salary to do what she loved most, Molly had little money left over at the end of the month after paying bills and the mortgage on her tiny house. Any extra cash went into her "Antique Investment Fund," which consisted of a roll of bills stashed inside a pottery vase. Right now, she was saving to buy a chest of drawers for her bedroom and a $150 speeding ticket coupled with a hike in insurance payments would take a big bite out of her cache.

The trooper approached the door of her Jeep in a spotless and pressed uniform with knifelike creases on his dark brown pants and a pair of black boots that shone like glass in the midday sun. He was short and stocky with thick arms and legs. Dark stubble framed his leathery, tanned cheeks and his brown hat covered up most of his hairless head. Removing his mirrored sunglasses, he looked at Molly with dark, stern eyes and an unsmiling mouth.

"License and registration," the trooper demanded, carefully examining her front windshield.

Molly followed his gaze and noticed that her inspection sticker was expired. Her shoulders drooped as she remembered that she had chosen to hang out at a bookstore instead of getting her car inspected the day the tag had expired. Thinking of her evaporating antique fund, Molly handed the officer her license while she continued searching her glove box for her registration.

"I'll find it," she assured him, noting that his gleaming name tag read Jim Johnston.

Officer Johnston frowned. "Do you know how fast you were going, miss?"

Molly hated that question. Of course she didn't know the

exact speed, just that it was obviously too fast. "No, Officer," she answered, deciding she had best be polite.

"I clocked you at seventy-seven miles-per-hour. This is a sixty-five-mile-per-hour zone. Did you happen to notice that?"

"Not really, sir," Molly said meekly.

"What's your rush then?" he asked emotionlessly.

Molly finally found her registration and handed it to the trooper. "Honestly, my mind was just wandering. I didn't even notice how fast I was going. I *do* have to be someplace by three o'clock though," she added feebly.

"Oh? And where's that?" Johnston spotted the issue of *Collector's Weekly* on her front seat and displayed a trace amount of curiosity. His upright composure seemed to relax a fraction.

Molly followed his gaze. She picked up the paper and held it out. "I work for this paper. I'm going to cover the taping of *Hidden Treasures* in Richmond."

Officer Johnston's face lit up like a Christmas tree. "I love that show! I've been dying to bring some of my collection in for their experts to appraise."

"What do you collect?" Molly asked, surprised by the man's instant change in demeanor. Would his interest in collectibles get her out of a ticket?

"Couple things," Johnston answered proudly. "Coca-Cola advertising, Hot Wheels, Lionel trains, and tobacco tins."

"Well," Molly said, thinking furiously, "I'm sure I could get you into the show." She handed him her business card. "That's my cell phone number. Give me a call and I'll try to get someone to look at one of your collections. I don't think you can bring everything you own though," she added hesitantly.

"I'll just bring the Hot Wheels," Johnston said, looking extremely pleased. He took his own card out of his wallet and handed it to her. Then, he remembered his duty. "Look, I've already called in your plate, so I've got to give you a ticket for something. I'll write you up for your expired inspection if you promise not to speed in my state anymore."

"I promise!" Molly exclaimed, sinking back into the seat with a sigh of relief. She wiped her clammy palms on her pants and exhaled loudly. As she waited for Officer Johnston to write her up, she turned the radio back on. The Temptations sang, "Heard It through the Grapevine," and Molly hummed along, deciding not to share this anecdote with her mother who would certainly berate her for almost receiving another speeding ticket. Her mother, Clara, also wanted Molly to invest in antiques. She never failed to offer her opinion when Molly purchased something Clara deemed a complete waste of money, such as an Ann Taylor sweater set or a spa pedicure.

She could almost hear her mother saying, "Now, if you had gone on to be a lawyer like *I* thought you should be, it wouldn't take you a year to save up money for one piece of furniture."

Officer Johnston returned, holding out a clipboard so that Molly could sign her ticket. She noticed that the fine for an expired inspection was only twenty-five dollars.

"Thanks so much," she told Johnston gratefully.

"See you at the show, miss," he tipped his cap. "And don't let me catch you speeding on your way home to North Carolina," he added firmly.

"No, sir!" Molly started her engine in time to Van Morrison's "Brown-Eyed Girl." Before pulling back onto the highway, she glanced gratefully at the folded copy of *Collector's Weekly* and smiled.

"Thank God for collectors," she said aloud in jubilant relief and once again headed north for Richmond.

Molly pulled up in front of a stately brick row house in the heart of Richmond's Fan District. A wooden sign reading TRAVELLER with a painted silhouette of Robert E. Lee on horseback welcomed guests to the quaint bed-and-breakfast.

The front of the house had gleaming bay windows topped by small, horizontal panes of multicolored stained glass. An orderly garden filled with English ivy, red and yellow dahlias, fuchsia coneflowers and budding chrysanthemums was alive with the frantic hum of bees and a cluster of skittish monarch butterflies. Molly lifted the brass horseshoe door knocker and rapped twice.

The door was quickly opened by a short, plump woman rubbing flour-encrusted hands on a polka-dotted apron. Her light gray hair was cut in a bob, accentuating full, pink cheeks and the two dimples which sprang into place as she smiled.

"Mrs. Hewell?" Molly asked.

"That's me, dear," the woman drawled in a genteel southern accent. "Come in, come in. You must be Molly."

"Yes," Molly replied, looking away from the friendly woman to inspect the sunny hall. Her eyes fell on a Victorian coat rack decorated with vintage hats. Nearby was a porcelain umbrella stand filled with antique wooden walking sticks. Photographs and framed prints of Lee and his famous horse, Traveller, lined the walls.

"You're in luck," Mrs. Hewell bustled her forward, "I've just finished making my famous cinnamon scones. We have teatime here at Traveller. Don't let it be said that Richmond doesn't have class. Let me show you to your room first."

Mrs. Hewell led her up a curved mahogany staircase to a wide hall with two doors on each side and one on the end.

"How many bedrooms do you have?" Molly asked.

"Five. Mr. Hewell and I live out back in the converted garage. That's where you can find us if you ever need anything," Mrs. Hewell chirped, opening the second door to the right. A placard on the door read *THE FLOW BLUE* in delicate script.

"All the rooms are named after porcelain," Mrs. Hewell explained. "I've been collecting for years and it seemed like a good theme for the guest rooms. I do like displaying my goodies for everyone to see. There's no point in having them locked up inside some china cabinet. Besides, no guest has ever broken a single piece, and we've been running this place for twenty years."

Molly stepped into her room. The first thing she noticed was a large four-poster bed covered in an off-white quilt with a cobalt and white plaid coverlet folded neatly over the bottom half of the bed. Dark blue and white toile curtains with sheer shades allowed soft light to fall upon a large and plump blue floral side chair sitting next to a cherry drop-leaf side table. Above an antique chest of drawers, three plate racks held Mrs. Hewell's collection of Flow Blue dinner plates. Rimmed with deep cobalt, the plates had pink and yellow rose designs blooming in the center. Above the small mahogany writing desk was another set of plate racks holding serving platters with the same pattern. A thick indigo and cream plaid rug covered most of the hardwood floors.

"The Flow Blue in the bathroom is just a reproduction set, so don't worry about how you handle it," Mrs. Hewell said.

Molly loved her room. The soft light combined with all the whites and blues made her feel immediately cozy.

"It's wonderful!" she turned to her hostess. "What are the other rooms like?"

"Take a look for yourself," Mrs. Hewell beamed. "A gentleman is staying in Wedgwood, but the guests staying in Limoge and Blue Ridge haven't checked in yet. I believe all three guests are appraisers on that lovely TV show about antiques. The doors are all unlocked, as I've been misting the rooms with some delightful hyacinth-scented room spray. The Majolica suite, the big room at the end of the hall, isn't being occupied until tomorrow. Come down when you're all settled in and have some tea."

"Thanks," Molly smiled. She was so glad she had persuaded Swanson's secretary to spend the extra twenty-five dollars a night to book Molly at the Traveller instead of the humdrum chain hotel originally chosen for her. Molly had insisted that if she stayed at quaint bed-and-breakfasts, she might discover material for another article. Digging her digital camera out of her suitcase, she knew that her hunch about staying at the bed-and-breakfast had paid off. She decided to write a short piece on Mrs. Hewell's charming establishment and thought she should quickly photograph the other rooms before their occupants checked in.

The room directly across from her was the Wedgwood room. Completely forgetting that it was supposed to be occupied, Molly opened the door and was surprised to see such a completely different room from her own. The bed was a tall sleigh bed made of deep mahogany with a scrolled headboard and footboard. The coverlet was smoky green and a fluffy, white shag blanket was folded at the base of the bed. All of the furniture was more ornate than hers. Heavy, dark pieces with an abundance of decorative carving gave the room a more masculine air. Plate racks covered every wall, displaying Wedgwood plates and platters in pale olive greens and grayish-blues. Molly peered closer at the classical figures embossed in white on the plates. Most were of cherubs or couples kissing.

A Wedgwood vase on the dresser showed the procession of a group of harpists wearing togas. A thick bunch of dried lavender tied with a purple ribbon scented the room. Molly took several pictures then looked around once more to see if she had missed anything.

"Beautiful," she sighed.

"From where I'm standing, I would agree," said a deep male voice with an English accent.

Molly jumped and turned to see who had snuck up behind her. She came face-to-face with a man of equal height with sandy hair, honey-brown eyes, and thin lips pulled aside to reveal a neat row of square white teeth. He looked to be in his mid-thirties and had a healthy tan. His lean body was clad in jeans, a white button-down shirt, and a red tie patterned with fleur de lis.

"Inspection complete?" he asked, grinning. "Shall I do a twirl?"

Heat rushed to Molly's face. She had been scrutinizing him as if he were another attractive object in the room. She dropped her eyes to the leather tote bags in his hands.

"I'm sorry. Is this your room?" she asked, still flush with embarrassment.

The man put down his bags and held up a set of keys. "Right-O. Mrs. Hewell is setting up for tea, so I told her I'd find my own way," he said glancing around the room quickly before his eyes settled back on Molly's face. "And you must be Ms. Appleby, the talented writer for *Collector's Weekly*."

"How did you know that?" Molly was startled once again.

Instead of answering, he smiled enigmatically and presented a strong, square hand for her to shake. "I'm Garrett Huntington. I'm one of the researchers for Britain's *Hidden Treasures*. I'm here for a few weeks to observe the American version of *our* show," he said teasingly.

"Nice to meet you." Molly returned his easy smile and shook his hand. Garrett held hers for a long moment. He exuded a powerful aura of sexual intensity and electricity that seemed to surge through his hand. Eventually, Garrett released her and moved towards the bed. He tossed his bags carelessly on the coverlet. Every movement of his body spoke of confidence and effortlessness. He turned a grinning face toward the mirror and examined his reflection.

"You see, we're trying to figure out how to make ours a true road show. For the moment, we're based in the London area. We do a few episodes in Birmingham and Edinburgh to spice things up a bit, but things have turned rather stale. And . . . speaking of stale"—he gallantly proffered his arm—"let's not allow those delicious scones to cool. Shall we go down to tea?"

The tantalizing smell of cinnamon filled the dining room as Molly poured Garrett a cup of tea. Trying to reclaim some poise after being bedazzled by the Englishman's magnetism, Molly averted her eyes from him and focused on the charming dining room. Other than a walnut sideboard the room's only other furniture consisted of two gateleg tables, each surrounded by armless upholstered chairs. Only one table was set for tea with a linen-colored lace tablecloth and an ivory and pink floral Limoge tea set. Lovely silver-plate utensils with roses spiraling up the handles sparkled in the afternoon sun. Molly's fork parted the warm, flaky layers of her scone and a waft of melted butter caressed her nose. She dreamily noticed the generous drizzling of cream cheese icing before completely delighting her salivating taste buds.

"Splendid," said Garrett appreciatively. "I could eat a dozen of these," he patted his flat stomach.

Molly had been thinking about helping herself to a second scone, but one look at Garrett's trim waist reminded her that not everyone in the room was in perfect shape. Instead, she poured a second cup of tea and helped herself to two raw sugar cubes using sterling silver tongs.

"Do you know the rest of the crew?" Molly paused. "Or, I guess I should call them appraisers."

"Sure. I've been to the American set before lots of times before this." Garrett took a sip of his tea, the floral teacup looking fragile in his wide hand. "The major players are Victoria Sterling, the host, Frank, who appraises furniture, Jessica who does jewelry, Borris is books, Alicia is the art matron, Clarke is china, Lindsey is linens, and Tony is the Toy Man. There's also the managing director for the show, another Brit named Alexandra. Of course there are loads of assistant appraisers, but you won't need to interview them, as they never get camera time. And don't worry about last names. Nobody bothers with them."

Molly laughed, "There's an awful lot of alliteration in that group. Are any of those real names?"

"Just Victoria, Jessie, and Borris. Jessica and Borris are staying here, too, by the way."

Molly dabbed at her mouth with a cloth napkin, trying

her best to appear dainty and feminine, two traits she had never been associated with. As much as she would like to spend the remainder of the afternoon gazing at Garrett's Adonis-like features, she was scheduled to meet with Victoria Sterling at 3:30.

"I'd better head over to the set," Molly said as she began to stand, unaware that the hem of her long skirt was pinned under the chair leg. Trying to straighten up, she instead flounced back in her chair with an ungraceful thud.

"Oh, my, too much tea?" teased Garrett in a friendly manner. Then he suddenly leapt from his chair with the grace of a jaguar. "Where are my manners? M'lady?" he lifted the chair leg off of her skirt. As they stood facing one another, Garrett gave her another deep stare and asked, "Could I give you a lift to the set?"

Molly was feeling overwhelmed by his attention. She was unused to flirting, especially with bold, intense, confident men. She was used to Mark. Sweet, awkward, adorable Mark. And thinking about Mark made her feel guilty about being so attracted to Garrett.

"Thanks, but no." Molly smiled, feeling uncharacteristically shy. "I'm sure I'll see you there."

Garrett performed a deep bow. "Until then," he said, then grabbed a scone from its china platter and took an enormous bite out of it. His cheeks were completely stuffed with pastry as he gave her a closed-mouth grin. In the blink of an eye, he had transformed from a debonair gentleman into a mischievous scalawag. The man was quite a chameleon.

Molly didn't know what to make of him.

Hidden Treasures would be calling the Richmond Science Museum home for the next week. Formerly a railroad station, the building had turn-of-the century architecture on the outside, complete with dated cornerstones and wide arches for entryways. Enormous red and white banners announced the museum's current exhibit called "Science and Medicine of the Civil War." Inside, the cavernous halls were incredibly spacious, well lit, and modern—everything seemed to be made out of white plastic or chrome, a true contrast to the thousands of antiques that would soon be filing in through its doors.

Workmen wearing black *Hidden Treasures* T-shirts were busy placing signposts, which would soon be used to direct the large crowds. Doors wouldn't open to the public until Wednesday, but Molly was told by one of the producers that the crew would use Monday for setup and Tuesday to film some high-quality pieces from local antique dealers or established collectors as a security measure.

"We can't have an hour-long show filled with junk," the producer had scoffed over the phone a few weeks ago. "And believe me, you'll see plenty of *that*. We have to make arrangements to film a few *real* antiques ahead of time, just in case Local Joe doesn't bring any."

Molly took out the *Hidden Treasures* ID badge that had been mailed to her and showed it to a man creating a queue using brass stanchions and velvet rope. When she asked for Victoria, he pointed down a long hall leading off to the right. Passing by bright cloth banners depicting Civil War medical instruments and a variety of weapons, Molly entered a large space sectioned off into a series of screened areas. It looked like a massive beehive. In one of the white-screened areas, a group of cameramen was testing the lighting. They focused the object before them—a woman in an office chair. As the woman gracefully swiveled the chair around to face the cameras, Molly recognized Victoria Sterling.

On television, Victoria always looked immaculately groomed. Her ash blond hair was pulled back into a controlled French twist and her careful makeup drew attention to her catlike green eyes. Her thin frame was always dressed in what Molly and her mother decided were the worst couture suits available but at prices which undoubtedly left great dents in Victoria's bank account. Molly could never tell what Victoria's height was as most of her television shots were close-ups.

After getting the thumbs-up from the cameramen, Victoria began recording her sound bytes for the opening scene welcoming the viewers to Richmond. Her rose-colored suit featured a white vintage blouse whose sleeves poked out several inches beyond the suit jacket. The high neck rose in a series of pearl buttons, opened to reveal an attractive cameo brooch made into a necklace. A black and white striped scarf dangled from the suit pocket and gold filigree drop earrings finished off the ensemble.

Molly sat down off to the side and waited while Victoria repeated her lines a dozen times. Each repetition sounded exactly the same. The famous television host looked completely bored.

"That's a wrap, Ms. Sterling," one of the men said and moved his camera off to a different location.

Victoria barely issued him a nod before turning towards Molly.

"And you are?" she asked coolly, her green eyes stagnant as an algae-covered pond.

"Molly Appleby, with *Collector's Weekly*." Molly extended her hand.

Victoria slipped a limp, cold hand into Molly's and then let it flop back down against her body like a dead fish. "Well, let's start by introducing you to the rest of our head appraisers."

Molly hustled alongside Victoria. She noticed that her host was quite tall, almost six feet in fact, and strode with a quick, decisive walk toward the middle of the massive room. Her toneless voice and limp hands directed Molly. "This is where the filming will take place. We'll select pieces from the Great Hall—that huge room you first walk in after entering the building—and bring the pieces, along with their owners, in here. The Great Hall is where the public will line up to meet with the regular appraisers. Only head appraisers and their crews will be back here."

As they approached another curtained section, Molly saw a short, balding man, with thin strips of greasy black hair combed over to form the pattern of a garden rake, snap a latex glove onto his right hand. Frowning, he pulled a respirator mask over his mouth and nose and bent over to examine the back of a southern blanket chest.

"This is Frank." Victoria weakly gestured. Everything about her spoke of boredom and lethargy. "He's head appraiser for furniture."

"Hello." Molly offered a quick greeting, her eyes glued to the lovely, dark brown patina of the blanket chest. "Walnut?" she asked the masked man.

"Yes." Frank drew down his mask, a pleased look appearing on his pallid face. He raised the lid of the chest and pointed to the unfinished interior wood. "With southern yellow pine secondary."

"Of course." Molly smiled. "Is it Virginia-made?"

Frank looked at the piece thoughtfully. "This is an unusually deep blanket chest with an interior compartment for storage," he began in a nasal voice, sounding exactly as he did on television. "The compartment has a hinged lid with the original hardware. The blanket chest rests on the original bracket feet. It is generally hard to find original feet in good condition and without restoration." He paused. "I'd date this piece circa 1830 and give it a provenance of western North Carolina." Frank turned to Molly as if waiting for applause.

"Why the mask?" she asked instead of gushing her approval.

"Oh! I have terrible, terrible allergies. I'm allergic to *so* many things . . . dust, pet hair, pollen, peanut butter, milk—"

"Oh, you are *not* allergic to milk," Victoria interrupted crossly, finally demonstrating that she was capable of human emotion. "You just *want* to be allergic to everything. You aren't happy without some new *drama*, so now it's milk."

Frank stood over the blanket chest and put his hands on his hips defensively. "I am simply a sensitive person, unlike *some* people who could turn hot springs into ice."

Molly quickly interrupted the pair before their argument could become any more combustible. She introduced herself properly to Frank and asked him to remove the mask so she could photograph him with the lovely chest. Victoria made a snort of disgust and walked away towards the cafeteria.

So much for my guide, Molly thought.

"This is certainly a prime piece to photograph." Frank gestured at the blanket chest. "But I am going to start off my segment with a fabulous slant-front pigeonhole desk. Would you like to see it?" he asked.

Molly nodded and Frank peeled off his latex gloves with a loud snap and dropped them on the ground in repulsion. Kicking them repeatedly with his feet as if they weren't dust-covered gloves but a pair of scorpions, he managed to maneuver them away from the chest. He stuck his mask in the front pocket of his brown pants. "Too many English reproductions in Richmond," he said dismissively, leading Molly out of his cubbyhole. "I hope the local viewers learn something from this show."

Molly followed Frank behind another curtained partition to an area cluttered with stands, bucket benches, cleaning materials, and unused spotlights. Here, a slant-front desk was positioned on a raised platform covered in gray carpet. Two men were rubbing the desk with soft cloths, pausing every now and then to reapply dabs of wax to their cloths. Molly immediately noticed how hot it was beneath the row of floodlights that the men had erected in order to perform their tasks.

"Randy and Chris." Frank introduced Molly to the men. "They're my cleanup crew. I simply can't get near a piece until they've cleared off the dust and waxed it up. I can't tell you how many brands of wax we went through until we found one I wouldn't have a reaction to."

As Frank droned on about his allergies, Randy, a short, wiry man wearing a Nascar T-shirt with cutoff sleeves and black tattered jeans rolled his narrow eyes at his partner.

Chris, a smooth-faced man in his mid-twenties with a sculpted body and powerful-looking hands, returned Randy's sneer with a shrug. Chris had shiny blond hair and aquamarine eyes that seemed unnaturally bright. Molly wondered if he wore colored contacts. She was having a difficult time tearing her gaze away from the rippling muscles on Chris's forearms as they carefully stroked the surface of the desk.

"Gorgeous, isn't it?" Frank asked expectantly, watching the men work. Molly thought he was talking about Chris and she was about to agree when she realized he was talking about the desk. Before she could answer, Frank suddenly threw his hands in the air and snapped, "Rub that evenly, Randy! It will look like garbage on camera if you don't rub along the grain! How many times do I have to tell you that?"

Randy shot Frank a menacing look. "Oh, just quit for now," Frank said disgustedly and shooed the two workers away. "Go chew some tobacco or whatever it is you do when you're not waxing incorrectly."

A flush crept up Chris's neck as he dropped his cloth and grabbed Randy's skinny arm, leading him away from Frank. Randy shot Frank a look of pure venom before Chris was able to successfully maneuver his angry coworker out of the exhibit area. Molly stared after their sweat-stained backs in sympathy. There were some real divas in the antique world and it looked as though *Hidden Treasures* had a few of its own.

Molly took a good look at the desk. The base was comprised of four graduated drawers with brass pulls. The center of each drawer had inlaid escutcheons made of delicate bone or ivory. Molly pulled down the "slant front" which created an instant writing surface when resting on the two slide supports and drew in a breath. Opening the desk had revealed a dozen shaped pigeonholes, the small caches carpenters created in order for their patrons to store letters, ledgers, quills, or other correspondence-related items. Some of these pigeonholes were simply empty spaces meant for stacking documents and some were filled with small drawers given the same inlaid escutcheons as the outer drawers.

"And . . . can you believe it?" Frank whispered reverently. "I have the original set of keys for the four drawers. Now, shall we talk about this unbelievable wood?"

"It really glows." Molly was impressed. "Is it cherry?"

"No. Black walnut with yellow pine secondary. See? If we pull out a drawer you can see to the back." Frank removed two of the top drawers. "The whole case is actually made of pine. Most southern slant-front desks were made of walnut or mahogany, but this piece has the most gorgeous lines. All original hardware, original escutcheons, and nary a major repair in sight. It's a killer piece. Probably Williamsburg made, circa 1780."

"No major repairs?" She arched her brows at Frank. "I don't even see any minor ones. Can you show me?"

"Certainly." Frank preened. "There's nothing noticeable, fortunately. Here's the first one." He pointed at the back leg of the case. "Looks like someone broke off the bottom and replaced it with a newer piece of wood. It's a good repair, though, and at least one hundred years old, so it won't affect the value of this piece, which is *significant*."

Molly nodded, having no idea what Frank meant by significant. "And the second repair?"

"That's even older, I'd say," Frank answered, sliding out one of the supports that held up the writing surface when the desk was opened. "There's a square patch here, too. Not very big and it's got almost the same patina as the desk. I can't imagine what happened to damage a piece of wood that sits *inside* the body of the desk, but I guess we'll never know."

"Any secret compartments?" Molly asked, intrigued. From her experience at auctions she was well aware that desks with pigeonholes often had drawers with removable backs or sliding walls which revealed secret hiding places. A few years ago, Molly's mother, Clara, was examining the lower drawer on a secretary desk she had purchased at auction to sell in her antique shop. Clara's elbow had accidentally jarred into a rectangular strip of wood set above a pigeonhole. The thin piece of veneer broke loose and fell to the ground. Clara reached into the empty cavity to gleefully discover a signed note by the maker of the desk, a well-documented carpenter from Georgia. In that second, the piece of furniture she had just paid $2,500 for rose in value to over $15,000.

"I haven't gone over it completely yet," Frank said. "It was just delivered here this morning and now I'll have to wait until those two clowns are finished prepping it. I simply can't take the dust. However, I have a feeling that this piece is going to be the star of the show. Shall we take some photographs of the blanket chest in the meanwhile?"

Molly followed Frank back to the niche where they had first been introduced. She took out her digital camera and snapped a few pictures. Although the blanket chest photographed beautifully, its warm, molasses-brown patina glowing beneath the multitude of overhead lights, Molly had a difficult time finding a "good side" to Frank. She could see that he had earned his spot as a *Hidden Treasures* appraiser through his expertise, not his looks.

The opposite might have been said for the next appraiser Frank introduced her to. Tony the Toy Man was an adorable, energetic man in his late twenties with a mop of brown hair, freckled cheeks, and wide, hopeful eyes. He was just shy of six feet tall and was wound like a spring. He practically leapt around the table to shake Molly's hand and as he did, a cluster of dimples sprang into his rosy cheeks. He looked like a grown-up Gerber Baby.

Molly spoke to Tony briefly before he excused himself to unpack the box of toys he planned to open his spot on the show with. Suddenly, she remembered that she had Officer Johnston's card in her pocket.

"Tony?" she asked. "Any chance you'd be interested in seeing someone's Hot Wheels collection?"

"Depends." Tony grinned after examining the card. "Is this a 'get out of jail free' card?"

Molly laughed guiltily and then told the amused toy man about how she almost got a ticket. Tony amiably agreed to call the trooper during a coffee break.

Frank led Molly around another barrier of white exhibit walls to an empty space with a lectern where a man and woman were bent in deep concentration over an open book.

"Jessica? Borris? This is Molly Appleby from *Collector's Weekly*." Frank introduced them, and then turned his head away to sneeze. "Ohhhhh," he moaned, digging a wad of tissues out of his pants pocket. "That book must be *filled* with dust." He turned to Molly, his eyes watering, "I'll just leave you here. I can't take more than a few seconds in the book area." And with a loud honk into the tissue, Frank scurried away.

Borris had a square jaw and a Roman nose and bore a strong resemblance to a bust of Julius Caesar. He ran a hand through a thick mane of snow-white hair and shook his head quizzically. "Barely qualifies as a man, that one. Don't know how he found himself in this business with all those allergies."

Jessica, a short, chic-looking woman with cropped, spiky gray hair, a hooked nose, and deep brown eyes, fingered the amber beads of her vintage necklace. She swatted Borris playfully on the arm. "Borris, what will Molly think of us? Don't mind him." She pointed at Borris, and then at the book on the lectern. "He's just disappointed that these botanicals aren't hand-painted."

Molly leaned over to examine a bookplate detailing the medicinal uses of lavender. "It's still lovely," she offered, but Borris made a very Caesar-like dismissal with the flick of his wide hand and turned his dignified shoulders away to dig for another book from a pile at his feet.

Jessica turned to Molly. "You have an unusual name for this day and age. Kind of old-fashioned. Is there a story behind it?"

"Not a good one," Molly laughed. "My parents were on their way home from a camping trip in the Smoky Mountains. The car broke down in this little two-horse town. I was conceived in a roadside hotel named The Molly Arms. This was a big surprise to my ma, who liked neither camping nor kids. My parents didn't stay together long after that night, but I guess the name stuck with her, even though my dad didn't."

"Sounds like a story I can relate to," Jessica said bitterly. "Your mom was probably better off raising you alone."

Molly shifted, uncomfortable with the subject of her parents' infinitesimal marriage. "So are you the jewelry appraiser?" she asked, hoping to turn the conversation back to matters at hand.

"Sure am," Jessica said proudly. "I come from a long line of Jewish jewelry experts. I'll be opening the show with a marvelous set of vintage cat's eye pieces. A ring, necklace, and earrings. A local dealer has had them on display for months with no luck getting them sold, and she's hoping that getting the set on TV will help them sell."

"That's nice of you." Molly approved of antique people helping one another out. In fact, she liked both Jessica and Borris immediately. "Are the rest of the appraisers around here?"

"No," Borris said. "They've already knocked off for dinner. We're all supposed to meet at the Mexican place down the street. Want to join us?"

"Sure. I love margaritas," Molly said, happy to be included as another member of the show instead of an outsider. She often felt alienated when she was interviewing the close-knit groups of dealers exhibiting at shows.

Borris beamed. "Finally, a woman I can drink with! Jessica here is strictly a Perrier gal. I always feel like the poster child for A.A. when I eat out with her."

"Not for A.A. You're the poster child for crotchety, old book appraisers," Jessica teased.

"Let's go." Borris ignored Jessica's jibe, though Molly

could see the pair had a comfortable camaraderie that usually only developed between two people who have been friends for a long time.

As Borris bent to retrieve a book from the floor, Jessica reached down at the same time to grab her purse. Their heads collided with a resounding thud.

"Ow!" Jessica cried as she rubbed her temple.

"Ow yourself." Borris smiled. "You'd better stop abusing me. You're acting like Victoria does to Frank when he complains about his allergies."

"Those two really don't seem to get along," Molly observed.

"Don't get along? That's a polite way of saying they'd like to strangle one another at least once a day," said Jessica laughingly.

"Someday, one of them will figure out a way to bump the other one off," Borris jested, making a goofy slashing motion across his throat.

"But they're just coworkers," Molly mused. "How did they grow to dislike one another so much?"

"As someone who's survived a horrible marriage and a *very* nasty betrayal which led to divorce, I'll give you a simple answer," Jessica said as she opened the front door leading outside and gestured for Molly to pass through. "They don't dislike each other because they're coworkers. There's absolutely no competition between them as host and appraiser. They want to kill one another for the best reason of all, which is this . . ." She paused, breathing in the crisp evening air. "They're married."

Chapter 2

Above all, keep a sharp look-out for signs of attack by fungi and woodworm. Train your nose to differentiate between the dusty and the musty.

—THE ILLUSTRATED GUIDE TO FURNITURE REPAIR
AND RESTORATION

Once Jessica and Borris discovered that Molly was also staying at Traveller, they insisted on driving her to Casa 'Rita, the Mexican restaurant where the head appraisers were gathering for a casual dinner. Borris was clearly looking forward to having a margarita partner.

"We need to take advantage of Jessica's sobriety," Borris said, holding the rental car door open for Molly. "She'll drive us *both* home."

"I still can't believe it," Molly began saying as Borris turned onto Broad Street and drove past one strip mall after another. He closely tailgated a Jeep Wrangler whose upside-down bumper sticker read, IF YOU CAN READ THIS, PLEASE TURN ME OVER. Clutching the door handle nervously, Molly looked out the window and continued, "Victoria and Frank are married. I mean, they don't exactly strike me as a well-matched pair."

"I'll explain it to you, dear," said Jessica, settling into her storytelling mode. "Victoria Sterling was formally

Vicky Jiminski. She was a waitress at this place called The Terrapin Diner and lived in a run-down apartment complex south of Baltimore. Back then—we're talking about ten years ago—Frank owned a successful antique shop in Baltimore and another in Alexandria, just south of D.C. He was having unbelievable success as a furniture dealer and soon developed a reputation on the East Coast for being an expert in his field."

"Victoria knew nothing about antiques," Borris continued as Jessica took a swig from her water bottle. "But she knew Frank had money. He used to stop at The Terrapin because he loved their catfish platter. Vicky often waited on him and was shrewd enough to realize that Frank had the potential to provide her with a comfortable life."

"Vicky was a looker." Jessica regained command of the story. "With her tight skirts and long legs, it was easy to flirt with wimpy allergic Frank and, of course, he was bowled over. It didn't hurt that she was ten years younger either. They got married after two months of dating and then he quickly began transforming his new bride. Vicky the waitress gets her hair done, buys a new wardrobe of designer clothes, is given speech and acting lessons, and *wham*! she becomes Ms. Victoria Sterling."

That's why her clothes are so frumpy and mismatched, Molly thought. Victoria's never known what stylish clothes are. She just buys clothing with the highest price tags.

"How did she ever get on TV?" Molly asked.

Jessica snorted. "Frank knew some people on the local network who gave her a spot hosting a home makeover show. Trouble is, Victoria's attractive, but she isn't too knowledgeable about decorating or antiques. Still, she's a fast learner, can memorize her lines instantly, and does a decent delivery. And let's face it, she has the right look for our show, a sense of conservative, though dowdy elegance that people find nonthreatening."

"How do you guys know all this stuff? Wouldn't Victoria want to hide her background?" Molly asked.

"Nah," said Borris. "One night she was two sheets to the wind and told us the whole story. She even told us that she and Frank have separate bedrooms at home."

"I asked why she stayed with him," added Jessica as they pulled into the parking lot of another strip mall behind a white convertible with cowhide seat covers and a bumper sticker that read, *SAVE A COW, EAT A VEGETARIAN*. "Victoria said that she liked her lifestyle and had no interest in sex, so Frank was the perfect husband."

Molly mumbled, "How romantic."

"Romance is a Hollywood notion," Jessica said dismissively as she turned off the ignition. Molly saw a flicker of sadness surface in Borris's eyes as he watched Jessica exit the car.

Inside Casa 'Rita, long tables covered by vinyl cloths decorated with red chili peppers were crammed in a haphazard pattern on top of a perspiring terracotta floor. Waitresses, who all seemed to be local college students, wore tight citrus-colored T-shirts bearing the text, *MILK STINKS. GOT MARGARITAS?* Festive piñatas shaped like chili peppers, donkeys, and sombreros dangled from the ceiling. Jessica was hailed by Tony the Toy Man and the threesome moved forward to join the other head appraisers.

Molly sat down at the end of a table with Jessica, Borris, and Tony. She waved to Garrett who was seated next to a middle-aged Asian woman with glistening, ebony hair and an unlined face. The woman broke off her conversation, smiled warmly in Molly's direction, and called out, "Hi! I'm Alicia. I'm art." Alicia gestured to the man seated on her right. "This is Patrice. He's porcelain."

Patrice turned a bearded face toward Molly and smiled thinly. He had a prominent nose, sunken eyes, a long chin, and pointy ears. "My pleasure," he drawled in a French accent. Molly thought he resembled an elf.

Jessica kneed Molly under the table. "That accent is totally fake," she whispered. "But it works on TV."

Frank was seated at the other end of the long table, talking animatedly with a homely-looking woman in her late fifties. Her brown hair, woven with gray, was falling out of a low bun. She continuously poked at a pair of owl-like glasses as they slid down her small nose. Next to the owl-lady, Victoria was drinking a margarita on the rocks and looking about the restaurant with her usual indifference.

Borris and Molly ordered frozen grande margaritas, chili con queso, and sizzling fajitas. Jessica chose a vegetarian appetizer of bean quesadillas followed by a spinach and cheese enchilada.

"Who is that lady Frank is talking to?" Molly asked Borris.

"That's Lindsey. She's linens. Kind of ditzy, but a real doll. Knows her stuff, too."

"There's an empty chair next to Tony. Is anyone else coming?" Molly asked. "I don't know if I can remember any more people."

Jessica snickered. "That chair is for Alexandra Lincoln. She'd prefer a throne, however. She appraises coins, stamps, and clocks. She'll be fashionably late and make a grand entrance, even in this setting."

"But her name doesn't have the alliteration everyone else's does," Molly pointed out.

"No, she refused to play along. Apparently"—Jessica broke out into a haughty British accent—"she is from the *Lincolns* of *Lincolnshire*. Her father is a baron. A broke one, but still, a title is a title. Alexandra said it was insulting to have a television pseudonym," Jessica said dismissively as she bit off the corner of a blue tortilla chip. "The rest of us peasants don't mind. A paycheck is a paycheck. You can call me Penelope Pitstop as long as the money's good."

Just as their margaritas were delivered, a stunning woman walked through the front door. Wearing a tailored designer suit in crisp white with an expensive Gucci bag and matching pumps, the woman tossed a shiny wave of copper-colored hair professionally streaked with glints of gold over her shoulder. As most of the men in the restaurant looked in her direction, she turned a carefully made-up face toward the appraisers. Molly noted the woman's shapely legs, the alluring sway of her hips as she walked, and the poise of her movements as she approached Tony and issued him a smile that was not reflected in her cold eyes.

"Save me a seat?" she asked Tony. Unlike Garrett's, Alexandra's British accent lacked charm. It simply elevated the air of condescension about her.

Alexandra turned golden eyes toward Molly and gave her a queenly nod. Molly felt instantly snubbed. Over the rim of her margarita glass, Molly watched Alexandra suddenly brighten as she spoke to Garrett.

"She's had a crush on him for years," Jessica whispered.

"And not a chance in hell." Borris sniggered.

Garrett wasn't attracted to that gorgeous creature? Molly found herself smiling demurely in his direction. Garrett flashed her a dazzling smile in return. Molly felt a warm glow spread through her body as a result of his attention, two delicious margaritas, and the restaurant's festive atmosphere.

"I *like* you two," she said as she clinked glasses with Jessica and Borris. "I think this is going to be such a cool assignment."

Suddenly, Frank clanged a fork against his water glass in order to get everyone's attention.

"Listen, folks." He sniffed, clenching a tissue in his fist. "As some of you are aware, my mother passed away a few months ago and she left me her townhouse. It's here in Richmond, on Strawberry Street, just a few minutes walk from the museum. Mother lived in Florida most of the year, so her place has been empty for over six months now." He turned his head aside to sneeze. "Are you wearing perfume?" he asked Lindsey accusingly.

"Just a little," the homely woman admitted guiltily. "But it's from this morning."

"Ugh, my nose is *so* sensitive." Frank honked into a tissue. "Anyway, I'm going to auction everything in her house, but if anyone would like to see what she's got before it gets packed away, you're welcome to join me tomorrow morning to go through the house. Of course, I know what the furniture is worth, but my mother had oodles of smalls and I don't want anything *priceless* to go to auction."

Several of the appraisers smiled appreciatively at Frank. There was nothing antique people enjoyed more than poking their noses around other people's houses—especially ones in which all the contents were to be sold. Molly was terrified of being excluded. "I can suggest an excellent auctioneer for the job!" she shouted a bit drunkenly from her end of the table. "When are you going over?"

Frank stood and made his way over to her end of the table. "Tomorrow morning before filming starts. Say, nine o'clock?" he asked the group, dabbing at his raw, red nose. Murmurs of assent rose from the appraisers who were distracted by the arrival of their food.

"We'll meet you at the front door of the museum," said Jessica. "Sounds fun."

"Good. Fine," Frank replied as the waitress arrived and Molly's fajitas were placed in front of her. As Jessica bit into her enchilada, a long string of cheese trailed from her plate to her mouth. Frank's eyes widened in panic as he stared at the cheese. Jessica giggled, but Frank dashed after the departing waitress to inquire if the burritos he had ordered contained any milk-based cheese products.

From the corner of her eye, Molly watched Garrett excuse himself and head off to the men's room. As soon as he was gone, Alexandra's stiff smile melted away and she scowled at her plate of quesadillas.

"You Americans consume such rubbish," she announced. "No wonder your country is filled with obesity."

Molly was amazed that everyone ignored the barb. The other appraisers simply continued their conversations as if no one had spoken.

"Look at this dump," Alexandra continued, "bloody disgusting."

"Cheer up, mate," Tony mocked her by using an exaggerated Cockney accent. "You could be eating alone at your hotel."

"What? And miss your witty banter! Never." Alexandra's voice dripped with sarcasm. "And do try to dress better than a country bumpkin for tomorrow's shooting, Tony. You look a mess, as usual."

Tony stuffed his mouth with salsa-drenched tortillas and bowed his head. "Thank you, Your Majesty."

Garrett returned from the restroom and headed straight for Molly.

"Can I offer you a lift back to our hotel?" he asked, his eyes twinkling.

Molly could feel the heat of Alexandra's angry stare burning a hole through the back of her head.

"No, thanks." She smiled, feeling that everyone was listening. "I came over with Jessica and Borris, so I'll just go back with them."

"It's your life," Garrett teased. "Jessica is a real New York driver. Tailgates, curses, holds up a particular finger if—"

"Oh, I do not!" Jessica threw her napkin at Garrett.

After a dessert of fried ice cream drizzled in warm honey, Molly and her two new friends rose to leave. Molly decided to quickly introduce herself to Alexandra and get it over with. She would rather not talk to her at all, but as a head appraiser, Alexandra could hardly be avoided, royal snob or not.

Alexandra deliberately picked up her water glass as Molly held out a hand in introduction. She muttered, "Charmed," in her belittling way and turned her face away from Molly in order to tease Garrett about being back in the States.

"She's going to be a pleasure to interview." Molly sighed as she slid into the back seat of Borris's rental car.

"She's a bitch all right," said Borris as they drove off. "Just ignore her. We all do."

"If she hates America so much, why is she here?" Molly

asked, eyeing a blue minivan stuffed with children as it eased itself into their lane. The van's bumper sticker proclaimed: *I'M EMBARRASSING MY CHILDREN—IT'S A FULL-TIME OCCUPATION.*

Jessica scowled. "Does anyone use a turn signal anymore?" She adjusted the rearview mirror. "Alexandra got demoted from the British version. She used to be a talented director. I heard she slept with a fellow director over there. Problem is, he was married."

"Yeah"—chuckled Borris—"to the daughter of the network president. Oops!"

The trio laughed in wicked merriment. Back at Traveller, they said their good nights and Jessica went into the Blue Ridge room as Borris entered the Limoge. Molly made a mental note that she would need to photograph their rooms for her article before the week was over. Yawning widely, she changed into a pair of green cotton pajamas covered by a pattern of pink steaming coffee cups and fell back onto a plump, soft pillow.

What a great assignment this was turning out to be, she thought happily before falling asleep.

The next morning Molly heard stirrings in the hallway and realized she only had thirty minutes to get ready to meet Frank. She had completely forgotten to set her alarm clock. Quickly showering and dressing in beige linen slacks, a light blue shirt, and a sterling necklace in the Greek key pattern, Molly decided she had just enough time to phone the office and see if there was any news about Mark.

When a young female voice answered with, "*Collector's Weekly*, how may I direct your call?" Molly was momentarily taken aback.

"Hello?" the voice asked again.

"Where's Mrs. Goodbee?" Molly finally stammered, asking after the crotchety elderly lady who had worked the reception desk since the paper's inception twenty-five years ago.

"Who may I ask is calling?" the voice asked in false sweetness.

"Molly Appleby, I'm a staff writer."

"Oh, *Ms*. Appleby," the girl placed special emphasis on the title. "I've actually met you already. It was over two years ago. I think you and I may have applied for the same job. You know, as a staff writer." She giggled briefly and without a trace of merriment. "Guess you landed it since you're out there writin' away and I'm here answerin' the phones. Anyways, no hard feelings." She paused and Molly was certain there was a plethora of hard feelings. "And about *Mrs*. Goodbee . . . *she* quit yesterday."

"What? Why?" Molly asked in surprise.

"I'm afraid that's personal information," the girl replied firmly. Molly disliked her immensely.

"Has *Mr*. Harrison called in?" Molly asked, nastily copying the girl's tone.

"Oh yes, he asked to speak to you, actually."

Molly's heart skipped a beat. "And? Did he leave a message? Did you give him my number?"

"No, I didn't have your number. And no, there was no message," the girl replied with evident satisfaction.

"Did he leave *his* number?" Molly demanded testily.

"Let me see here." The girl shuffled papers loud enough for Molly to hear. Then she picked up a message pad and ripped off the top sheet containing Mark's number in Ohio. Luckily for her, Molly couldn't see the wicked smile that sprouted on her young face as she balled up the paper and threw it in the trash. "No, no number. Sorry."

Molly sensed the girl was lying. "Let me speak with Clayton, please."

"Oh, he's out. My . . ." The girl giggled. "We're not doing too well here, are we?"

"What's your name?" Molly asked, trying to control her temper.

"Brittani, with an *i*."

"Well, Brittani with an *i*, I am going to leave my number again, since it must have walked away from your bulletin board which is where I hung it yesterday." Molly recited her number and hung the phone up roughly. Brittani sounded like a manipulative, nosy little twerp. Molly would have to phone Clayton at home to find out more about her. Before she could get any more worked up about the new receptionist, there was a knock on her door.

Garrett stood outside her door looking refreshed and handsome. He wore white pants with a salmon-colored shirt and a tan suede jacket that begged to be stroked. He smelled of earthy cologne and just a hint of hazelnut coffee. Molly stared at him and tried to ignore the heat rushing throughout her body.

"Can I offer you a lift?" he asked brightly. "I've got to head over to the set and I know you want to meet up with Frank and the gang to poke through his mum's digs."

Before Molly could open up her mouth to accept his offer her stomach issued a long and loud growl. Trying to stifle the sound with her hands, Molly covered her soft middle in embarrassment.

He laughed and held up a small berry basket filled with an enormous blueberry muffin, a banana, and a glass of orange juice in a lidded cup. "I thought you'd be too short on time to join us for breakfast, so I asked Mrs. Hewell to pack you a picnic basket."

"Oh, thank you." Molly inhaled the muffin's scent gratefully.

"And I wouldn't forget your coffee." Garrett held up a small thermos. "Light and sweet, right?"

"Right." Molly smiled, once again unnerved by her attraction to this man. Mark *was* trying to reach her, and she resolved to keep *that* close in mind and Garrett Huntington more at a distance. Still, it was difficult to get her mind to listen when her body was longing to throw itself into his strong arms.

Garrett chatted amiably about how much he expected the Civil War exhibit to really impress the American home viewing audience. Molly was too busy enjoying the freshly baked muffin while trying not to get crumbs down the front of her shirt to focus on much else. As they pulled up in front of the museum, it was Victoria, not Frank who awaited the group of appraisers.

"Morning," Victoria greeted Garrett and Molly flatly. She was dressed in a gray suit with a light blue blouse. A triple strand of pearls dangled from her chest and once again, a black and white handkerchief stuck out of her jacket pocket. Molly thought it was one of Victoria's better outfits. At least it was an improvement over the one she had worn yesterday.

"Frank's getting the car," Victoria said, gesturing feebly toward the parking garage across the street.

At that moment, Jessica and Borris walked over from the direction of the garage followed by Tony and Alicia. They all greeted one another with raised coffee thermoses.

"Can we play hooky all day?" Tony asked hopefully.

"No, Frank's mother's townhouse isn't that big," Victoria replied flatly.

"The *mother-in-law*. Whoa. Did you guys get along?" Tony raised his eyebrows.

"Not really. She didn't want anyone to marry Frank. Ever." Victoria hastened to change the subject. "Look, you guys can head over, but Tony, there's no toys except for a few old dolls. Frank said the house should be easy to find because there's a café called Oodles of Noodles next door to the townhouse—"

"Don't you know where the house is?" Borris wondered.

Victoria frowned deeply, forcing unattractive lines to spring out across her forehead and around her mouth. "I've never been there myself. Mrs. Sterling and I weren't *exactly* close. Ah, here's Frank now." Victoria actually looked relieved to see her husband.

"Isn't Strawberry Street within walking distance?" Garrett asked, eyeing the car.

"Yes." Victoria seemed to be growing impatient. "But Frank wants to stay out of the fresh air and I'm not wearing my running shoes."

"What's the house number? We'll meet you there," Borris suggested.

"Four hundred and sixteen. Make your second right up at that light." Victoria waved a languid hand at the intersection just east of the museum.

"Have fun!" Tony waved as the unlikely couple drove off. He turned to the rest of the appraisers. "You guys go on. No toys, no Toy Man." Tony poked Molly playfully in the arm and said, "By the way, your trooper is meeting me inside. Hope he's got something good!"

"Your trooper?" Jessica asked curiously. Borris put his hands on his hips expectantly.

"I'll tell you later," Molly said as Patrice, Alicia, and Garrett joined them. Alexandra also arrived, looking gorgeous and sophisticated in a black pantsuit with a chartreuse blouse. She eyed the group, mumbled something about American collectibles being junk, and sauntered inside the museum.

After a short walk on the fractured sidewalks of Broad Street, the group turned south onto Strawberry Street and were instantly granted shade by a row of old live oaks. Neat row houses with small front gardens lined the street. Ten blocks into their walk, Borris spotted number 416. Frank and Victoria were waiting in their sedan in front of the two-story row house with cracked stucco siding and peeling shutters painted ages ago in Williamsburg Blue.

High grass speckled with dandelions covered the small garden area and the brick stairs leading up to the wooden front door were crumbling in places. Brown leaves were scattered under the shelter of the front porch and a pile of old newspapers in dirty, blue cellophane wrappers were thrown carelessly on the two wicker rockers. Frank dug a set of keys out of his pocket and opened the front door. It creaked in protest.

Following Victoria in, Molly couldn't see much in the dim light until Frank switched on the lights and moved off to the room on the left to raise the shades. Molly was immediately struck by a feeling of cold dampness within the house. A layer of dust covered the floor and a large cobweb had been erected across the chandelier hanging above their heads. The rest of the appraisers filed into the hall and waited expectantly.

Frank returned, his respirator mask covering his mouth and a pair of latex gloves garbing his hands.

"How long did you say this house has been empty?" Molly asked, her voice echoing eerily in the high hall.

"Over six months," was Frank's muffled reply. "I hired a handyman service to cut the grass and tidy up in here, but I think I should ask for a refund."

Molly followed Frank around the downstairs while the others took their time investigating items in each room. Frank focused on examining the furniture while Molly took a mental note of Mrs. Sterling's collections. The front room contained a china cabinet loaded with Hummel figurines. In the dining room, every possible surface was covered by pieces of Cranberry glass. The kitchen featured a collection of bright Fiestaware, and the office was crammed with leather-bound books and dozens of pieces of Staffordshire.

A set of very narrow stairs led to the top floor, which held three bedrooms and two baths. One of the bedrooms, decorated in yellows and blues with antique oak furniture, contained Mrs. Sterling's immense collection of Royal Doulton figurines. The second room, decorated in sage greens with heavy Victorian furniture, boasted a souvenir spoon collection displayed in dust-covered spoon racks.

"This was my mother's room," Frank said, leading Molly into a room that was an explosion of pink and white. The wallpaper was a riot of pink roses, the bed was pink satin with a frilly white dust ruffle and all of the country furniture was white with pink tassels hanging from the knobs. Pink and white checked curtains hung from the windows and pieces of pink and green Depression Glass covered every flat surface.

A display case with four deep shelves featured a beautiful collection of antique dolls. Each doll stood erect on her own stand and varied in style from the Madame Alexander Little Women, to a grouping of celluloid Kewpie dolls, to valuable bisque dolls with human hair and nodding eyes made in Germany.

Molly noticed that the feeling of dampness had increased within Mrs. Sterling's bedroom. A stale, musty odor permeated the stagnant air. Peering into the bathroom, Molly saw that the skylight had leaked, leaving brown water stains all over the toilet and bathroom floor. The tub faucet was leaking in a slow and steady drip and the basin was covered in a black, moldy stain. The same blackness had completely discolored the wallpaper, crawling up the height of the wall like an army of small roaches. The room exuded a powerfully fetid smell.

"Yuck," said Victoria, who stood behind Molly. Frank appeared next to his wife's shoulder and shrieked like a little girl confronted by a spider.

"Oh, my God, look at all that mold!" he squealed through the mask. "Tour's over!" he shouted down the hallway and began to usher the dumbfounded appraisers out of the rooms.

"What's the matter?" asked Borris crossly as Frank gave him a firm shove out onto the front porch. "I was looking at a nice first edition Kipling in there."

Patrice was the last person to be extricated from the house and he wailed as Frank locked the door, "But I didn't even get upstairs!" Molly noticed he had more of a Boston accent now than a French one. "And that Royal Doulton! Frank, I *need* to get back in there!"

Standing by his car, Frank inhaled deep breaths of air and dabbed at his eyes with a tissue. "I'll never be able to go in there again! What am I going to do?"

Molly jumped forward. "You can still have all the contents

cleaned and put up for auction," she said soothingly, her mind racing. "You don't need to go back in there."

"But I want to sell that stuff right away. I need to take care of this before I leave town."

"I know an auctioneer who could handle everything for you," Molly suggested calmly, thinking of her friend, Lex Lewis. If Lex came up to view Mrs. Sterling's estate, he would certainly bring Clara with him. Molly *would* have a companion to eat out with in Carytown after all.

"Do you? Oh, that would be great. How soon do you think he could look the place over?"

"I'll call him as soon as we get back to the museum," Molly promised. "He is an excellent auctioneer and will do his best to get you top dollar for your mother's things."

"Don't you want to keep any of it?" asked Jessica in surprise.

"No." Frank waved his hand dismissively. "I'm not interested in her smalls and my furniture at home is of a much higher caliber. I can't stand that Victorian garbage. Oak, oak, oak. Yuck. Now, I need to get back to the set." He turned to Molly. "Let me know when your friend can get here."

While Frank and Victoria drove off, Molly walked a bit behind the rest of the group as they headed back to the museum and excitedly dialed Lex's number. Lex answered on the third ring.

"Hey Lex," Molly greeted him, speaking loudly over the rumbling of a garbage truck, "feel like coming to Richmond?"

"Molly? Speak up! I can barely hear you."

Molly scowled. She hated cell phones, but she explained the immediacy of the situation and described some of Mrs. Sterling's collections. By the time she had finished her descriptions she had reached the museum. Just as she was easing herself into a comfortable bench outside the front door, Lex agreed to drive up and take a look.

"Any luck?" Frank suddenly appeared in front of her and Molly jumped. She pushed her cell phone back into her purse and stood. "Yes. They'll be here tomorrow afternoon. Is that okay?"

Frank sneezed. "I'll be a bit tired as it's the first day with the public tomorrow, but I suppose I'll manage."

"You can give me the keys if you're too tired," Molly suggested as they walked toward the front door.

"Good idea." Frank handed her the key ring with his thumb and forefinger as if it were a contagious disease.

At that moment, Molly stumbled on a turned up corner of the rubber doormat and the keys clattered to the concrete floor among three pairs of shoes. Garrett was smoking a cigarette with Frank's cleanup boys, Randy and Chris. As Garrett smiled widely at her, Randy bent his thin body over to retrieve the keys. He dangled them in front of his chest, his narrow eyes boring into Molly's. There was something cold and menacing about the intensity of his stare as he dropped the keys into her open palm.

"Don't you have work to do?" Frank demanded in annoyance, and Chris immediately stumped out his cigarette and hastened inside. Randy looked away and continued smoking leisurely until Frank began to cough. "Nauseating habit." Frank threw his comment back over his shoulder as he headed into the museum.

Disappointed to discover that Garrett was a smoker, Molly quickly followed in Frank's sneezing wake. Molly didn't mind the smell of pipe smoke. In fact her grandfather had once puffed merrily away at a lovely rosewood pipe as he told her stories of undersea kingdoms and magical forests filled with tamed dragons or vindictive fairies.

On the other hand, cigarette smoke reminded her more of the packed rooms at country auctions, where stale air and a floor littered with butts, which occasionally floated in the spittle that was the result of a flavorless hunk of chewing tobacco, made a five-hour auction a trying affair. Molly had often turned a few shades nearer to yellow as her contacts protested and burned as she squinted uncomfortably at the item being sold through a circulating fog of cigarette smoke. Taking notes for an article during one such auction, Molly decided that she was simply not paid enough to endanger her health every week, but then a miniature fire pole whose tapestry had been woven by a seven-year-old girl in 1862 came up for sale and Molly forgot all about her cigarette-induced complaints.

Back inside the smoke-free museum, Molly spent the morning happily interviewing Alicia and photographing a fabulous folk art portrait of a young girl holding a gray kitten. Next, she spent some time with Lindsey whom she photographed with a Baltimore quilt done in reds, greens, and golds on an ivory background. Hoping to catch Jessica and Borris for lunch, Molly headed in their direction. On her way to their stalls, she dropped off her heavy bag filled with her camera and her interview equipment in the staff room. Everyone else had left purses and briefcases in there, so she figured her camera was perfectly safe.

Borris spotted her approaching their exhibit area and headed her off, "Lunch is in the cafeteria. Jess is already down there. It's just sandwiches, but rumor has it there's homemade chicken salad."

"Yum." Molly's stomach rumbled agreeably. She joined the other appraisers at a long cafeteria table and helped herself to a chicken salad sandwich, a bag of sour cream and onion potato chips, and two chocolate chip cookies. Feeling guilty, she replaced her soda with bottled water. Molly was chagrined to see that Alexandra was eating only the turkey, lettuce, and tomato from her sandwich and had neither chips nor cookies by her plate.

"How was your visit to Strawberry Street Manor, proud neighbor to Oodles of Noodles?" Alexandra teased Garrett as he slid into the empty chair next to her. Since Frank and Victoria had yet to join the group for lunch, Molly felt free to embellish on the neglected state of the house, especially in regards to Mrs. Sterling's upstairs bathroom. She thought her lively descriptions would draw Garrett's attention away from Alexandra.

"That much mold?" asked Lindsey, crinkling her nose. "I'm amazed Frank is still among the living."

"I saw it for a second," Alicia added with a grimace, "before Frank threw us all out. It was like the bathtub had been painted black."

At that moment Victoria arrived and joined in the complaints about the state of the bathroom. Molly noticed that at the next table over, Randy had stopped eating and had fastened his beady eyes on Victoria's face with a look of intense longing. Suddenly, he stood and flung his uneaten food in the trash. Without a backward glace, he stomped out of the room.

After a few more lighthearted digs at Frank's expense, the group grew bored with his allergies and returned to swapping stories about the spectacular antiques that would be filmed over the course of the day. Even Alexandra looked animated as she boasted about a collection of carriage clocks she was putting in the spotlight.

"The largest is almost . . . oh, let me convert this to your silly American measurements . . . thirteen inches tall and the smallest is about five inches. All are signed on the dial and in perfect working order. Lovely bunch."

The group ate quickly, eager to begin filming their segments. Molly, who was an extremely fast eater, had finished her entire lunch before Jessica had even started on the second half of her pimento cheese sandwich. Jessica inconspicuously eyed Molly's empty plate and noted the impatient tapping of the younger woman's left foot.

"Go visit with Tony." She kindly shooed Molly into motion. "He's dying to show you that cop's set of Hot Wheels and I need to clean the pieces we'll be filming. We'll meet you back at our pens at three."

"It's a date," Molly answered. "I hope you two have something exciting to show me as well."

"I've got an anatomy book the likes of which you've never seen," Borris said smugly.

"That sounds like a come-on line," Jessica teased.

"Only for you, my dear." Borris winked and Jessica smiled at him fondly. Molly could see that the pair had already forgotten about her, but she didn't mind. Those two should just get over their relationship hang-ups and admit they're crazy about each other, she thought.

Molly spent over an hour with Tony as he meticulously reviewed the highlights of the Hot Wheels collection he had filmed that morning.

"This is all Officer Johnston's!" he exclaimed, his boyish smile lighting up his face. "This is one of the best collections I've ever seen."

"Whew!" Molly laughed. "I'm glad I didn't waste your time."

"No way. These are the first ones ever released," he gushed. "All of the packaging is mint. And see here"—he pointed to a row of yellow-green and pink cars—"these two colors, the vaseline and pinks, are much more rare than the other colors."

"I'm surprised they even made pink for boys to play with," Molly said, taking photographs.

"Exactly! That's why they're more unusual," Tony enthused.

"What's this collection worth?"

Tony swept his arm over the group of cars. "Close to six grand. Officer Johnston is going to keep them for his son. I told him he'd better get them insured and to store them in plastic bins. He's the nicest state trooper I've ever met, probably 'cause I wasn't behind the wheel of a car. He'll be here for the show on Friday. I gave him two tickets. I think he mentioned something about bringing some Coca-Cola memorabilia."

"That's great, Tony."

After photographing all the Hot Wheels, Molly got some coffee from the vending machine downstairs and drew up an outline for her piece. She decided to write a side story on what people choose to do with their items once they were given their estimated values by the appraisers of *Hidden Treasures*. She could follow this line in an interview with Trooper Johnston. Her readers would love to discover that members of law enforcement were collectors as well. Molly checked her watch. She still had a half hour of free time before she met with Jessica and then Borris, so she decided to check out the exhibit on Civil War antiques.

As Molly walked through the Great Hall, she felt a bit lost among the bustling mass of activity. Curators and staff members from the Richmond Confederacy Museum were frantically putting the finishing touches on the exhibit they had put on loan. Molly paused next to a formidable statue of Stonewall Jackson on horseback. The top of Jackson's hat was twenty feet off the ground and the enormous haunches of his mount could easily hold four regular-sized riders. Molly admired the sculpted muscles of the horse's forelegs and the wrinkles meticulously carved into lifelike creases on Jackson's pants. Just as she reached out a hand to touch the tiny lines creating the horse's marble mane, the lights went out. The windowless hall was completely enveloped in darkness.

A woman began to scream.

Chapter 3

With their crushing inferiority complex about English furniture, the Early American cabinetmakers called cherry American mahogany—and usually stained it to look like mahogany. This is something like gilding a lily with mud.

—George Grotz, *The Furniture Doctor*

Molly stood with one hand on the marble mane and her body pressed against Stonewall Jackson's cold but reassuringly solid leg. The woman's panicked screaming was close enough to force goose bumps to erupt up and down Molly's arms. She felt vulnerable and frightened as the screams echoed in the rafters of the high ceilings.

"Stop it, Ellen!" a man's voice suddenly yelled and the screaming abruptly stopped. "For Christ's sake! It's just a power failure."

"But I *hate* the dark," the woman wailed and began to sob like a child refused its night light.

"Anyone have a flashlight?" another voice called out timidly and Molly allowed herself to breathe.

"Just sit still!" the first authoritative voice yelled again. "These things never last long."

People in the exhibit space began whispering animatedly. Molly slid down the statue and sat on the ground in the protective gap underneath Stonewall's mount and calmed herself. For some reason, the blackout had seemed particularly ominous, as if the lights were going to snap back on only to reveal a bloody corpse.

"Been reading too many mysteries," Molly mumbled to herself. She was amazed that she could see absolutely nothing from where she sat, but then she remembered that the exhibit hall had no windows. She strained her ears for any unusual sounds, but only the nervous whisperings of the people around her could be heard.

Suddenly, she thought she saw a pinprick of light coming from the direction of the display cases against the wall. It bobbed up and down once, then again, and then disappeared. Molly blinked. Had she really seen anything or were her eyes playing tricks on her in the dark?

Five minutes passed, but it seemed more like twenty when the lights were finally restored. Weak cheers arose from the people grouped in the Civil War exhibit and Molly looked quickly around to make sure that her strange hunch about bleeding cadavers was incorrect.

No bodies hung from the track lighting or lay sprawled at the feet of the imposing Robert E. Lee statue nearby, so Molly released a deep breath and her hold on Stonewall's booted foot. As the museum workers returned to their tasks and a feeling of normalcy resumed, Molly decided to take a quick look at the display case near her before her meeting with Jessica and Borris.

A selection of letters, diaries, and daguerreotypes occupied the first of three large display cases. Molly looked carefully at the black and white images of the young Confederate soldiers. Some of them were mere boys, beardless and skinny, their eyes beaming with pride in their innocent uniforms—so clean and pressed and unprepared for the grit and blood of a real battle.

The next case held musket balls, decks of playing cards, domino boxes, and currency. There were several types of Confederate bills displayed on rectangular pieces of black velvet along with an array of coins. A special case boasted a

series of rare gold coins that had been found on the uniden-
tifiable body of a Confederate officer. The coins had a
greenish-gold luster and the face of Lady Liberty on one
side with a crown of laurel leaves on the reverse.

Molly read the exhibit notes in horror and fascination.
The soldier had received two shots to the face, erasing his
identity forever. No letters or personal documents were
found on his body—just a scorched locket with the rem-
nants of a woman's photograph and these six gold coins.
According to the labels affixed below the coin display, each
coin was a three dollar gold coin minted in Dahlonega,
Georgia in 1854. To date, only a handful of these coins were
known to exist. The soldier wouldn't have been using them
for currency, and since they were hidden away inside his
pocket Bible—holes had been cut through the pages in order to hide the coins—he may have carried them for luck,
but they were otherwise a mystery.

"Didn't prove very lucky," Molly said to herself.

"Guess not," agreed an elderly man with a white mous-
tache, gold spectacles, and a blue seersucker suit leaning
on a wooden walking stick. He smiled and his face creased
in every direction, but his pale blue eyes sparkled with in-
telligence. "Each one of those coins is worth at least eighty
thousand dollars. They're all AU Dahlonega coins with unusually high eye appeal. Only one thousand one hundred
and twenty were minted and one hundred are known to still
exist. And they are in unbelievable condition, despite the
young man's unfortunate fate."

"Are you a numismatist?" Molly asked, trying to sort
out the jumble of coin terminology.

"Used to be. I gave my collection to my grandson."

Molly returned her glance to the coins. "What does AU
mean?"

"About Uncirculated. Circulated coins have received
wear. Mint coins are perfect with no wear. AU coins exist
in the realm between extremely fine and mint." The man
chuckled. "But I certainly could never afford that level of

coin. One of those sold in New York last year for one hundred thousand dollars."

"Wow! So there's almost half a million dollars worth of coins here? Shouldn't there be a security guard watching them?"

The old man pointed with his cane to an empty chair across the aisle. "That's where he's supposed to be, but I imagine he went off to check on that power failure. Plus, we're all here working and watching. Speaking of work, guess I'd better get back to supervising my interns. Enjoy the exhibit."

Molly cast one more appreciative look at the coins and the photographs of battlegrounds. Civil War displays always made her feel depressed, so she hastened along to find Borris and Jessica. As she passed by Frank's screened niche, he hailed her over with a wave.

"The slant-front desk is ready to be photographed," he told her. "And I thought you might like to be here when I check for hidden compartments. After all, I owe you a favor for finding me an auctioneer so quickly."

Molly couldn't resist the possibility of discovering something within the desk, so she ran over to Borris's exhibit area to tell him that she would be late, but the camera crew was already filming him with a large, leather-bound anatomy book. Victoria was standing by to film the segue between the segment on the anatomy books and the next commercial break.

"Can you tell him that I'm with Frank and I'll be back?" Molly asked Victoria, who issued a bored nod in response.

The slant-front desk had been expertly polished and waxed. Its red patina radiated age and beauty as Frank ran his hands tenderly over its surface.

"No gloves?" Molly teased.

"Not on camera!" Frank answered shrilly, oblivious to her jesting. "Take some pictures, then we'll dig around inside."

"Hasn't the owner already searched for secret areas?"

"I doubt it. The owner's an old lady who has had this piece in her family for years. She just wants the appraisal for insurance purposes as she's going to leave it to her daughter in her will. Said she just kept a bunch of letters in it and it was kept closed most of the time. That's why the inside has a deeper red than the outside. It was exposed to less sunlight over time."

After shooting several photos, Molly took a seat in a chair next to Frank as he switched on a penlight and began working his fingers inside each pigeonhole. Watching him, Molly could sense his deep appreciation of the workmanship it required to craft the desk's nooks and drawers, careful dovetails, and detailed inlay. Frank closed his eyes as if in a trance, letting his hands search and pry as he tried to get a sense about an extra large hollow space or a thinning of an area of wood.

As Molly leaned closer, she detected a faint, musty odor beneath the heavy smell of furniture wax. It was oddly familiar, but she couldn't quite place it. The interior of the desk had a small, central cupboard surrounded by pigeonholes and drawers. Frank was carefully examining one of the pillar-like pieces of wood that created a fluted border between the cupboard and the pigeonholes.

"Here!" Frank breathed, pulling one of the pillar-like pieces away from the body of the desk. It slid out, revealing a small vertical space in which documents or other thin objects could be stored. Mesmerized, Molly waited while Frank put his pale face against the opening and he flashed his tiny beam of light into the cavity. He began to frown.

"What is it?" Molly asked.

"Someone forced this," Frank replied angrily. "And recently, too. See these scratches." Frank handed her the piece of wood that had formed the fake pillar front and then shone the light beam on similar scratches within the cavity. "Those are made with a screwdriver. And there's fresh wood dust in the opening. If there was something in here . . ." He broke off as a powerful coughing fit racked his body. Swallowing great gulps of air, he searched his pocket for tissues. He blew his nose loudly before finishing with, "It's gone now." He looked at the desk angrily. "Some moron in the owner's family must have rifled through this piece in case there was anything of value inside. Damn amateurs."

Molly sat with him as he searched the rest of the pigeonholes, but no more secret compartments were discovered. She felt sorry for Frank, odd as he was, for missing out on the desk's treasures. She was disappointed, too. After all, it would make a great article if she had been an eyewitness to the finding of some rare document or precious gem.

Handing the fake drawer front back to Frank, she noticed black smudges on her palm. Frank's hands were also dusted with black smudges and a long streak of pale black darkened the tip of his nose and upper lip. His eyes had begun watering and just as Molly was about to tell him about the marks on his face, he jumped up, rubbing vigorously at his eyes and said, "I've got to get my nasal spray! Excuse me."

Molly watched him scurry off down the wide aisle between exhibit areas. Then she picked up the discarded penlight and directed the beam around the pigeonholes. Black smudges were everywhere, but without direct light on them, they could barely be seen. Molly wondered why Randy and Chris had not done a better job cleaning the inside. Putting down the pen, she went off to the restroom to wash her hands.

Just as she was drying off, Jessica entered and headed for a stall.

"We're all eating Italian tonight," she said from inside the stall. "Garrett's found us a place in Carytown that is supposed to have delicious, authentic Northern Italian cuisine."

Molly examined her full and curvy figure in the mirror and frowned. "I could do without all those heavy sauces," she answered.

Jessica appeared next to her at the mirror and began to apply some lipstick in a brownish-rose shade. She ran thin hands through her cropped hair and asked, "Got a boyfriend?"

"There's someone from work I'm interested in. We've tried to date, but our schedules seem to be keeping us apart."

"Take it from me, honey"—Jessica spritzed on some light perfume with a fruity bouquet—"my husband got too busy for me. Too busy with another woman, that is. That's why we're divorced. You don't want a man like that."

Molly opened her mouth to defend Mark but instead asked, "What's the deal with you and Borris?"

Jessica immediately began to fumble in the depths of her hemp purse. "We're just friends."

"I think he'd like it to be more than that," Molly suggested gently.

"Well, I'm not going down *that* road again." Jessica quickly changed the subject. "Oh, listen to this. Just before I came in here, I overheard one of the security guards saying that the power failure was intentional."

"Someone hit the switch, so to speak?"

"Yes. I wonder why. Nothing's missing or anything. Probably Tony, playing a prank," Jessica said, rubbing a fragrant herbal lotion on her hands and forearms. "Come on, let's go eat."

Molly thought about the pinprick of light she had seen. It had been right near the display cases housing the rare coins and the daguerreotypes. A shiver ran through her, but she pushed thoughts of the blackout away. Someone had a penlight and nothing was missing. What was there to worry about when good food and Garrett's handsome face awaited her?

The head appraisers were all gathered just inside the museum's front doors. Garrett was handing out sheets of directions to Ristorante Amici.

"Everyone set?" he asked.

"I'm not coming," moaned Frank who was sitting in a

chair with his head propped back against the wall. He looked even paler than usual and sounded completely congested. Beads of sweat had sprung out on his forehead and a damp ring was forming around the neck of his shirt. His eyes watered and his shoulders were slumped with fatigue. "I'm going to the hotel to lie down," he whined as he rose gingerly and walked off slowly in the direction of the parking garage. The other appraisers watched him silently.

"He looks awful," said Alicia sympathetically, her kind, wide face turning toward the group. "He might really be sick this time."

"Nonsense," replied Victoria dully. "Let's go."

"I'll ride over with you." Alexandra sidled up to Garrett and grasped his arm possessively. Molly stared enviously at Alexandra's trim figure. She looked sophisticated and cool in a bisque-colored linen pantsuit with a chocolate brown silk blouse. Her hair shimmered beneath the track lighting and her makeup accentuated her high cheekbones and smooth lips.

Molly again carpooled with Jessica and Borris while the other appraisers divided themselves amiably between the two other rental cars.

"Take Monument Avenue so we can show Molly the sights," Borris suggested to Jessica.

"The architecture of the historic houses on this street is stunning," Jessica said, turning left onto Monument. "Many of these are million-dollar homes."

Molly's eye was immediately drawn to a statue of a Civil War soldier on horseback. It looked just like the statue she had hid beneath during the blackout, but in a much larger scale. "Is that Stonewall Jackson?" she asked.

"Indeed, it is," Borris said. "The statues on Monument are all dedicated to Civil War heroes, except for the most recent addition of Arthur Ashe. All great men, I would say, but many Richmonders are upset over the latest addition. I've got a friend who lives here and he thinks the Civil War theme should have been left . . . uninterrupted."

Molly gazed in awe at the enormous mansions lining both sides of the city street. Wrought iron gates surrounded the small yards of four thousand square feet, three-story homes that sat on wide haunches behind tree-lined sidewalks. Even though the rows of large houses seemed uniform, Molly noticed that upon closer scrutiny, the architectural styles were actually quite varied. A colonial was neighbor to a Spanish villa, which bordered a traditional Georgian. Ancient magnolias and oaks stretched their arms out over the neat lawns or front gardens and well-dressed pedestrians walked dogs and exchanged friendly greetings.

"Up next is the monument to Jefferson Davis," Borris continued his role as tour guide. Molly craned her neck in order to view a pillared arc with an obelisk rising from its center. She was more interested in watching the homes pass by, but Borris pointed out Lee sitting astride Traveller and finally, another general on his mount, J.E.B. Stuart.

"Are you a Civil War buff, Borris?" Molly asked.

"Not really. I just pick this stuff up by default. Hazards of the occupation so to speak."

"You mean, becoming a tour guide is your occupational hazard?" Jessica teased.

"No, being smarter than everyone around me is."

The women laughed as Jessica pulled into a parking space on Main Street, right in front of one of the many Carytown antique stores. Molly noticed a long row of boutiques, specialty shops, and eateries lining both sides of the quaint downtown street. The whole area had a lively, colorful atmosphere. No wonder Clayton loves this part of town, Molly thought.

The restaurant featured a narrow downstairs room seating couples only and a cozy upstairs with larger tables crammed next to one another in the style of traditional European cafés. Molly dipped a thick slice of warm Italian bread into olive oil seasoned with parmesan cheese and sipped a glass of smooth red wine. Jessica, Borris, and Tony enlivened the meal with stories of the most ridiculous objects the public had brought them to be appraised.

"A box of used *Playboy* magazines. And I mean *used* . . ." Borris was saying.

"Ha! What about that beehive wig someone brought me in San Francisco?" Lindsey burst in on his story. "That thing was full of bugs!"

Molly enjoyed her homemade gnocchi in creamy pesto sauce and the delightful chatter of the head appraisers. Over coffee, she also remembered that Lex and her mother would arrive tomorrow. All she needed was Mark, and all would be right with the world.

Sensing that Jessica and Borris were going to linger over a second cup of decaf, a fatigued Molly joined Victoria and Alexandra in Garrett's car.

"Three lovely ladies in my car, how lucky I am," Garrett said as he drove towards Victoria and Alexandra's expensive and modern hotel near the museum.

At the front door, Victoria bid them a brief good night while Alexandra seemed to hesitate. Shooting Molly a nasty look, she asked Garrett to pick her up in the morning.

"Can't put up with a quick ride with Frank and Victoria?" Garrett teased.

Molly watch Alexandra's stiff face force itself into a grin. "It's just nice not to be surrounded by sneezes and tissues for a spell."

"Right-O, see you in the morning."

During the brief car ride back to the bed-and-breakfast, Molly asked Garrett to compare the British and American versions of *Hidden Treasures*. He pointed out that most of the objects brought to the British show were far older than the ones he saw in America. He mentioned several items from Portuguese side tables to Delft tiles and before Molly knew it, they had reached their rooms. She looked at her watch and was amazed to see that it was after midnight. Normally, she was in bed every night by ten with a book and her two cats, Merlin and Griffin. Turning the key in her door, she was even more surprised when Garrett laid a restraining hand on her arm.

"Nightcap?" he asked. "I've got some lovely brandy in my room."

Brandy, Molly thought. Who drinks that? Having a nightcap in America only meant one thing: sex. Molly wondered if it meant the same thing in Britain, too. But when she raised her bent head to tell him she was too tired, his face was suddenly inches from her own. Molly could feel the warmth of his body as he leaned in against her. She felt frozen in place. She was so attracted to this man, but yet, did she really want to kiss him? What about Mark?

With Garrett's lips approaching hers, Molly knew that her indecision was about to lead to a kiss, and she resigned herself to being swept away by the moment. However, her lips remained untouched as another one of the guest room doors creaked open and Garrett immediately leapt back to a respectable distance.

Borris stepped out of his room still wearing his suit jacket. He and Jessica must have returned just minutes before Molly and Garrett. Looking at them in concern he said, "Listen, I've got Victoria on the phone. Frank never returned to their room. You didn't see him on your way home or anything did you?"

"No," Garrett answered while Molly tried to discern the gravity of the situation.

"Has he ever stayed out all night before?" she asked nosily, thinking about what Jessica had told her about Frank and Victoria having different bedrooms at home.

"No," Borris answered. "Well, I'll tell her we have no news. He may have gone back into the museum for some reason."

"Could he have gotten locked in?" Garrett asked.

Borris looked thoughtful. "Don't think so. All the night guards would identify him by his *Hidden Treasures* badge. He could get in or out if he really needed to. Well, let me get back to Victoria. Good night."

"Good night," said Molly to both men, rushing into the safety of her room. Adrenaline was surging through her veins as she pictured Garrett's face moving closer and closer to her own. Garrett had almost kissed her and she had wanted him to!

Molly averted her own eyes as she stood before the bathroom mirror brushing her teeth. She wondered whether Frank could truly be missing. He had looked absolutely awful as the group left for dinner. Maybe he really was sick. Maybe he drove himself to the hospital instead of going back to the hotel.

Molly wondered briefly if she should suggest this possibility to Borris, but felt too ridiculous to go through with calling his room. After all, Borris knew Frank much better than she did. Frank would probably be in the exhibit area in the morning as usual, blowing his nose and barking at Randy and Chris. Sliding under the rosewater-scented covers, Molly was sure Frank was absolutely fine.

She couldn't have been more mistaken.

Chapter 4

*When a tree is cut down its life support system comes to a halt.
Even the parenchyma sapwood cells gradually die as the wood is
dried. In no sense can wood be said to breathe after it is dead.*

—*The Art of Making Furniture*

The next morning was an exciting one. Molly arrived at the museum happily satiated by a three-cheese omelet, crisp bacon, and two slices of raisin toast homemade by Mrs. Hewell. She was amazed to see the throng of people lined up for the opening of *Hidden Treasures*. The show had pre-sold over three thousand tickets, with one thousand people arriving per day. Those lucky few possessing rare or extremely valuable objects would be invited back for further filming on Saturday morning.

After that, it would take the road crew another two days to dissemble the show and pack the hundreds of tables and chairs, lighting fixtures, booth structures, and the show's signage into an eighteen-wheeler before heading to the next city. Jessica had previously mentioned to Molly that the appraisers were looking forward to a week off before opening the next show in D.C. After working in Tampa, Charlotte, and Atlanta with no break, everyone was ready to go home, however briefly. For Jessica, home was Charlotte, North

Carolina. Borris lived in Wrightsville Beach and Tony was from Baltimore. *Hidden Treasures* made its headquarters in Washington D.C. and most of the appraisers lived south of the Mason-Dixon line. Victoria and Frank had remained closest to D.C., living in Alexandria, where Frank's successful antique store thrived on tourists visiting the charming waterfront.

"I could have worked for Southeby's, but there's no good sweet tea in New York," he had stated the other night at Casa 'Rita. Most southerners would agree with Frank that strong sweet tea was an important part of any southerner's diet.

Molly longed to see what items the public had chosen to bring for appraisal and wanted to slowly walk along the line of ticket-holders, but Garrett hustled her forward. Once inside, they flashed their ID badges to the security guards and, after being eyed curiously by those waiting in the front of the line to be called by an appraiser, headed for the Great Hall. Before they could reach the Civil War exhibit, Victoria intercepted them with a frantic wave. She quickly spoke to a group of cameramen and then approached Molly and Garrett in long, rapid strides. Victoria's face looked drawn and haggard. Even a careful application of makeup didn't disguise the bluish, swollen bags beneath her eyes.

"Frank never came back last night!" she exclaimed with an uncharacteristic display of emotion. "We can't spare any of the other appraisers looking for him." She tapped her watch face. "The show starts in five minutes! Can you two help?"

"Of course," Garrett assured her in soothing tones. "But where do we start?" he lowered his voice. "Did he ever return to the hotel last night?"

"No." Victoria eyed the front door nervously. *Hidden Treasures* crew members wearing black T-shirts were lining up in order to show the public which queue to go into upon entering the museum. "I even checked with the front desk. No one saw him. And you know Frank, with all his sniffing and coughing, he's . . . well, hard to ignore."

"Where's his car?" Molly asked. "We dropped you off

last night, so he had the car, right? Was it in the hotel parking lot?"

A spark ignited in Victoria's eyes. "No! At least I didn't see it. I last saw him when all of you did. He could be anywhere!"

"Well, when we all last saw Frank he was heading for the car," Molly said calmly, though inside she was growing excited about the possibility of finding the missing appraiser and winning the undying admiration of all the other appraisers. She conjured up a rosy fantasy of them toasting her around a dinner table while Garrett beamed at her adoringly. Taking a firm hold of Garrett's arm, she announced, "We'll check the parking garage first and go from there."

At that moment, the front doors were unlocked and people carrying a myriad of different objects began flooding into the entrance hall. "I've got to get going." Victoria turned away. "Thank you," she shouted over her shoulder as she hustled off.

Garrett turned to Molly. "Sherlock? Shall we?"

"Carry on, Watson," Molly replied, then flushed guiltily for she remembered having called Mark "her Watson" just a few months ago when she had tried to unravel the mysterious death of a pottery collector. Following Garrett out of the entrance past a middle-aged woman holding a large Delft platter, a young man carrying a tiny Tunbridge box, and a pair of white-bearded twins each bearing a lamp with Tiffany poinsettia shades, Molly's heart began to race at the sight of hundreds of intriguing objects flowing into one building.

Itching to take photographs and stick her nose among the queue lines, Molly was torn between looking for treasure and searching for Frank. After a moment's hesitation, in which the pull of the objects almost turned her from her task, Molly squared her shoulders resolutely and quickened her pace toward the garage. She tried to remember if the boatlike sedan she had seen Frank drive was dark blue or black. Unfortunately, the garage was packed with cars.

Not a single spot was empty. Even the handicapped spaces were all taken.

"Why don't you take the top floor and I'll start on the bottom," Molly suggested. "We can meet somewhere in the middle."

"A woman who takes charge. Very sexy." Garrett smiled roguishly and headed for the elevator.

Molly walked slowly up the first row of cars, marveling at the number of minivans and SUVs squashed in the narrow parking spaces like bloated cows stuffed into corrals meant for sheep. Of course, it was impossible to be a collector without owning some kind of vehicle with what Molly's mother called "schlepping ability." Because the cars were so tall, Molly couldn't see over to the next row, so she had to walk up and down every aisle.

Finally, she headed for the next floor. On this deck, half of the cars were under cover and half were exposed to the elements. She decided to begin with the row of cars baking beneath the powerful September sun and get it over with. Frank's dark blue rental car occupied the last spot of the long row. Molly hastened over to the driver's side and stopped dead in her tracks.

Frank was inside. Hunched over the steering wheel, his face was completely hidden. Molly rapped timidly on the window, afraid of startling Frank awake. She was close enough to see the dandruff flakes clinging to the few thin strands spread over his pasty scalp. Molly began to sweat. Why didn't Frank move? Was he drunk? Had he passed out from the heat? She knocked again, harder this time.

"Frank!" she called, wiping sweat off her brow. Then, she noticed his hands.

Clutching the base of the steering wheel, Frank's two hands were bloated to twice their normal size. Their color was completely alien in appearance. No traces of pink skin or thin rivers of blue veins created contrast on those colorless canvases. They were stark, pale white, like two large hunks of Havarti cheese.

"Did you find him?" Garrett yelled from three rows away, startling Molly.

Molly turned and stared at Garrett blankly, her mind not registering that someone was calling to her. She turned back to Frank's hands, unable to take her eyes away from them, unable to digest their grotesque shape and color.

"Molly!" Garrett began sprinting towards her.

The heat surged through Molly's clothes and robbed her lungs of air. She sagged against the side of Frank's car and stared up into the cloudless sky.

Garrett gave her a little shake and she could hear him speaking as if from far away, but none of the words made any sense.

"He's dead," Molly muttered to the heavy air, and then she fainted.

Chapter 5

All day long the machine waits: rooms,
stairs, carpets, furniture, people
those people who stand at the open windows like objects
waiting to topple.

—ANNE SEXTON, "THE HOUSE"

When Molly came to, she heard the sounds of Garrett's voice as if she had sunk underwater in her hotel room's deep claw foot bathtub. She slowly became aware that her head was nestled in Garrett's lap and that she had been moved into the shade. As her senses returned, she could smell the musky scent of Garrett's cologne and feel the rise and fall of his chest as he spoke. Pebbles from the concrete dug into her thighs and her first thoughts were irrationally about the wrinkles that must be forming on her linen pants and whether or not her mouth had been hanging open during her faint as it often did during sleep.

"Hang on a tick, she's coming 'round," Garrett said softly into his cell phone and looked down at her with a concerned smile. "Feeling better?"

Molly tried to sit up, but felt immediately dizzy so she sank gratefully back into Garrett's lap.

"Don't get up just yet," Garrett cautioned. "I'm on hold with the police. You just stay where you are for the moment."

He placed a cool hand on her forehead and gently stroked her damp hair until her entire body relaxed under his touch. "Right, we'll be waiting in the car park," he said confidently into the phone and then stuffed it into his shirt pocket.

"Awful fright," he said tenderly. "That the first corpse you've seen?"

Molly eased herself into a sitting position. Suddenly feeling awkward and shy, she looked around, taking in the fact that they were both seated in an empty parking space just under the cover of the deck. "No, it's actually not the first time I've seen a dead man," Molly answered as she stared fixedly at a chipped nail on her left foot. "At the beginning of the summer I saw a well-known pottery collector collapse at a kiln opening. Turns out he had died on the spot. Later, I discovered his wife's body in their mansion. She had been shot in the chest." Molly shivered, despite the intense humidity. She wanted to change the subject, as she had no desire to rehash those dramatic events with a relative stranger.

"You don't say . . . ?" Garrett couldn't prevent the curiosity from stealing into his placating tone. "So you've actually seen two dead bodies?"

"I'd rather not go into details if you don't mind. In fact, I'm feeling much better now." She smiled weakly and stood up slowly, dusting off her pants, which were now both dirty and wrinkled. "I think the shock and the heat just got to me. Trust me, I'm not exactly the swooning type."

"No," Garrett agreed as he sprang lightly to his feet, "I don't imagine many of you American girls are."

Molly realized they were suddenly acting rather callous considering the body of a celebrity appraiser was baking away in a nearby car. She reasoned that shock had made them both rather mute in regards to the dead man. But the image of Frank's bloated hands was firmly imprinted in Molly's mind. That unnatural shade of white belonged to a lump of unbaked bread dough, not to a human.

"Poor Frank!" she exclaimed as the wail of approaching

sirens burst through the thick and heavy air of the parking garage. "I wonder what happened to him?"

A mournful look appeared in Garrett's eyes. "He wasn't feeling well yesterday, remember? He may have had some kind of heat stroke."

"He must have been in that car all night," Molly reasoned, her eyes glued to the back of Frank's sedan. Her voice sounded much calmer than she felt. "He didn't come with us to dinner and he never made it back to his hotel. Poor man. To die alone like that! It's awful!" Unexpectedly, tears sprung into her eyes.

Suddenly Garrett's arms were around her. "It'll be alright," he soothed her.

Molly felt safe and comforted in his arms, breathing in his earthy scent. Just then, the sirens grew piercingly loud as two police cars and an ambulance drove up the curve of the parking deck and came to a stop in front of the waiting pair.

Garrett immediately took charge. He introduced himself and Molly then led the officers over to the car. Molly followed the group of men, watching in fascination as one of the policemen easily forced a long metal bar inside Frank's window and unlocked the driver's side door. A putrid smell like rotten cheese mixed with sun-baked garbage immediately burst from within the car, and Molly quickly covered her nose with the sleeve of her blouse. Garrett pulled a handkerchief from his pants, clapped it on his nose and backed away. Curiosity quickly overcame repulsion, however, and Molly found herself moving closer to the car in order to watch the police at work.

A tall man wearing a navy T-shirt with the words CORONER printed on the back bent over Frank's body. He tried to ease Frank's head back off the steering wheel, but rigor mortis was making the task difficult. Finally, with the help of a burly-looking policeman with a shock of red hair, the two men managed to extract Frank's hunched body out of the car and onto a gurney. Molly was thankful Frank's eyes were shut. It was bad enough to stare at his impossibly white and waxen face without having his sightless eyes staring back at her.

"Was it heat stroke?" she asked the man wearing the coroner T-shirt.

He eyed her carefully before answering. "Are you his wife?"

"No . . . um, I was working with him," Molly stammered, suddenly thinking that Victoria was inside greeting the public with no idea that her husband's corpse had just been loaded into an ambulance.

"Well, we'll need to do a complete examination before we can state the cause of death," the man explained hastily as he shut the rear doors to the ambulance. Matters were obviously in the hands of the police from here on out.

The robust redhead took a second peek inside Frank's car and then approached Molly and Garrett. He introduced himself as Officer Combs and led them away from the car back into the shade. After shaking both their hands with a crushing grip, he politely thanked Garrett for calling and then flipped opened a small black notebook and began scribbling in what looked to be indecipherable shorthand. Finally, he looked up and asked them to explain how they had discovered the body.

Molly gave her statement first, describing how Victoria had asked them to search for her husband, who had not returned to the hotel the night before. She also gave Officer Combs the details of Frank's illness the day before. Blushing with embarrassment, she mumbled through her account of seeing Frank's bloated hands, feeling the oppressive heat of the sun, and finally, of having fainted. Garrett grabbed Molly's hand and quickly concluded the narrative. He relayed how he saw Molly crumple to the ground so he carried her into the shade and used his cell phone to call 911.

"I tried the door on Frank's car before I called," Garrett added. "I didn't think he was alive, but I gave it a go anyway."

"So his wife, Victoria Sterling, is inside the science

museum right now?" Officer Combs asked. "Will you take me to her?"

"Certainly." Garrett nodded. "I think it would be better if I fetched her and brought her into one of the staff offices so she can hear the news in private."

"Of course," Combs agreed pleasantly, then turned to his men. "Finish going over the car and I'll be right back."

Molly watched the other officers as they began to examine the interior of the car.

"You *do* think it was an accident, right?" she asked Officer Combs.

He glanced at her briefly, his hazel eyes intelligent and calculating. "Sure, but we're just covering the bases. We always examine the scene around every cor— . . . um . . . person who has passed away."

"Do you think whatever killed him happened quickly?" Molly asked as they headed for the museum.

"What makes you ask that?" Combs asked as one eyebrow rose in a tawny arc.

Molly glanced at him in surprise. "Because he didn't even have the energy to take his hands off the steering wheel!"

The noise inside the museum was deafening. Hundreds of excited collectors talked to their neighbors in line as they clutched plastic bags or carefully balanced a treasure-laden cardboard box in their arms. Walking past them, Molly's eye spotted bright flashes of hooked rugs, brass lamps, shimmering crystal, and the warm glow of pottery as she and Garrett led Officer Combs deeper into the museum where the head appraiser's niches were.

"I'm going to need names and permanent addresses for the whole crew," Officer Combs said to Garrett as they arrived at one of the museum's staff offices which had been emptied for the use of *Hidden Treasures*.

"I'd better fetch Guy. He's the producer." Garrett turned to Molly. "You'll have to bring Victoria here. She'll be filming now, so think of something to get her away without alarming her in front of the others."

"What should I say?" Molly asked, panicking. How could she be expected to make up some silly excuse to pull Victoria off filming when the woman's husband was dead?

"You'll think of something," Garrett said kindly and rushed off. Combs was no help either. He simply shrugged and disappeared into the office to wait.

"Lord," Molly mumbled as she headed down the lane of screened booths. She found Victoria filming an introduction for Patrice. A round woman in her fifties whose proud face beamed into the camera sat next to Patrice behind a small, velvet-covered card table. Their attention was fixed upon a jade green Lalique vase with two macaw heads jutting out of each side.

Victoria introduced the owner as Mrs. Claudia Zimmerman and then gestured gracefully toward the iridescent object on the table. The camera moved away from her face and focused in on the vase.

"Zis is a rare vase," Patrice intoned nasally in his fake but convincing French accent. "See zee beautiful plumage, non? Only ninety-nine pieces were made in each color. Zis vase is a limited edition and is in *absolutely* perfect condition." He turned to the beaming owner. "What do you sink zis is worth?"

"Oh." The woman's eyelashes fluttered for the camera. "I have no earthly idea."

"Zee current market is verry, verry good for zis piece right now. And I see you have zee original box. Bien. What do you think of this vase being worth, oh . . . say . . . how about a leettle guess?"

"Two thousand dollars?" The woman flushed.

Patrice puffed out his bony chest and stroked his elfin chin thoughtfully. "No!" he shouted dramatically as the woman jumped in her seat. "How about eleven thousand dollars?"

"Oh, my stars!" the woman cooed, hugging Patrice as if he had just saved her life. The camera turned its eye back to Victoria who promised another fabulous find awaiting the viewers after the following commercial messages.

Molly touched Victoria on the sleeve as the cameramen headed farther up the aisle. "Excuse me, Victoria. Can I speak to you for a moment?"

"Did you find Frank?" Victoria's face showed genuine concern.

Molly began to walk up the aisle away from Patrice's booth. "Um . . . can you come with me to the staff office for a second? Garrett needs to see you."

Victoria followed her into the next booth and then stopped. She stared intently at Molly. "You *did* find him. What's wrong?"

"He's . . ." Molly quickly looked away, her cheeks growing warm with discomfort. What could she say? "Please, just come with me and you'll hear everything."

Victoria refused to budge. "He's dead, isn't he?" she asked in a whisper. "I can see it in your face."

To her frustration, Molly's eyes grew watery with tears. "I'm sorry."

Outwardly, Victoria remained composed. Only her eyes betrayed that she was trying to digest the news that her husband was dead. "How?" she finally asked in a very soft voice.

Molly took her arm and began to steer her toward the office. "I really don't know. There's a policeman in here who will explain everything to you." Molly opened the office door and Combs jumped to his feet.

Molly turned to Victoria. "Can I get you anything?"

Victoria shook her head and Molly closed the door quietly.

Wandering toward the cafeteria, Molly decided she would have a long coffee break and collect herself before interviewing members of the public. The cafeteria was crowded and noisy and Molly found herself desperately in need of some quiet, so she took her coffee to a bench outside the museum entrance where she watched the line of anxious collectors shuffle forward in agonizing slowness. After taking a few sips of creamy coffee and a healthy bite of a chocolate almond bear claw, Molly felt herself beginning to relax.

Just as she was brushing crumbs from her lap, Garrett walked out of the front door and joined her on the bench.

"How are you feeling?" he asked.

"Better. How is Victoria?"

"Fair. She feels guilty about not phoning the police last night, but she didn't suspect anything was *that* wrong." Garrett's eyes rested on the throng of people baking beneath the late morning sun. "It's no secret theirs was no love match. But they had a comfortable if somewhat unconventional partnership and I think she's a bit overwhelmed thinking about life without him."

Molly stood and dropped her coffee cup in the trash bin, callously thinking that Victoria would probably marry again as soon as possible. Women like her needed a man in order to define themselves. "What will happen with the show?"

"Oh, the show *will* go on. Guy and Victoria decided not to inform the crew until the show's ended for today. Victoria's gone with Officer Combs to make a statement, but she says she'll be fine to carry on as host for the rest of the show. Bet she can do it, too; the old girl's tough," Garrett said with sudden admiration. "What will you do with the rest of your day?"

"Interview some of the dedicated crowd," Molly replied. "Then I meet my friend Lex, the auctioneer, and my mother over at the townhouse—" Molly abruptly stopped. "Do you think I should still go ahead with the auction arrangements?"

"Absolutely." Garrett nodded. "Victoria won't want any of that stuff. She'd rather have the cash, I'm sure."

Molly couldn't help prying further. "Did Officer Combs say when the authorities would know the cause of death?"

Garrett looked at her closely. "By tonight or tomorrow morning. Why?"

"Just wondering," Molly said as a memory flooded her mind. She excused herself and quickly made her way over to Frank's booth. Frank had been healthy until he had examined that desk. Not long after that he had become congested, weak, and pale. What if that material they had found on the desk was to blame? It wouldn't affect her because Molly had no allergies. She could roll in a field of ragweed, cat dander, and dust and remain impervious to all of the above, but Frank was ultra-sensitive to allergens.

Pulling aside one of the white screens, Molly gazed at the slant-front desk as it sat in the dark, its warm colors dulled by shadow and its pigeonholes gaping like black teeth from inside its empty room. She pulled a small flashlight from her bag and aimed the beam into the pigeonholes. There were no traces of the black powdery material both she and Frank had touched the day before. Even the piece of false drawer front had been completely cleaned. The desk smelled strongly of fresh furniture wax.

Molly switched off her flashlight and backed nervously out of the booth, making sure that no one was watching her leave. She proceeded with her interviews with only a portion of her consciousness. Normally, her full attention would have been devoted to a pencil drawing signed by Picasso or a walking stick carved with skulls that held a hidden, but fully functional, miniature pistol within its wooden handle. Jotting down names and captions for her photographs, Molly kept seeing an image of the black powder smeared on Frank's face. As she walked over to Strawberry Street to meet Lex and Clara at the townhouse, her mind focused on one thought that buzzed inside her head like a fly caught between the window screen and the glass.

The black powder was purposely put there, then just as intentionally removed, the thought buzzed. That newly polished desk carried all the feeling of destroyed evidence. It had been polished before Frank and Molly examined it, so why polish it again? There was only one explanation. The person who cleaned it needed to leave no trace of black powder behind.

And that person was a murderer.

FREDERICKSBURG, VIRGINIA 1778

"We've got the French! We've got the French!" Thomas's young apprentice, William screamed. "It's all over town. They're our allies now!"

"That is fortunate indeed," answered a mellifluous voice from Thomas's doorway.

A tall young woman with blond hair and intelligent blue eyes stepped into the shop. A maid trailed behind her, giggling nervously.

Thomas recognized the pretty young woman immediately. "Miss Tarling." Thomas bowed low and hid his stained hands behind his back. "I remember you. I saw you in your father's carriage outside Samuel Chauncey's shop in Williamsburg."

"I remember that well." The blue eyes flashed coquettishly and Thomas felt his neck grow warm. "I am here on an errand from my father. He wishes to commission a new dining table and chairs. He does a great deal of entertaining and our current table has proved insufficient in size as *our house in Williamsburg was much smaller. Will you come out and measure the room?"*

"Certainly. Right now if you should desire it, miss."

Miss Tarling issued a grateful curtsy and waited for Thomas outside. They walked several blocks in comfortable silence before the young lady glanced sideways at Thomas and began to speak. *"My name is Elizabeth, but most people call me Elspeth. I don't know anyone here. We only just arrived last week. My father says that the Rappahannock River will make trading easier and allow him to get"*—she lowered her voice to a conspiring whisper—*"essential messages to our commanders in the north."*

Thomas almost tripped in surprise. Perhaps old Samuel Chauncey had been right. Men could fight the war for freedom in different ways. Luckily, his lack of grace went unnoticed by Elspeth. She paused before the wrought iron gate surrounding a large brick house and waited while Thomas swung it open for her.

Inside the front hallway Thomas admired the scrolled carving on the stairway banisters and marveled at the size of the dining room. It would take a large table indeed to fill such a long room. Thomas caught Elspeth watching him in one of the room's enormous gilt mirrors.

"I made your father's desk," he stammered, uncomfortable before her frank gaze. "I hope he has found it satisfactory."

"Truly." Her face lit up with interest and a trace of mischief. "Well then, let me show you how it has fared."

Elspeth led Thomas to a masculine room filled with books and maps. His eyes fell on the slant-front desk and he longed to open the lid and see how Captain Tarling had filled the drawers and pigeonholes Thomas had so meticulously crafted. The dark walnut glowed warmly in the afternoon sun and Thomas was pleased to see how dignified his piece looked among the captain's objects collected by means of his wealth and trade connections.

"So I guess you know all about the secret panels, since you built them."

Thomas met Elspeth's gaze for the first time. "Yes, miss. I know where they are." And then he boldly asked, "Do you?"

Elspeth pulled out the two slide supports located on the sides of the top drawer and placed the lid gently upon the supports. This created the writing surface of the desk and revealed the pigeonholes. Ignoring the documents neatly arranged in the pigeonholes, Elspeth quickly showed her knowledge of the secret compartments within. "They're always empty though. What good is such wonderful craftsmanship if you have nothing to put inside? No love letters, no treasured photographs, no details of where the redcoats will attack next . . ." She laughed lightly. "Though I guess with my mother gone, my father's life is all business."

Elspeth suddenly looked so forlorn that Thomas longed to make her smile again. Against his better judgment he whispered, "You've missed one. There is another hiding place."

"Where?" she asked breathlessly. "Please do show me. My father is in Washington, so we need not fear his wrath." She drew herself up proudly but with a trace of self-mockery. "I am mistress of the manor today."

Thomas hesitated, but the pleading blue eyes of his hostess broke down his resistance and he gingerly closed the lid and began to pull out the slide support on which the writing surface rested upon.

"Behind there?" Elspeth peered into the narrow opening.

Thomas shook his head with a smile. "The secret is in this piece of wood." He pulled at the hidden end of the support and a piece of wood measuring a mere four inches came off in his hand.

"But no one could have known that was there. There are no marks, no lines!" Elspeth exclaimed. "I see a tiny grove now, but you made it along the grain so it is impossible to see." Elspeth took the piece of wood from his hand. "Look! There's a piece of paper hidden within!"

For some unknown reason, Thomas felt a wave of dread pass over him as Elspeth unfolded the paper. Minute handwriting covered the page and as Elspeth read, her face grew alarmingly pale and her breathing slowed almost to a standstill.

"Miss? Are you ill?" Thomas looked around for the maid.

Before he could move to aid her, Elspeth crumbled onto the ground, the paper clutched in her hand.

Beads of sweat lined her ashen forehead and wisps of honey-colored hair clung to the dampness. "Miss? Shall I get help?" Thomas asked pleadingly.

"Help?" Elspeth whispered. "Only God can help me now. My father is a traitor!" She thrust the paper towards Thomas. "A traitor!"

"I cannot read," Thomas answered softly, ashamed.

"I shall tell you who has written it then," Elspeth hissed vehemently. "These are orders from His Majesty's Humble Servant, General Henry Clinton."

"Clinton!" Thomas exclaimed. "Word tells that he plans to march on Philadelphia. He is a great enemy to our cause!"

"Yes, he is a great enemy." Elspeth held the letter aloft and her blue eyes blazed with the anger of betrayal. "But at least we knew him as such, unlike my father, who has pretended to help us when all this time . . ." She trailed off, her overwhelming emotions prohibiting her from speech.

Thomas leaned on the desk, remembering the day he had applied the final coat of polish to the smooth and sculpted wood. How proud he had been when it had been loaded onto Captain Tarling's coach and several townsfolk had stopped to admire its dignified beauty. It had been betrayed as well. It was Virginian black walnut and pine, the nails made from the local blacksmith, glue from animals living in the forest. Every piece of it, from its case to its drawer pulls, was made in The Colonies. The desk's very lines marked it as an American; there were no flourishes or ornate feet as with pieces from The Continent. It should have graced the home of an honorable, industrious gentleman. Instead it had become the property of a dangerous and loathsome man who placed the direst of secrets within its innocent nooks.

Chapter 6

*But the trouble with pine is twofold. First, it doesn't have the
strength to stand up under use in thin members in chairs. Second,
the wood is so soft that it is easily dented.*

—George Grotz, *The Furniture Doctor*

Clara stepped down from Lex's cargo van with a
deep scowl. She quickly embraced her daughter and
whispered in her ear, "Lex has been on the phone with
Kitty for two of the two and a half hours it took to get here.
I've never heard so many *darlings* or *sweetums* in my life!
I'm going to strangle him!"

Lex and his wife Kitty were known for their outward
displays of affection. Even though they worked together at
their auction company and therefore spent every waking
moment with one another, the second one of them was out
of range for more than an hour, a phone call would have to
be placed in order to touch base.

Molly and Kitty had once taught together at the same
private school. One day, Molly had invited Kitty to work at
one of Lex's weekend auctions. It was love at first sight between Lex and Kitty and they were married a year later.
Kitty quit her job as the school's art teacher to help manage her husband's auction company, alongside Clara. Clara

had once owned her own antiques shop, but the burden of holding regular store hours combined with the hassle of dealing with unreasonable customers forced her to close her doors. When Lex approached her to join his staff as floor manager, she leaped at the opportunity.

As Lex dug around inside the van for his briefcase, Molly shook her head in mock sympathy and asked softly, "What do they talk about?"

"Nothing!" Clara rolled her gray eyes and put her hands onto her crown of short and thick brown hair. As she was several inches taller than her daughter she had to lean forward to ask rhetorically, "How many times can you ask someone 'How are you, dear?' or 'Do you miss me?' when you've just seen them?"

"They're just in love, Ma," Molly said as she tried to ignore the typical stab of jealously she experienced whenever she thought about the couple's happy marriage. "That's how people in love act."

"Love!" Clara snorted. "Love is a twenty-pound apricot tabby named Tiny Purr who will sit on your lap all night while you watch the Discovery Channel and make biscuits on you in the morning when it's time to get up or . . ." She trailed off as Lex came around to their side of the van and looked at Molly expectantly.

"Hey, Moll. Got the keys?"

"Right here," Molly said, handing over the key ring.

As soon as the trio entered the house, Lex sprinted ahead to turn on lights and open blinds. Molly followed closely on her mother's heels as Clara inspected the contents of the downstairs rooms.

"Not bad," Clara said as she examined the collection of Staffordshire in the office. "I just love a pair of Staffordshire poodles, don't you?"

"Ma, I need to talk to you," Molly began.

"In a minute, cupcake." Clara replaced the poodle on its shelf and headed upstairs. "You know I can't concentrate on anything when there's a house waiting to be rooted through." Lex was busy in one of the front rooms examining an oil on canvas of two women in Victorian gowns gazing at a caged canary.

Once upstairs, Molly followed her mother around one of the guest bedrooms and practically fell on top of her when Clara stopped abruptly to examine a piece of carnival glass from the 1936 World's Fair held in Cleveland. Irritated, Clara swung around and squawked at Molly. "Stop hovering! You're acting like a man in the mall! What is with you?"

Feeling admonished, Molly took a step back and whispered, "I'm just impatient to talk to you. You see, there's been a murder. One of the appraisers . . ."

Clara's eyes flew open wide. "What? Oh! I hope it was that intensely annoying, overly pompous Frenchman who drools over the *worst* pieces of porcelain."

"It wasn't him." Molly put her finger to her lips in an effort to keep her mother's voice down. "And he's not really French. It was Frank, the furniture appraiser."

"No!" Clara was shocked. "He had such wonderful taste! Think of all those pieces of southern furniture he highlighted. The man did wonders for the furniture of our region. Oh that *is* a shame."

"Ma." Molly was exasperated. "Never mind his loyalty for southern furniture. Did you not hear the part where I mentioned *murder*? And *I* found his body?"

Clara's interest now seemed divided between examining the last room left in the house and listening to the details of her daughter's story. Hesitating, she was finally drawn by the mysteries awaiting her in the master bedroom where she went straight for the display case of dolls.

"Wait until I finish this room," she told her fidgety daughter, "then we'll go back to your hotel and you can tell me everything over a cocktail." Clara wrinkled her nose. "This house smells worse than most."

"Fine." Molly sighed in resignation, knowing her mother was immoveable when faced with a house loaded with collectibles. She found herself gravitating toward the biology experiment growing in the master bathroom.

As she pushed open the bathroom door, she stared in renewed horror at the extent of mold growth on the walls and tub. For the first time she looked down at the pink carpet and saw that black splotches of mold surrounded the base of the tub and gave the appearance that the carpet had been burned. The smell that hung about the house was only a hint of the powerful, musty odor within the bathroom. It was so strong that it distracted Clara as she peered beneath the petticoat of a bisque doll in search of the name of its maker.

"Good Lord, what *is* that stench?" she asked, putting the doll gently back into its stand. Her lip curled in disgust as she came to stand beside Molly. "That is one *serious* mold problem."

"I think it's more than a problem, Ma," Molly said, looking down at the black dust on her fingertips where she had touched the bathroom door. "I think it's the murder weapon."

Molly had asked Mrs. Hewell if she and Clara could take their tea upstairs in her room. The cheerful proprietress had agreed and arrived moments later with a tray laden with tea service and a plate of fresh lemon squares. Molly was vigorously scrubbing her hands with soap and scalding water for the second time when she came bustling in.

"What a lovely establishment!" Clara praised Mrs. Hewell as she gazed appreciatively at the Limoge tea set. "Are all of your rooms occupied?"

"Not anymore, dear. The couple who booked the Majolica suite had to cancel, poor things. The young wife got her heel caught in a sidewalk grate and twisted her knee. They won't be rafting on the James this week, that's for sure."

"That's why *I* only wear sensible shoes," Clara said smugly. "Could I have that suite then?" She turned to Molly and whispered out of the side of her mouth. "After all, *Lex* is paying."

"Of course you can, dear." Mrs. Hewell's smile grew even more magnanimous. "Enjoy your tea and I'll give you the key when I come to fetch the tray."

Clara picked up a lemon square and took a bite. Powdered sugar drifted like snow onto her navy T-shirt. "Delightful woman," she said, brushing off her shirt. "I thought I'd stay here while we pack up Mrs. Sterling's house. Lex can stay at one of those chain hotels, but I need a good breakfast in the morning and I have a feeling I won't be disappointed here."

"Is Lex still taking inventory over at Mrs. Sterling's?" Molly asked.

"Yep, but he's almost done. We have a clear enough picture to draw up a simple contract. I hope you're right about Victoria being willing to go through with the auction."

"I'm positive she'll want to sell everything." Molly poured two cups of steaming tea. Setting her cup on a side table, she sank into an overstuffed chair with a lemon square in hand.

"Now, tell me what's going on," Clara said as she sipped her tea.

Molly polished off a lemon square in record time and loaded a second onto her plate. "Do you remember the day we went to the Valley of the Kings?"

Clara's eyes lit up. "Do I? Our whole trip was like a dream! The cruise up the Nile, the pyramids, our gorgeous guide . . ."

"Focus, Ma. Do you remember what our gorgeous guide told us was probably the real cause of Lord Carnarvon's death?"

"Instead of the mummy's curse? Let me think." Clara stared at her teacup, wishing she could instantly transform it into a Waterford tumbler containing a nice cocktail as she recalled their visit into Tutankhamen's tomb. "Are you referring to the theory that the fungus trapped within the tomb caused the death of Carnarvon and possibly others as well?"

"Yes! And I think that black mold we saw at Frank's mother's house might have caused *his* death. You see, it was deliberately put on a piece of furniture where he was sure to come in contact with it." Molly explained Frank's allergic sensitivities and how he had displayed flulike symptoms the last time she had seen him alive. She went on to describe how she and Garrett had found Frank's body. Then Molly told her mother how she had retuned to reexamine the slant-front desk, only to find that the mold had been completely cleaned off, destroying all evidence of foul play.

"So you're the only one who believes there's been a murder?" Clara asked coyly. "I must say, I'm much more interested in this Garrett fellow you've mentioned. Visiting from London? Knowledgeable about antiques? But the real question is"—Clara leaned forward with a mischievous gleam in her eye—"whether or not he's single."

Molly rolled her eyes toward the ceiling. Her mother was relentless in her pursuit of a suitable husband for her only daughter. "No sign of foul play will surface until the autopsy is complete. As far as Garrett goes—" Molly's decision to praise her new friend was cut short by a burst of staccato knocking on her hotel room door. She opened it wide.

"Thank goodness you're back!" Garrett said breathlessly and nearly tripped into the room. "You won't believe . . . oh!" He stopped as he spotted Clara sitting regally in one of the room's wing chairs. "Forgive me, I'm interrupting."

"Nonsense." Clara beckoned toward the chair Molly had occupied. "Join us for tea. I'm Clara Appleby, Molly's mother."

"Charmed," Garrett boldly kissed Clara on the cheek. "You two could surely be mistaken for sisters."

Clara glowed. Molly sighed in annoyance. She often heard that statement from men trying to get on Clara's good side. "What's going on?" she demanded of Garrett.

He turned his honey-brown eyes toward her and instantly, his face became grave. "Victoria's been picked up for questioning. The police are holding her as the primary suspect in Frank's murder case. It's absurd, of course," he explained to Clara. "This woman is no killer. However, I'm afraid we've all been summoned to the station in order to give statements. That includes you as well, Molly. I came to offer you a ride. It's bound to be an unpleasant experience, so I thought we might at least muddle through it together."

Garrett threw another winning smile at Clara who clucked in sympathy, and then loaded Garrett's plate with the two remaining lemon squares. "How awful!" Clara exclaimed. "What on earth will you two do for dinner?"

"I, for one, plan to take both of you lovely ladies out for dinner. Just as soon as we're done we'll come pick you up. Until then . . ." Garrett bowed.

Molly rolled her eyes again. Garrett was going a bit over the top, though her mother didn't seem to mind.

"Let's get this over with," she mumbled ungraciously and headed out of her room without waiting to see whether Garrett was behind her or not.

Detective Robeson was, without a doubt, a giant of a man. His six-foot-five frame was made up of 260 pounds of bulky muscle and dense bone covered by espresso-colored skin dressed in a tight black T-shirt tucked into gray pants. Molly couldn't tear her eyes away from his massive biceps. This man could crush another man's head by simply raising his wrist to his shoulder.

When he spoke, his voice carried a surprisingly gentle and very deep bass to her ears. "Now, Miss Appleby. Let's start with your arrival at the museum and go from there."

As Molly gave her statement, she felt herself growing excited about being given the opportunity to provide an invaluable clue toward solving the murder case. She had deliberately avoided telling Garrett anything about the mold.

If anyone was going to get credit for assisting the police, she wanted it to be her. Just think of the article she could write for *Collector's Weekly* with herself as the heroine!

"So what makes you think this mold on the desk was the same as the mold in the bathroom?" The deep voice broke her reverie.

"It had that black, powdery look and that same, musty odor."

"And there were no traces on the desk when you returned to examine it?" Robeson leaned his massive frame an inch closer to hers.

Molly wasn't sure, but she felt as though her starring role in solving the crime was not taking the direction she had planned. "No . . . sir."

He leaned in another inch, his wide nose flaring slightly and his dark eyes boring into hers. "And you didn't mention the sudden disappearance of the mold to Officer Combs at the time?"

"Well, I didn't know it was mold then, and . . . well, I had to go meet my mother. Once I was back inside Mrs. Sterling's house, I recognized the smell first, and then, when I went into the master bathroom, I saw it again. That's when I realized what the black powder really was."

Robeson raised his thick pointer finger in the air. One of the officers taking notes in the corner of the room immediately put down his pen and jumped to attention.

"Clarkson," Robeson said without looking away from Molly. "Get a team over to Strawberry Street. Pick up that desk on your way there. If there's a trace of mold on that desk, I want it found."

"Right away." Clarkson scurried from the room.

Orders given, Robeson settled his wide shoulders against the back of his chair and examined the lines on his palm for what seemed like an eternity.

"Um . . . do you mind me asking the cause of death?" Molly mumbled quietly.

Robeson flicked his eyes at her and then began studying

his short, clean fingernails. He seemed to be weighing whether or not he planned to answer the question. Finally, after inspecting each nail, he sighed and said, "He basically had a severe asthma attack that triggered both a massive heart attack and stroke at the same time. In short, the guy couldn't breathe and then his body just shut down. End of story."

"Can mold cause a reaction like that?" Molly asked bravely.

"Sure, if you're really allergic to it," Robeson shrugged. "The question is, did Ms. Sterling know what that mold could do to her husband?"

As Robeson relapsed into his silent mode, Molly pondered his question. Why would Victoria kill Frank? She couldn't think of a single reason. Locking eyes with Robeson, Molly finally responded. "I highly doubt she did, in fact. Look, I know I don't know this group that well, but I can't think of any obvious motive on Victoria's part."

"In these kinds of cases, nine times out of ten, the spouse has done the deed. Either it's money or it's jealousy that spurs them on. Ms. Sterling has no concrete alibi as she was alone in her hotel room and she gets all his money upon his death."

Molly shrugged. "She had his money already. They seemed like a contented, if not exactly *happily* married couple. The other appraisers seemed to think that even though they seemed mismatched, they had an amiable enough relationship going. And I can't imagine Victoria had anything to be jealous of where Frank was concerned."

Robeson slowly stood. "That's what Ms. Sterling said, too. Just so you know, she hasn't been charged with anything . . . yet. That'll be all for now. If you can think of anything else, here's my card." He dismissed her by opening the door to his office. Molly struggled to think of something useful to say, for some poignant question to ask, but she could think of nothing.

"Thanks," she said meekly and tucked the card into her

purse. So much for her dreams of assisting the police. But if Victoria was innocent, and Molly firmly believed that she was, since she was simply too indifferent to be a killer, there was still a murderer out there. That murderer had made one mistake already. He or she had not counted on Molly being with Frank when he searched the slant-front desk for hidden compartments. All she had to do now was subtly pry into the private lives of the other appraisers to see who had something to gain from Frank's death. She also had to find out who had access to the mold growing in the Strawberry Street house's bathroom.

Feeling reassured that her destiny as crime-solving reporter was firmly revived, Molly took Garrett's proffered arm and headed out into the balmy evening.

Chapter 7

Rotten wood cannot be carved.

—CHINESE PROVERB

The phone rang with a shrill determination that
pierced Molly's sleep, but not enough to make her remember that she was in a strange bed-and-breakfast in
Richmond and not curled up in her own bed with her two
cats, Merlin and Griffin, asleep near her feet.

Confused and groggy, Molly expected the phone call to
be from Mark in Ohio. Without opening her eyes, she
croaked out a "hello" and waited for Mark to begin speaking.

"Madam, are you up?" Clara's voice burst into Molly's
ear.

"Ma? What's going on?" Molly fumbled for her watch.

"Look. Lex and I have a lot to do today and we realized
that we can't get started without the wife . . . what's her
name . . . signing off on our contract. I mean, what if we
pack up that house and bring it back to Hillsborough for auction and she suddenly changes her mind or doesn't like our
percentage or—"

"Okay, okay, I get the picture," Molly said huskily. "So we need to visit Victoria at her hotel and get her signature."

"Exactly!" Clara trilled. "Now get up and let me in, I have coffee for you."

"Bless you, I think." Molly hung up the phone and stumbled to the door.

At Victoria's hotel, the desk clerk looked as though she had been deprived of a good night's sleep. Reluctantly, she noted that neither Molly nor her mother carried bags and were therefore not paying guests intending to check in but two women bent on giving her more work to do.

"We'd like to know what room Victoria Sterling is staying in please," Molly asked sweetly.

Happy to be able to deny Molly's request, the clerk shook her head until her wispy bangs shot back and forth across her forehead and issued a thin, false smile. "Oh, we can't provide that kind of information. You may speak to her using our house phone, but I'll have to dial it for you."

"Fine," Clara said curtly. "Dial away."

The clerk gave Clara a dirty look, but punched in the numbers using long purple nails airbrushed with silver flowers. Molly found herself mesmorized by the flash of the woman's fingertips.

"No answer," the clerk informed them triumphantly. "I'm sorry."

Molly dug out Detective Robeson's card and quickly formulated a lie. "I need to see Ms. Sterling this morning. I am assisting this detective with a case and have important interviews at the museum in another hour for which I cannot be late," she added with what she hoped sounded like the authoritative tone of a very busy important person. "Please dial the room until someone answers."

The desk clerk eyed the card carefully, and then seemed

to be sufficiently impressed by Robeson's card and Molly's snappish manner. "Let me just try again."

"Thank you." Molly smiled smugly.

Victoria answered the phone on the first ring and the desk clerk handed the receiver to Molly. Molly quickly explained the nature of her visit.

"Come on down to my room," Victoria said blandly. "No wait, I'll come get you. Give me five minutes to get properly dressed first."

"Sure. We'll grab some coffee in the lobby," Molly said and hung up.

As the two women sat at a square wooden table sipping cups of burnt, lukewarm coffee in the small lobby, Clara dug a multi-grain cereal bar out of her purse and held it out to Molly.

"Hungry?"

"No, thanks." Molly drummed her fingers impatiently on the table. Finally, Victoria appeared looking tired and fragile. Wearing wrinkled slacks and a plain cotton T-shirt, she looked much more vulnerable than usual. Without her designer clothes and makeup, Victoria seemed to have shrunk overnight.

"I'm surprised to get a visit from you," Victoria said as she led them to her room. The double beds were both made and the couple's clothes were hanging neatly in the closet. Two suitcases sat side by side on the floor and the nightstand held a copy of *Antiques* magazine and a romance novel. Victoria gestured for Molly and Clara to sit down on the two side chairs while she sank onto the nearest bed.

"I admire your composure." Clara held out her hand and introduced herself. Victoria listened halfheartedly to Clara's request for a signature, signed the contract without reading a line of it, and then turned her weary, green eyes to Molly.

"I didn't kill my husband, of course. I don't have much time to talk, though. My lawyer drove down yesterday and will be picking me up in a half an hour to go with me to the station. They've got nothing to hold me on except for not having a solid alibi, but they plan to question me all over again today. I'm not looking forward to getting grilled. I'm still in shock over the whole thing."

"I'm glad you'll have your lawyer there," Molly offered by way of comfort. "Of course I didn't think you did it."

"Well, that's nice," Victoria replied dryly, "but in the meantime, someone else will be doing my job until this gets straightened out." She brushed her knotty bangs off her forehead. "I wonder what gave Frank that attack. True, he got on my nerves on a regular basis, but I never wanted him dead."

"The police didn't tell you what killed him?" Molly was surprised. She decided there was no harm in filling Victoria in about the mold.

"But who would do that? I know Frank was annoying with his constant health problems, but I'm the one who lived with his . . . persnickety habits."

"But someone else must have had a reason to hate your husband," Molly pointed out. "Can you think of anyone?"

Victoria shook her head. "If he offended someone that much, I don't know about it. He was extremely fair over the prices of furniture in his shops and he never insulted people who brought him bad pieces of furniture to appraise, even if the pieces were complete fakes. He had too much respect for his role as the Great Educator to be rude to anyone who brought him a piece of furniture to look at." She sighed. "I just don't get it."

"Did anyone else go inside Mrs. Sterling's house except for the group of us that came with you?" Molly asked.

"Not that I know of. Frank told me he gave *you* the keys."

Molly started. "That's right! Well, that narrows the group down to Jessica, Borris, Alicia, and Garrett. Besides myself, they were the only ones who knew about the mold."

Victoria waved her hand in dismissal. "No motive there. That group gets along with everyone."

At that moment there was a knock on the door. "Mrs. Sterling?" a deep voice called. "Are you in there?"

"That's my lawyer." Victoria stood up. "Come in!" she

called and the door was opened by a portly man wearing an expensive-looking business suit. "One moment, Mr. Fielding." Victoria told the lawyer before turning back to Molly. "I'll see you at the group dinner tonight. I sure could use a good meal," she added with an attempt at brevity, but Molly thought her eyes looked heavy with worry. Molly said goodbye to Victoria, exited the room with Clara, and closed the door. In the lobby, she linked arms with her mother.

"I'll drop you off at Mrs. Sterling's house. I've got a lot to do today at the museum. I've got to photograph antiques, get a few more interviews, and somehow find out who had it in for Frank."

"And tomorrow is the last day of the show, right?" Clara asked.

"That's right. I'm running out of time!"

"Just be careful," Clara warned. "Maybe you should take that handsome Garrett along when you start doing your snooping."

"But he was in the house," Molly said as she got in her car. "He could be a suspect."

"So no one mentioned the mold afterwards?" Clara asked.

"Oh!" Molly slapped her forehead with her palm. "It *was* mentioned. In the cafeteria, in fact. Everyone was listening to *me* talk about how nasty the bathroom was. I went on and on about how it had taken over the entire room. Half of the cast and crew were sitting right there as I described everything in detail. Oh, now I'll *never* find out who did it!"

"But someone still needed those keys," Clara pointed out. "Did you have them with you the whole time?"

"No. I put my bag in the staff office while I had lunch. I have no valuables in there except for my digital camera and I didn't think anyone would mess with it."

"Well . . ." Clara pulled down the sun visor, checked her reflection in the mirror, and added a coat of rose-colored gloss to her lips. "Try to think who *wasn't* in the lunchroom with you. That person took the keys from your bag, got into the house, and brought the mold back to the museum while you were eating. Think of who was missing."

Molly pulled up in front of Mrs. Sterling's townhouse where Lex was pacing on the front lawn like a dog on a short leash. He was talking animatedly into his cell phone. He wore a vexed look that instantly evaporated when he spied Clara who waved the contract out of the car window like a victory flag.

"Thanks, Ma," Molly said, patting her mother's free hand. "You've given me a place to start."

"Sure thing." Clara slid out of the car and then leaned in the open window. "But like I said, be careful while you're snooping. Guilty people are most unpredictable."

It was after opening time when Molly finally arrived at the museum. The crowd had already begun to filter their way inside and the rest of the people were looking at the sky with justifiably anxious expressions. An ominous tier of thunderclouds had begun to gather above them and a hint of a breeze began to tickle a strand of hair here or pluck at a scarf there. A breeze in Richmond in September can only mean a storm is about to arrive and the waiting members of the crowd were wondering whether their clever foresight in bringing an umbrella would be enough to prevent any rain from getting on their precious possessions. Those without umbrellas were looking desperately ahead as if willing the line to move faster.

Molly decided to interview members of the group who had already made it inside. They would be much more relaxed than the sky-watching group outside. She was immediately drawn to a young, black woman in her early twenties who held the hand of the most beautiful little boy Molly had ever seen. The boy had creamy brown skin, the color of a rich latté, huge blue-green eyes winking with excitement, and a mop of unruly, frizzy hair that bobbed up and down as he danced a jig in place.

"I'm sure you hear this all the time, but your son is so cute," Molly said, staring at the little boy. She then introduced herself to the mother and asked if she could conduct a short on-the-spot interview.

The woman seemed a bit uncomfortable. She was Molly's height, almost five feet nine inches, but while Molly was all curves, this woman was bone-thin and had the long, languid legs of a flamingo. Her bright, brown eyes looked downcast and she put an arm around her son.

"I really don't know anything 'bout this stuff. My late husband left me a coin and I've never thought of selling it 'til now, but I need the money. He said it was in his family since before the Civil War and if I ever needed money, to go sell it. Otherwise, he wanted Erik here to get it."

Molly gazed into Erik's merry eyes. "Well, you definitely need to find out how much it's worth before you try selling it. It was smart of you to come here." Molly complimented the nervous woman and she seemed to relax.

"I'm Jasmine," she said. "Jasmine Jones. Yeah, it was a good idea, but Erik's getting awfully antsy and I've got to get to work. Here's the coin." Jasmine unwrapped a small, dingy bandana.

Molly picked up the coin and examined it. She was no coin expert, but she recognized the bust of Lady Liberty. Stars surrounded her head and below her shoulders the coin's date was stamped 1836. Turning it over, Molly saw an eagle grasping an olive branch in the left talon and a bunch of arrows in the right. A shield covered the feathers of his breast. The text read "United States of America 50 Cents." The coin was shiny and looked as if it were newly minted.

"I can't believe what good shape this is in," Molly said as she returned the coin. "I know the woman who does the coin appraisals. She won't mind if I let you skip this line. I think it would be the best thing for you to get her opinion of what it's worth and where you should sell it. Just follow me."

Jasmine's grateful smile rendered her instantly beautiful. "Thanks!"

Molly led Jasmine and Erik through the complicated stanchion maze until they had reached the next room where the head appraisers were meeting with members of the public or waiting for a camera crew to arrive. When Molly and her companions reached Alexandra's area, she was surprised to find Garrett seated at the table instead. He was peering intently at a coin with the aid of a jeweler's loop.

Garrett straightened and returned the coin to its owner, an attractive middle-aged man wearing a neatly tailored light blue suit.

"I'll take it, Jared. I'll drop by your shop later this afternoon to see what else you've got. Put this aside for me, will you?"

The older man nodded as he and Garrett shook hands.

"Friend of yours?" Molly asked.

"He's a coin dealer. He's got a small shop in a place the locals call the Bottom. I'd hate to even ask . . . I see you've picked up some locals of your own. Keeping busy, are you?" Garrett smiled kindly down at Erik.

"Actually, I'm looking for Alexandra. This young lady has a coin that needs to be appraised."

"Then look no further." Garrett puffed out his chest. "I am here to save the day. Let's have a look-see."

"You?" Molly stammered.

"Sorry to shock you, but Alexandra has taken over the hosting spot and as I told you a few days ago, coins are one of the things I collect." Garrett faced Jasmine. "If I can't give you a value, I shall send you to Mr. Freeman, the dealer I was just speaking to. He is a fair and honest chap, to be sure."

Jasmine, won over by Garrett's easy manner, handed him her red bandana. Garrett examined the coin carefully using his jeweler's loop and though Molly studied his expression closely, she couldn't tell what he made of the coin's value just by watching his face.

Suddenly, Molly heard her name being called from farther down the aisle. Alicia was beckoning her excitedly.

"Excuse me a minute," Molly told Jasmine and hustled

toward Alicia's area. Propped on an easel was the most detailed and colorful painting Molly had ever seen. The scene
was of New York City, complete with billboards, taxis, and
hundreds of tiny pedestrians walking the sidewalks. In the
distance, a folksy Statue of Liberty held a bright light bulb
aloft as glossy tugboats surrounded her in the harbor.
Every inch of the painting was covered in bright, shiny
paints—down to the tiny skyscraper windows and the
waves in the water.

"This is wonderful!" Molly exclaimed. "Folk art, right?"

"Yes, a contemporary piece by a North Carolina artist
named Benny Carter. This is one of his early pieces. I
thought it would make a nice addition to your story. Mrs.
Wilbur here only paid two hundred dollars for it over ten
years ago, and I'm about to tell her that she should insure
this piece today for five thousand dollars."

"Oh, my!" Mrs. Wilbur exclaimed as Molly dug out her
camera and began to take pictures. As she was writing
down how Mrs. Wilbur had bought the painting from the
artist's house for $200 plus a six-pack of his favorite beer,
Molly looked up and caught Alicia smiling at her.

Was Alicia at lunch when I was? Molly tried to remember. Yes, she had been there. Molly remembered that Alicia
had sat across from her with Lindsey on one side and
Patrice on the other. Garrett and Alexandra had been there,
too. Borris and Jessica had not arrived until after Molly
had already started her lunch. Had either of them had
enough time to get to Mrs. Sterling's house and back?

Returning Alicia's smile, Molly thanked her and then
headed back toward Garrett to see what he had determined
about Jasmine's coin. Before Molly reached his table, she
could see him counting out a pile of twenties and slipping
them into Jasmine's hand. Jasmine hugged him quickly and
then stuffed the money in her purse.

"Thanks again!" she said as she scooped up her son and
turned toward the exit. "I've got to go! Bye!"

"Well, that looks like a happy customer." Molly remarked

as she moved to Garrett's side. She watched Jasmine hastily maneuver her way through the crowd. "Was the coin worth anything? I hope so, because she really seemed to need the money."

Garrett looked grave. "I know, she told me that, too. Unfortunately, her coin was a fake. A good one, but still a fake. I didn't have the heart to tell her that, though, poor mite, so I just told her it was of small value but that I could sell it to a friend of mine."

"So you paid her for it even though it was a fake?" Molly was astonished.

"What's a bloke to do?" Garrett blushed and looked away.

A warm feeling rushed through Molly and before she knew what she was doing, she had thrown her arms about Garrett's neck and planted a fat kiss on his lips. When he remained rigid, Molly was mortified at her forwardness and she immediately detached her arms and crossed them over her chest in embarrassment.

"Well! I say," said Garrett teasingly. "I'm going to get involved in all sorts of good works if *that's* the result it produces."

"That was so sweet of you, Garrett." Molly gave him a shy smile and settled for squeezing his hand as a means of illustrating her admiration. "Why did Jasmine rush away in such a hurry?"

"Had to push off for work. She's got a shift at the hospital starting in an hour. Nice of you to hustle her through the queue like that. I should be kissing *you* for being so sweet." Garrett took her hand.

At that moment, Molly longed to confide in Garrett, to tell him all about the mold on the desk and ask him to help her find Frank's killer, but for some reason she kept silent. She released his hand in order to grab her notebook from her bag.

"I'd better get back to work. Oh, I forgot to tell you. Victoria says she's going to rest after being grilled this afternoon but will join us for dinner. That means the police haven't charged her with anything. Isn't that good news?"

"Topping," Garrett agreed brightly. "I didn't think they had any hard evidence on the gal. Where are you off to next?"

Molly thought about Jessica and Borris and their tardiness at yesterday's lunch. "I think I'll check out what's going on in the book and jewelry area. See you at dinner."

At the furniture area, a local dealer and one of the staff appraisers were filling in for Frank. Molly stopped to watch them as they looked over a stunning tilt-top table. She felt a sudden sadness come over her that Frank, with his deep passion for antique furniture, was absent. She also missed the warm beauty of the slant-front desk. Was it sitting in some dark room down at the police station? Did its owner know that their antique had been an accessory in a murder?

Off to the side, partially hidden from view by a curtain, Randy and Chris sat at a table playing cards. Molly assumed the men were kept nearby in case a piece of furniture needed to be lifted or polished for the benefit of the camera's eye. She stood watching Randy. Apparently he had just lost his hand, for he threw down his cards with a slap as his lip curled in frustration.

"Now there's a man with some anger," Molly murmured as she turned her back on him. Randy had no love for Frank. Maybe he just meant to play a nasty trick on his employer—a trick that had ended up killing him. Molly needed to know more about this hot-tempered assistant. She decided to pay a visit to the producer, Guy, who had set up his temporary office as far away from the clambering crowd as possible.

Lucky for her, Guy was on the phone when she arrived, bellowing into the mouthpiece. "A replacement for Frank has to be in D.C. for the next show . . . I don't care whether he's under contract or not, just get him!"

Guy was an all-around average guy. Nothing about his height, weight, or looks made him stand out in any way. He wore square reading glasses that he was constantly placing on his head of dull brown hair while he squinted through flat blue eyes at the world.

"Who are you?" he asked impatiently.

"Molly Appleby, from *Collector's Weekly*. We spoke on the phone last week."

"Ah, yes," Guy nodded, his voice thawing notably.

"Thank you so much for letting me visit with the show. This is going to make a great piece. In fact, I have so much to write about that I think I'll do a whole series."

All producers love publicity and this one was no exception. Guy was words away from eating out of her hand.

"I'd love to do a side piece on the crew, a behind-the-scenes kind of thing. Now that the show is wrapping up tomorrow, I'm not sure if I'll have time to get backgrounds on all of the crew members. Do you have anything like that with you?"

Guy frowned. "Nah. Personnel files are back in New York. We'd have to fax stuff to you."

That was a disappointment. "Well, can you tell me what you know about Frank's crew? For example, who will be replacing him?"

Guy looked at her suspiciously. "I'm trying to get a dealer from Atlanta on board. He's a greedy bastard though and wants more money than we're willing to pay. You're not writing a piece on Frank, are you? You know that was an accident," he added with a growl.

An accident? Molly ignored her instinct to laugh at such an outrageous statement. "Of course I'm not writing about Frank," she lied. "Now, how about his assistants, Randy and Chris."

"Don't know." Guy was obviously bored with the direction of their conversation. "Frank hand-picked those guys."

Molly gave up. She wasn't going to find anything out from this man. He didn't know a thing about the people who actually made his show work. She stood up to leave when she had a sudden flash of inspiration. "Just one more thing. With all of these people working here, where does everyone park?"

"Oh, we're borrowing Krispy Kreme's lot for the week. They're closed for renovations."

At the name Krispy Kreme, Molly's stomach issued a loud gurgle, reminding her that she had not eaten anything for breakfast. A fresh jelly donut would certainly hit the spot. Too bad the shop was closed.

"Frank didn't park there, though," she wondered aloud, quickly trying to cover up the sounds of her protesting stomach.

"Frank said that there might be traces of asbestos in the air from the donut place's renovations. He refused to park there." Guy sighed and stood to leave. "He'd have parked in the handicapped spot if he thought he could get away with it. Now, I need to make a call and my cell phone doesn't work well in here, so if you'll excuse me, I'm going to head outside."

"Of course. Thank you for your time," Molly said politely, noting that the shape of the object in Guy's hand looked much more like a pack of cigarettes than a cell phone. Fortunately, Guy's need to indulge in his habit would leave her alone in his office. Once he was out of sight, Molly moved as quickly as she could and grabbed the portable file case behind his desk. Rifling through the papers, she discovered a list of employee cars and plate numbers.

"Gotcha!" She smiled, stuffing the paper into her purse. She then headed for the nearest exit. She had spied a barbeque restaurant next door to the Krispy Kreme and she wasn't going to go one step further into her investigation without a nice order of baby back ribs with baked beans and slaw.

Molly had no idea what she expected to find by walking around the lot where the crew of *Hidden Treasures* parked. While most of the head appraisers were given the use of rental cars in each city, the crew members were expected to drive their own vehicles to every show. Apparently there were less perks involved in being a member of the crew. They certainly didn't stay at the same quality hotels as the appraisers, and even if she tracked down Randy's hotel, Molly had little expectation of being able to break into his hotel room if his car gave her no indication of whether or not he was a murderer.

Scanning over the list, she read that Randy drove a black Ford F-150 with Alabama plates reading N2BASS. The front grill was outfitted to hold at least six fishing poles and the rear bumper was completely covered by fishing bumper stickers reading: *WOMEN LOVE ME, FISH FEAR ME; THE QUESTION OF FISHING IS NOT A MATTER OF LIFE OR DEATH—IT'S BIGGER THAN THAT; 'CARPE DIEM' DOES NOT MEAN 'FISH OF THE DAY';* and *SAVE THE BASS—SHOOT A LAND DEVELOPER.*

The back window was covered with fishing stickers and catch-and-release badges. A silver wide-mouth bass dangled from the rearview mirror.

"So this is your passion," Molly said. She peered through the tinted passenger window into the cab and grimaced at the mass of fast-food cartons, balled-up napkins, and empty soda cans that littered the floor. The front seat was completely obscured by maps, fishing magazines, and what looked like a well-read issue of *Playboy* featuring a sexy pro-wrestler on the cover.

A fat drop of rain splashed down onto Molly's hand as she pressed her nose against the glass.

"Great," she complained to the dirty truck. "What was I thinking I would find? A written confession propped up on the dashboard?"

Sighing in self-disgust, she decided to take a quick look through the small cab window at the back seat bench. It too was littered with old food containers and yellowed magazines, but just as Molly was about to give up and seek shelter from the rain, which had begun to dot the surface of the truck with more regularity, she spied a balled-up rag soiled with what looked like black stains on the driver's side of the bench seat.

Hoping against hope that the stains were not created by furniture polish, Molly dashed over to the other side of the truck and peered down at the rag. Her heart began drumming faster as she stared at the powdery-looking black stains. It was the mold. It had to be.

"I knew it!" Molly declared and pulled out both her cell phone and Detective Robeson's card from her purse. She punched in his number excitedly and almost jumped for joy when he answered on the third ring.

"Robeson speaking." The deep voice rumbled through the earpiece. Molly quickly explained her discovery and described exactly where Randy's truck was parked in the Krispy Kreme lot.

"This'd better be the real thing," Robeson mumbled to himself after he hung up. He untied a red-and-white checkered apron and turned off the oven. He then watched in dismay as his undercooked soufflé fell inward on itself. "So much for my day off."

In the parking lot, the rain had picked up its tempo so Molly headed for shelter beneath an overhang on the backside of the Krispy Kreme building. Thick clouds blotted out the weak daylight and hung closely to the ground, creating the effect of an early twilight. Goose bumps erupted on Molly's arms as she listened to the growling thunder.

Suddenly, a fork of lightning flashed across the sky and as Molly turned to look at it in nervous fascination, the lanky, wet figure of Randy appeared like a ghost from around the corner of the donut shop.

Before she could even react, he had taken three impossibly quick strides and now stood before her, water streaming from his ratty hair. His thin arms were covered with cobra tattoos that crawled up his arms like black vines as he reached up to wipe moisture from his face.

"Whatcha doin' poking around my ride, girlie?" he asked, leaning in towards Molly's face. She could smell beer and cigarettes on his breath.

Molly shrank back against the concrete wall. "Uh . . . just admiring your bumper stickers." She tried to relax and act more casual, but her body would not cooperate. "I . . . um . . . think fishing is a great hobby."

"You do, do ya?" Randy dropped his soaked cigarette on the ground and placed his hand on the wall next to Molly's head. "So you're lookin' for some action from a real man, not that English punk I've seen you hangin' all over."

Molly twisted her face away from his breath and the hungry look in his eyes. She tried to laugh, but the sound came out like a strangled whimper. "Nothing like that. I've . . . got a boyfriend back in North Carolina."

Randy touched a strand of Molly's hair. "Sure you do, sweet thang."

A wave of anger flooded through Molly's body. Why was she just standing there? This puny man wasn't about to take advantage of her. "Look!" She stood up and pushed his hand off the wall. "You'd better back off."

Randy rocked on his heels while a look of amusement played across his pinched face. He narrowed his weasel eyes ever further and said, "I think I'd like a taste of those nice lips. You don't have to play those games with *me*, girl." And he grabbed Molly's shoulders with both hands as he tried to kiss her.

Molly jerked her knee into what she thought was his crotch, but ended up being a bony thigh. Luckily, she applied enough force to imbalance him. She shoved him roughly aside as she freed herself from his hands. Surprised at Molly's resistance, Randy fell on the ground and sat stunned for a moment before his face reddened with rage and he took off after her fleeing figure.

Molly was not a fast runner, but terror increased her speed until she was flying through the rain back towards the museum, the sounds of her pursuer yelling at her egged her desperately onward. As she dashed from behind a large delivery truck parked in the barbeque restaurant's lot, she ran headlong into an immoveable black wall. It was Detective Robeson.

"Oh, thank God!" Molly wailed and held onto Robeson's massive arms. "He's after me!"

Robeson issued the briefest of nods to the two officers standing next to him and within seconds, Randy was handcuffed and shoved, screaming obscenities, into the back of a patrol car.

Robeson held an umbrella over Molly's head and looked her steadily in the eye. "You all right?" he asked gently.

"Yes," she said as tears mingled with the rain on her face. She brushed them away in irritation. "I thought he was going to . . . you know." She looked down at the ground.

"But you got away?" Robeson handed her a napkin.

"Yeah," she said, wiping her face. "I was pretty glad to see you, though."

Robeson cracked a small smile. "Can you show me that truck?"

Molly nodded. Robeson gestured to one of the officers sitting with Randy. The man ran over to Robeson, sprinted back to the patrol car, and returned with the keys to Randy's truck.

Praying that the rag was really covered with the black mold, Molly led Robeson to the F-150. She pointed at the rag through the window and Robeson carefully retrieved it and plopped it in an evidence bag.

"Get this to the lab and tell them to put a rush on it," Robeson told his officer. He turned back to Molly and said, "I'll need you to come down to the station and make another statement."

She nodded wearily. "Can I stop at my hotel and get some dry clothes first?"

"Of course. Take your time," he said, again speaking quite gently. "We'll be busy with that fish for a while, anyway." He smiled and gestured toward Randy's bucking figure in the patrol car. He then walked Molly back to the museum.

Without bothering to go inside, Molly headed straight for her car and then for the bed-and-breakfast. She was hoping she could get Mrs. Hewell to give her some tea a little earlier than usual. A lemon square or two would certainly hit the spot about now as well.

"I deserve a treat," she told her sodden reflection in the rearview mirror as the fright began to be replaced by a powerful sense of triumph. "After all, *I* just caught a killer."

Chapter 8

Since the days of King Arthur, a table, and particularly a dining table, has been synonymous with royalty. Often to dine with a man is to make him your friend.

—PAUL BURROUGHS, *SOUTHERN ANTIQUES*

When Molly opened the Traveller's front door, she was greeted by the rich sound of her mother's laughter mingling with the familiar voices of a man and another woman. As she quietly approached the dining room, Molly lingered in the hall in order to allow the cheerful melodies of storytelling, teasing, and giggling to wash over her and drain some of the tension from her knotted shoulders.

Jessica and Borris were being regaled with one of Clara's favorite tales of woe from her days as an antiques store proprietor. Molly had heard the story dozens of times, but as she dropped her dripping purse on the dark green wool rug embroidered with roses that ran the length of the hall, she still couldn't help but smile.

"This old coot, T.J., would hang around my shop for hours bragging about how he had been around when people still built furniture with cut nails. He said he could tell if a piece was right just by looking at it, blah, blah, blah. So anyway, one day a customer came in and was *very* interested in my best piece of furniture—a gorgeous corner cupboard from Pennsylvania. I had picked it up for nothing at auction and was going to make a big enough profit on it to pay the bills for the next three months."

"So what happened?" Jessica asked.

"T.J. came in and I knew I was in trouble. Even though I lowered my voice, T.J. had superhuman hearing and when I told the customer that the piece came from a family in central Pennsylvania—which it did—T.J. started clearing his throat. Before I could reach him to shut him up, he drawled, 'Well, I donno 'about that bein' a Pennsylvania piece. Looks more like a southern piece to me.'"

"But didn't the woods make it clear where the piece was made?"

"Of course they did!" Clara nearly shouted. "That corner cupboard was made of maple with birch secondary! No way was it southern, but my customer was new to antiques, and all she saw was an old man who looked like he'd been around since the piece was made—somewhere around 1820—and I lost the sale!" Clara took a gulp of tea. She was really worked up now. "I could have *killed* that man! Every time he came in I stood to lose a sale, but I couldn't toss him out because he knew *everyone* in the business and wouldn't hesitate to blacken my name if I treated him rudely."

Molly finally stepped into the room and sank into the nearest chair.

"Hello, madam. Where did you come from?" Clara smiled at her fondly. She always called Molly "madam" when she was in a good mood.

"Hi." Molly poured herself some tea. "Telling war stories?"

Borris passed her a plate of heart-shaped linzer torte cookies. "These are baked with Mrs. Hewell's homemade blackberry and raspberry jam. Out of this world. They simply melt in your mouth."

"You've got powdered sugar all over your shirt, Borris." Jessica pointed at him, laughing.

Borris smiled in return and then asked Clara. "So you're glad to be out of the shop business? I was dreaming of getting into it. This traveling is wearing me down."

Jessica looked worried. "I'll tell you another shop owner's tale of misery and wretchedness from *my* days as a proprietor. I had these two lawyers across the street from my shop. Well, they decided to redecorate their offices with antique pieces and they came over repeatedly trying to decide what they would like for their waiting room."

Molly sank her teeth into the buttery, sugary heaven of a blackberry linzer torte and watched her mother and her two friends with pleasure. She felt safe and enveloped in warm coziness. Now, she could formally put Frank's murder behind her.

"You see the size of me, right?" Jessica held out her thin, petite arms. "I'm no Hercules, but those men used to get me to help them carry chairs and desks and tables across the street to their office. *Then* I'd have to help them arrange and rearrange the stuff while my shop stood unattended."

"Did they end up buying a lot?" Clara giggled.

"That's the thing! After all of that muscle work, they decided the *look* wasn't right and I had to help carry it all back. In the end, I think they bought one chair and one stand from me. All the heavy stuff got carried back to my store. Ergh!" Jessica held her clenched fists in the air. "I could have strangled those men with their own ties."

Borris was staring at Molly's blanched face and unfocused eyes. "Maybe we should change the subject, ladies. Molly here looks a little wiped out."

Clara took her first good look at her daughter. "What is it, sweetheart?"

Molly thought she was completely recovered from her afternoon scare, but she felt her eyes suddenly grow moist. She took a deep breath and told them all about her encounter with Randy. When she was finished, her mother's arms were around her and Jessica was fussing over her empty teacup.

"I'll teach that boy a thing or two when he gets out of jail," Borris threatened in a protective manner.

Molly smiled weakly. The concern and sympathy shown by her mother and her two friends restored her spirits enormously. "Thanks, Borris. Thanks to all of you, but I don't think any brute force will be necessary. I think Randy's going to be in jail for quite a while."

The skinny pencil lines forming Jessica's dark eyebrows rose up on her forehead. "Why do you say that?"

Molly filled her rapt listeners in on the details of the black mold and her discovery of the rag in the back of Randy's truck.

"Is Randy's motive strong enough?" Clara asked. "He disliked his employer, but so do thousands of workers."

Molly shrugged. "Maybe Randy just meant to make Frank really miserable. Maybe he didn't know how severely that mold would affect Frank. But there was another factor, I think. When we were all at lunch the day Frank was killed, Randy was really staring fixedly at Victoria." Molly broke off another piece of cookie and held it between her fingers. "His eyes were really boring into her, but with desire, not malice. Kind of like I'd look at this cookie before taking a bite out of it." She popped the piece in her mouth.

"But if he had feelings for Victoria, would he let her go to jail for a crime *he* committed?" Jessica asked doubtfully.

Molly frowned. "That would be pretty cold, wouldn't it? The good news is Randy's now in jail and Victoria's being released. The police have no reason to hold her anymore. Apparently, they've gotten a hold of her phone records from the hotel. She made several calls to New York from her room during the hours Frank most likely died, and she was never alone long enough that afternoon to put the mold on the slant-front desk. So she's in the clear. She said she'd be at the group dinner tonight."

"Where are we eating tonight?" Borris asked Jessica. "Or should I say, where are you driving me tonight, dear?" he added teasingly.

"A place called Elmo's. It's all the way out in the next county, but they're supposed to have these fabulous steaks covered with bordelaise sauce and melted blue cheese crumbles." Jessica smacked at Borris with her napkin. "What would you do without me as your chauffeur?"

"Be miserable," he answered softly with tender honesty. Suddenly, the room was filled with the tumult of the unspoken feelings between the two appraisers. Jessica flushed right up to the roots of her spiky hair and then quickly reached over and grabbed Clara's hand. "Come with us tonight. You and Lex. It'll be fun."

Clara squeezed Jessica's hand. "Of course we will. Who in their right mind could resist a good steak?"

After tea, the group headed up to their respective rooms for a little rest. Molly had difficulty focusing on the quaint Scottish village mystery she had brought. As she lay on her bed, her thoughts kept straying to her last date with Mark. She pictured his warm smile as he held her hand under the table and told her about his dreams of becoming a doctor one day.

Now he was somewhere in Ohio and he hadn't even tried to reach her. Garrett's face also appeared in her mind and Molly thought back to the moment she had kissed the dashing Englishman. For all his charm, there was still something missing in Garrett's personality. Molly felt that she really hadn't seen the *real* Garrett, while Mark was instantly and utterly sincere. Every emotion played across his sweet face like an open book.

Resolved to get in touch with Mark, Molly sat up on her bed, grabbed the phone, and punched in the numbers to Clayton's direct line.

"Mr. Fabulous speaking," Clayton answered.

Molly chuckled. "Now, that's an interesting way to answer the phone."

"Why beat around the bush?" Clayton drawled. "If it's that stud from the *Greensboro Times* calling, I want him to know exactly *who* he's dealing with. I've gotten quite a few hot dates answering the phone that way. People automatically ask me *why* I'm Mr. Fabulous and of course, I have to elaborate about—"

"—But you don't have to tell me," Molly said hurriedly as Clayton could go on for hours about his superior qualities. "I know that you're a fine vintage."

"Ugh, that makes me sound *old*, darling. I'm more like a bottle of 1990 Dom Perignon. Rosy-colored and *very* expensive."

"Clayton, any updates on Mark?"

"None that I know of, honey. Did you ask the new receptionist?"

"That little twerp? I already can't stand her," Molly complained as she recalled the strained conversation she had had with Brittani.

"Tell me about it! She's a cute little thang but those *clothes*! And the way she talks is right out of Alice's Restaurant. You're probably too young to remember that show. Ugh. I think she wore pants with a *polyester blend* yesterday. I nearly spit out my Café Americano!"

Molly smiled at Clayton's love of drama. "Can you see if Swanson knows anything? I'm getting worried about Mark. It's not like him to not check in and leave a number. Here's mine, by the way."

"Hold your horses, girl. Clayton doesn't keep a pen behind his ears, you know. Might mess up my perfect hair."

As Clayton wrote down Molly's information, the undeniable grumbling of their boss, Carl Swanson, could be heard in the distance. It seemed to be coming closer and closer to Clayton's desk. The next thing she knew, Molly was suddenly speaking to Swanson instead of Clayton.

"Appleby? That you?" he growled.

"Yes, Carl," Molly answered quickly. "How are you?"

"Who gives a damn how *I* am?" he howled into the mouthpiece. "I've been trying to reach you on your cell phone for hours! All I've been getting is your damned voice mail, which you apparently *never* check! You've got a dead appraiser up there and *I* have no article about it! What the hell is going on? Are you a reporter or not?"

Molly knew Swanson would track her down over this subject sooner or later. The death of someone well known in the antiques world always skyrocketed the paper's circulation, and a questionable death really sent subscriptions through the roof.

"Carl." Molly tried to soothe her boss. "The facts of the case aren't in yet. I mean, the cause of death is known, but the current suspect is—"

"You get me a five hundred-word teaser as of five minutes ago! I mean it! I am holding the presses on the front page until I get an e-mail from you. Now get off the phone and start writing! And the next time someone falls over dead around you, I want to be the *first* to know! You got that?"

Molly held the receiver away from her ear as this torrent of words was screeched at her. She could then hear grunts and an "unhand that phone, you brute," from Clayton.

Breathlessly, Clayton returned on the line. "Lord help us! If that man doesn't start smoking again I will *simply* die! If I didn't hate the smell so much, I'd cover my clothes in Eau De Marlboro just to tempt him back to the Land of Addiction."

Molly snickered. "He's worse than ever. I guess I'd better type something up. Clayton, please call me if there's any word from Mark."

"I will, sugar. Are you behaving yourself up there?" he asked and Molly felt a guilty flush rising up her cheeks as she thought about kissing Garrett.

"Mostly," she said before hanging up.

She booted up her laptop and got to work on a short piece concerning Frank's death. As she typed up the facts, she couldn't help but think about the slant-front desk. She knew she would have to e-mail Swanson a photo of the piece to go along with the article, but she hated to have it viewed as something negative. The desk might be seen as a thing of evil since it formed the palette for the murderer's weapon.

Where was the desk now? Was it sitting in some dark room in the police station? Did anyone there appreciate the piece's superb craftsmanship or recognize the loving toil that the carpenter had put into making it so many years ago?

Molly pushed thoughts of the desk out of her head and quickly finished her article. She e-mailed it along with a photo of Frank leaning over the slant-front desk and shut the lid of her laptop down with a satisfying thud. She never considered that she had spent more time grieving over an inanimate piece of furniture than for the dead man who was the real subject of her article.

Jessica and Borris led a small caravan of cars west on Highway 64 towards Charlottesville. Molly, Clara, and Lex followed in Molly's Jeep, while Alexandra, Patrice, Lindsey, Alicia, and Tony were packed into a rented minivan. Garrett went to pick up Victoria from her hotel. She had needed a few extra minutes to change and collect herself, so Garrett let Molly know that they would be at Elmo's about twenty minutes late.

"Save me a seat," he had said with the pleading tone of an elementary school student.

For the first time, Molly noticed that Jessica's rental car bore the bumper sticker EVE WAS FRAMED. Jessica and her car seemed well-matched, Molly thought. I bet she put that sticker on there herself.

After a fifteen-minute drive, the caravan got off at the first exit in Goochland County and drove into the parking lot of a strip mall.

"This town is loaded with strip malls," Molly complained.

"Most towns are," Lex said, "but you're only seeing one

side of Richmond. After all, we're still on Broad Street, the same street that the museum is on."

"That's true," Clara agreed. "Think of how charming the downtown area is near Monument Avenue. I simply love all those stately, old houses lining that road."

"Maybe I'll stay an extra day and really explore the place," Molly suggested more to herself than anyone else. Lex held the restaurant's glass door open for Clara and Molly and they were led into a private room by the hostess.

The room was painted in a warm mustard hue above the wainscoting and a cranberry red below. Oversized paintings of rearing horses were hung exactly in the center of each wall. Rotund marigolds and fern leaves filled the small vases on their table and tea lights flickered in welcome on top of a perfectly pressed white tablecloth. I would have never expected this kind of elegance tucked away in a strip mall, Molly thought.

After the group had taken their seats, bottles of wine seemed to magically appear on the table. Clara ordered her usual Crown Royal and club soda.

"No ice, please," she added and gave the waitress a look which translated to, "My drink better not be weak or you will hear about it."

When it arrived, alongside Molly's screwdriver and Lex's Jack and Coke, Clara took a sip and beamed at the waitress. "Perfect." She nodded her approval and took a pleasurable bite of Elmo's fresh bread covered by a sun-dried tomato spread.

If Molly expected the group to be subdued after Frank's death, she stood to be corrected. The news of Randy's arrest coupled with the flowing wine and delicious appetizers appeared to have put every member of the group in the best of moods. Clara was enjoying herself immensely. She stabbed a piece of her portobello mushroom appetizer cooked in a balsamic vinegar sauce and covered in four different cheeses while telling Borris about a set of medical encyclopedias she had at home.

Borris's eyes were alight with interest as he speared a shrimp cooked with butter, white wine, and garlic. Lex and Tony were laughing at the silliness of toy commercials over the years as they shared a plate of fried calamari. When they broke into song with the Slinky jingle, a few of the other appraisers joined them. Alexandra rolled her eyes in disgust and turned to Patrice for a bit of understanding.

"I know you only *pretend* to be French, but at least that shows you might be able to hold your wine without singing jingles from the telly. I might need to host tomorrow and I don't think that—"

"Not to worry, Alexandra dear," said a voice from behind Alexandra's chair. She swiveled her aristocratic chin and with a swing of gloriously shiny hair allowed her eyes to fall upon the figure of Victoria, looking refreshed in a white suit with a black and white polka-dotted blouse. Victoria gave an expressionless perusal of Alexandra's outfit, which included a form fitting, immaculately pressed silk cobalt blouse and a vintage Hermès scarf with an equestrian design tied into a perfect knot around her graceful neck.

"Nice scarf," Victoria said in her toneless manner before taking her seat at the head of the table.

Tony grabbed his wineglass and raised it toward Victoria. "Welcome! We knew you were innocent! Cheers to Victoria for holding up so well after a day of hard-core questioning!" Others joined in the toast and Victoria was greeted with a round of applause. Garrett took a seat next to Molly while Victoria tugged on her pearls and smiled.

While the group waited for the main course to arrive, Alicia described a portrait she had appraised earlier in the day.

"It was of Grant. Just a black and white drawing, actually. I saw it on my way out this afternoon. This woman was loading it in her car. It wasn't even signed, but there was something about it that just spoke to me. Grant was sitting at a campaign desk and was leaning his head against one hand, like the weight of all that was on his mind was just too much for him."

"Did you give the woman an appraisal?" Lindsey asked.

"Just a ballpark. Actually, I referred her to a Civil War art expert I know." Alicia took a sip of wine. "I see so much art every week. It takes something special to make me stop and really *feel* a piece. I haven't felt that in a long time."

"I know what you mean," Lindsey agreed. "I see all of these linens and quilts and every kind of embroidery imaginable, but then someone walks in with a piece that just makes my heart stop. That's why I'm here, I guess."

As sizzling steaks loaded with melted blue cheese arrived at the table, Borris began to tell the group about an interesting set of books he had appraised that day.

"Lee's biography in a four-volume set," he said, describing the books. "They're not that rare. Dated 1937. Good shape. I've seen a bunch of them. But these were the first set I've seen signed and dated by the author, a guy named Douglas Freeman. He also wrote an inscription in each volume. A quote from Lee."

"Which one?" Lex asked with interest. "I love this stuff! I've watched that Ken Burn series on the Civil War like twenty times."

Borris nodded. "The quote was 'A true man of honor feels humbled himself when he cannot help humbling others.' "

The group fell silent, digesting the powerful line along with their food.

"What is it with you Americans and this war?" Alexandra said and looked to Garrett for support. "Do you understand it? And this General Lee," she snorted. "You'd think he was some kind of demigod. There are monuments and shops named after him all over this city."

"He's much like your Lord Nelson," Clara said calmly, though Molly could see annoyance in the way her mother's lips had drawn into a thin line. "He was a great commander and a good man."

"Yes, but Nelson *won*," Alexandra sneered.

"I agree with you, Alex," Patrice shook his head. "That war needs to be forgotten down here—Lee along with it."

"Lee is a hero," Lex said, his voice thick with emotion. "He was honorable, courageous, and like the quote said, humble. He was just a man protecting his home. *I* was raised in Virginia, and I'll tell you one thing. If an army tried to invade Her today, I would stand on Her shores and fight them off."

"Well said!" exclaimed Borris and clanked his beer mug against Lex's wineglass.

"Did all of you look at those daguerreotypes?" Lindsey asked, a hand futilely trying to replace stray hairs back into her bun. "Some of those boys . . . it's painful to look at them and wonder if they made it through all those years of war."

The group murmured about the exhibit until Alexandra raised her voice once more. This time, her face was aglow with triumph. "I'll tell you what's painful," she began.

"What's that, dear?" Lindsey leaned forward, her owl-like face waiting expectantly.

"Painful is how bad those fake Dahlonega coins are." Alexandra pronounced and Jessica's hand abruptly jerked sideways, knocking an untouched goblet filled with red wine into her lap.

"Oh!" she yelped and jumped up as a ruby stain bled over her pink floral skirt.

"I left a message for the curator of the museum to call me at my hotel first thing in the morning," Alexandra continued as if nothing had happened. "It's insulting to be a part of an exhibit with such blatant fakes. *Someone* is bound to notice."

Garrett sat staring at Alexandra with his mouth hanging open. The other appraisers looked just as shocked.

"Are you sure?" Borris asked. "You haven't actually handled them, right?"

"No," Alexandra said flippantly as she beckoned the

waitress. "I'll have a decaf with nonfat milk. If you don't have nonfat I'll settle for two percent. Anyone else having coffee or dessert?" She turned her cold, lovely face to Molly. "Molly? I'm sure *you're* having dessert."

Molly struggled to contain the anger that washed over her body. That bitch!

"How can you be so certain that they're fakes just by looking at them?" Garrett rephrased Borris's question. Molly sank back in her chair, relieved that the focus was quickly taken off of her.

"Simple, darling," Alexandra cooed at Garrett. "The reverse should have a Letter *D*, for Dahlonega, but someone put a *P* there instead. Or it's a *D* with a tail. Either way, it's a major mistake that isn't some minting error. Once the curator really takes a look, he'll see that I'm right."

"Why do you know so much about American coins?" Lex asked, obviously deciding to play devil's advocate. "It doesn't sound like there's much you like about our country."

"I like coins." Alexandra sipped delicately on her decaf. "I like them regardless of what country minted them and I know my coins well."

"That's true," Victoria said quietly. "So it's a good thing you can get back to your regular job tomorrow as the show's coin appraiser then, isn't it?"

Alexandra shot daggers at Victoria while Garrett busily calculated everyone's share of the significant bill. The other appraisers were yawning as they handed Garrett money. Jessica was still blotting hopelessly at her skirt with a napkin dipped in ice water.

Molly looked over at her mother. "Score for Victoria," Clara whispered. Out loud she said, "Madam, you must taste my flan. It's just as creamy and smooth as your beautiful skin."

The science museum was quiet at night. The clamor that filled its enormous halls during the day died away by six o'clock in the evening. Except for the two security guards who made their usual rounds past the dark exhibits, no footsteps echoed noisily down the wide corridors. To save money, the museum administration had decided to keep lights on only in the entranceway, so the guards were forced to use powerful Maglite flashlights as they toured the vast building.

Just before midnight, the guards moved off to the small break room near the front door. The middle-aged guard named Mack poured two cups of coffee and emptied a packet of sugar into each cup. The second guard, a young man named Bruce, shuffled cards with the quick, practiced motion of someone who has played many rounds of poker.

"What'll it be first?" Bruce asked his partner.

"Let's warm up with Hearts," Mack said, placing the coffee cups on the table as Bruce dealt their hands.

"What did your wife fix you tonight?" Bruce asked as he examined his hand.

Mack peeled back the aluminum foil covering his sandwich and moaned. "Bologna and peanut butter again."

Bruce laughed. "I've got salami, ham, and swiss. Ah, the life of a bachelor."

"At least I've got the good chips this time," Mack said, ripping open a bag of sour cream and onion Ruffles. Over the noise of the crackling bag, the guards heard a pounding resound through the front hall.

"What the—" Bruce began, but Mack was already on his feet with his flashlight raised though not switched on.

"There's someone at the front door," Mack said, pointing toward a waiting figure.

As Bruce approached, the figure held up a *Hidden Treasures* identification badge and pressed it against the glass for inspection.

"Ah, just one of those nutty appraisers," Bruce grumbled. "Some time of night to be working." He wrestled with a large bunch of jiggling keys until he had succeeded in unlocking the door's formidable deadbolt.

"Evening ma'am." Mack smiled at the woman. She blinded him with a brilliant smile and her beautiful face immediately captivated both men.

"So sorry to trouble you both," she purred, holding open the heavy glass door, "but I suddenly recalled a mistake I must correct before the show opens tomorrow. I'll only be back there for an hour or so."

At that moment, the woman dropped her trendy, rectangular purse and several items spilled out and rolled hither and thither across the marble floor. Bruce bent to retrieve a lipstick case and a pair of sunglasses while Mack picked up an expensive fountain pen and a roll of breath mints.

"Oh, how clumsy of me!" the woman cooed, taking advantage of the distracted guards by quickly sticking a piece of duct tape firmly over the door latch so that the knob could not automatically lock when closed. She released the door and watched with satisfaction as it closed but did not issue the soft click indicating that it was locked.

"Thank you ever so much," the woman said as Bruce returned her purse with the gawkiness of a teenage boy. He watched the woman's model-thin figure as she walked with elegant grace in the direction of the Great Hall. She paused outside of the door leading to the Ladies Room.

"Ma'am?" he called after her. "You need a flashlight?"

"No, thank you," she called back over her shoulder. "I've got my own torch."

As the woman's figure melted into the blackness, Bruce looked inquiringly at Mack.

"What's a torch?" he asked his partner.

Mack returned to the office and took a healthy bite from his sandwich. "Means flashlight," he chewed. "She's English. They say things a bit different over there." After crunching on a handful of chips, Mack reexamined his cards. "Come on now. Let's get this game going."

"What mistake do you think she's fixing?" asked Bruce as he fanned out his cards. After a moment's thought, he placed an ace of spades in the discard pile.

"Who knows?" Mack replied, studying the ace. "Whatever it is, she can't get into too much trouble back there." He eyed his partner's lunch pail enviously. "You gonna share that banana Moon Pie?"

Chapter 9

The basis of any cabinet, sideboard, wardrobe, cupboard or bookcase is a carcass. . . .

—KENNETH DAVIS AND THOM HENVEY,
RESTORING FURNITURE

Mack and Bruce were relieved at seven by the next shift. Their replacements, a stocky Italian from New Jersey by the name of Paolo and a black woman in her mid-forties named Crystal, arrived with steaming cups of coffee and a dozen donuts from the local grocery store, being that Krispy Kreme was temporarily unavailable.

Bruce helped himself to a glazed donut as he related the details of their late-night visitor.

"When did she finally leave?" Paolo asked as he slicked a strand of slippery, black hair back into place behind his ear.

Mack shrugged as he collected his belongings. "Dunno. We did rounds about an hour after we'd let her in and she was gone, far as we could tell. 'Course we had the alarms turned off just in case she decided to let herself out. Good thing we did, too."

"Strange time of night to come to work," Crystal said, taking a deep gulp of coffee. "I heard these antique people were kinda crazy, now I know it's the truth."

Paolo, who was a closet collector of Marvel comic books, looked at the floor sheepishly and confessed, "I watch that show, *Hidden Treasures*." As he met the raised eyebrows of his three coworkers, he squared his shoulders and added in a whispered bravado, "Ever seen the host? She's a hottie. Me, I'm hoping to get a glimpse of those long legs in person today."

"Yeah, too bad she's been in jail for your other two shifts, Romeo," Crystal teased.

"Ah, I heard all that on the TV, but *I* never thought she did it. Now, I wouldn't put it past that French guy, what's his name?"

"Got me," Crystal said nudging him in the shoulder. "*You're* the one watches the old ladies' antiques show, not us. Plus, why you always gotta go dissin' the French guy? You remember last year when you swore off French dressing and French wine on account of that *French* girl who dumped you? That what got you so hung up on the poor French? Huh?"

Paolo stroked his stubbly chin. "Jacqueline. Now *she* was a beauty, mama mia."

Mack and Bruce clapped Paolo on the shoulder on their way out and smiled warmly at Crystal.

"You two enjoy your shift, ya hear?" Mack said, opening the front door for Bruce. "Bachelors before old married men." He bowed to his partner.

"You're just angling for your own salami and cheese tonight," Bruce said as he exited.

"Got *that* right," Mack replied as he released the door.

Crystal waited in the hall so that she could listen to the front doors automatically click shut, indicating that they were still locked. Paolo began whistling as he moved down the hallway, switching on the seemingly endless rows of overheard lights as he strolled along.

Assuming that she couldn't hear the lock click into place over Paolo's frenzied whistling rendition of "Stayin' Alive," Crystal settled down in the break room to enjoy her breakfast before she took her post at the front door. From her uncomfortable plastic chair, she would check the ID badges of everyone who tried to enter the building. No badge, no entry until the museum was officially open at nine. Crystal had six children and she had heard every fib known to man. She was impervious to tears and unrelenting when it came to abiding by and enforcing the rules, whether she was at home or at work.

So when Molly arrived at the front door just after eight, Crystal stood up from her stiff, gray chair and opened the door just wide enough to ask, "ID, please."

"Oh! Sure." Molly immediately began shuffling through her bag as Crystal looked on with the same patient, bemused expression she wore while waiting for one of her four daughters to finish getting dressed for church.

"I think I left it in the car," Molly said, unsure if this was indeed the case.

"Can't let you in without it, ma'am," Crystal explained using her pleasant, but official tone.

Molly took one look at Crystal and knew that trying to get in without a proper badge would prove impossible. When the badge wasn't anywhere in her car, Molly suddenly had a vision of it sitting on top of her nightstand back at the Traveller.

"This is what happens when I only have one cup of coffee," Molly grumbled crossly, and then headed back to the bed-and-breakfast to retrieve her badge.

On the way upstairs, she heard Jessica and Borris speaking in hushed tones in the hallway outside of their rooms. There was no sign of Garrett. Clara was already at the Strawberry Street house supervising the loading crew who would be packing up all of Mrs. Sterling's possessions over the next few hours.

Unable to control her nosiness, Molly slowed her ascent and listened to her two friends.

"You know we could make it work," Borris was insisting. Jessica sighed heavily in exasperation. "How? Are we going to sign a contract, exchange drops of blood, what? There's no guarantee!"

"Look, I'm just telling you that I want out of this whole greedy business."

"Oh, Boris," Jessica said gently. "Money *does* matter. You've got to be more realistic about that."

At that moment, Molly shifted her weight and one of the wooden stairs groaned loudly. She quickly ran to the bottom, open and shut the front door, and then began her ascent once more, this time making the appropriate amount of casual noise.

"Hi there," Jessica said as they passed on the stairs.

"Forgot my badge." Molly smiled. Jessica's face looked drawn. Behind Jessica's tiny figure, Boris looked slightly defeated, but still held his body with the rigidity of a determined general.

"See you down there," he mumbled.

Molly watched them leave, grabbed her badge from her room, and then returned to her car. She was perplexed by the odd conversation she had just overheard. Were Jessica and Boris discussing a personal relationship or a business matter? Molly couldn't tell.

When she arrived back at the museum, the line that had begun to form outside the front door instantly distracted her. It looked like several hundred of the thousand ticket holders had already staked their places. Eager faces with hands or arms grasping treasures waited to discover whether or not their valuables belonged in a museum or in their next yard sale.

"Have fun." Molly smiled at the first few men and women in line and raised her ID badge for Crystal's examination.

"Come on in," Crystal said cheerfully. "I don't think you missed nothin'."

Paolo had turned on all the lights. He should have returned to his station guarding the Civil War exhibit, but he could not resist the urge to speak with Tony the Toy Man, so he lingered on the fringes of Tony's booth, peering around the corner of the white screen in order to see what Tony was up to.

"Are you spying on me?" Tony asked kindly, without looking up from the tin toy price guide he was reading.

"Um, no." Paolo edged closer to the booth. "Expecting a big crowd today?"

"Yep. There's a guy outside right now with a suitcase full of Popeye tin toys. Thought I'd better check my references before I see him." Tony raised his merry eyes to Paolo's. "You collect anything?" he asked.

Paolo nodded enthusiastically. "Marvel comics."

"Oh yeah? Which ones?"

Paolo stood up as straight and tall as his stocky body would allow. "I've got the number one X-Men. From 1963. Never read. I've got it in a plastic cover. Thing's beautiful, man. Not a crease or a wrinkle in sight."

"That's a keeper," Tony agreed. "I saw one go on eBay for just under a grand last week."

Paolo's face radiated pride and he squared his shoulders as he shouted happily at Tony. "So I've got something good!"

"You certainly do, my friend," Tony said, clapping Paolo on his broad back. "Now, if you'll excuse me . . ."

"Oh, sure, sure." Paolo retreated out of the booth and began whistling once again. By the time he had made his way back toward the Civil War exhibit, members of the public were already streaming inside and arranging themselves around the velvet stanchions.

Paolo was just about to turn the corner and head for his appointed gray chair when he spotted Victoria Sterling greeting several members of the crew. She wore a formfitting pantsuit in sage green with a white blouse, her triple strand of pearls, and a black and white striped handkerchief. Her hair was puffed and sprayed in place and her makeup was far too heavy and dramatic for daytime wear, but Paolo thought Victoria looked absolutely stunning.

He smiled at her widely as she passed by him in a fog of musky perfume. Dumbly, he watched her pass and fantasized that she would suddenly stop, turn, and see him as the man of her dreams. But the sound that pierced his stupor was not a sexual invitation from Victoria Sterling's sensuous painted lips. The sharp sound was out of place among the echoed murmurs of the museum patrons.

Someone was shouting. A man. A man was shouting. No, he was screaming. "HELP! HELP!" Paolo's body finally jolted into action. He broke into a run as several other people ran past him in the opposite direction, clutching valuables and screaming.

Was there a fire? Paolo's mind raced. Where were the alarms?

"HELP!" the man shouted again, a plea then taken up by a woman who began screaming it over and over in a hysterical tirade.

When Paolo finally got to the source of the screams, he immediately reached out toward the man and woman in order to try to calm them down. He briefly noticed shards of some kind of pottery scattered across the floor. The man shoved him roughly aside and pointed at something above and behind Paolo's back. The women stooped, sobbing, and began to mindlessly retrieve the yellow-brown shards of pottery.

Paolo swiveled his broad shoulders, utterly confused.

"My God," he whispered as his eyes registered the terrible sight before them.

A larger than life statue of Robert E. Lee stood against a wall painted with the state flag of Virginia. Lee held a sword in one hand and his army cap in the other. Above his meticulously detailed beard, his mouth looked grim, his jaw locked in earnest determination. Only the eyes, nestled beneath shaggy brows, betrayed a look of proud gentility mixed with a trace of deep sorrow. His uniform was obscured. Not by a piece of marble sash or by the mane of his horse, but by the long, thin body of a dead woman.

Hanging from Lee's neck, to which she was tied with her own Hermès scarf, the dead woman's head drooped at a severe downward angle and her expensive, leather pumps had been kicked off and lay useless at the base of the statue. Black tracks from where the heels had scraped across the marble crisscrossed Lee's thighs, like fresh wounds, but he didn't seem to notice them.

Alexandra looked like a statue herself. She was white and cold and utterly still.

Chapter 10

*Most broken legs can be repaired, the simpler ones even replaced.
But if you come across an elaborately curved leg with a compound
fracture, involving splits down the grain and loss of timber, remember that you will not be able to mend or replace it yourself
unless your skills resemble those of the original maker.*

—*The Illustrated Guide to Furniture Repair
and Restoration*

Molly watched people whisk by as they raced for
the exit in a complete panic, clutching their valuables to their chests as they shoved one another aside. Murmurs that there was a dead body in the Civil War exhibit
flooded through the front hall like a swift wind.

Molly shot a nervous glance at Crystal, who was listening to Paolo's frantic garbling over the walkie-talkie as she
edged toward the phone in the break room. Molly pointed
toward the front doors.

"Should I lock them?" she mouthed to Crystal as she
twisted her hand in a pantomimed locking motion. Crystal
rapidly nodded while reaching for the phone.

"No one is allowed in!" Molly opened the door and
shouted at the curious group of people pushing to enter the
building. "There has been an incident inside! Please back
away from the doors!" She turned the deadbolt and took her
stand by the door, shooing away determined members of
the public who banged on the door or shouted to be let in.

Several members of the *Hidden Treasures* crew quickly took up Molly's cue and began ushering the people waiting in line within the front hall outside, making sure that no Nosy Nellies slipped through the doors while this mass exodus was taking place.

"Thanks, I got it from here," Crystal said, suddenly appearing at Molly's side. "The cops are comin'."

"I'd better make sure no one else slipped by," Molly offered helpfully as she hustled off toward the Civil War exhibit. Her motivation to see if the rumor about a dead body was true should have come from a professional desire to investigate the scene as any first-rate reporter would, but Molly didn't give a single thought to her job as she wondered what had happened deeper inside the museum. Pure and simple curiosity propelled her toward the dark-haired security guard who stood staring up at the dead body of a woman strung up on a statue of the city's most beloved general.

"Alexandra," Molly whispered and stopped short at the sight of the limp figure and the stream of copper hair that covered the dead woman's face like an inert curtain. Molly put her hand over her mouth as if to contain any sound that might bubble up uncontrollably through her throat as she looked from Alexandra's drooping head, to Paolo's gaping mouth, to a woman sitting cross-legged on the floor fondling a pile of yellow-brown and black pottery shards nestled in her lap. The woman's long skirt had formed a soft bowl for the pieces to sit in and the woman fingered them repeatedly as she glanced up at Alexandra's body.

As Molly bent over her, the woman cried, "My Rookwood floor vase!" She held up two shards with traces of floral decoration for Molly to see. "Ruined! And it was signed, too! I saw . . . I saw . . . and it just slipped from my hands! Oh . . . God . . ."

"It's going to be all right," Molly said gently, touching the sobbing woman lightly on the shoulder. She then marched over and grabbed Paolo roughly by the arm.

"Snap out of it, man!" she ordered. "Can't you see this

woman is in shock? Get her to the cafeteria and give her something to drink. Crystal's called the police. They're on their way."

Paolo finally blinked as he looked away from Alexandra and turned his wide brown eyes toward Molly. "Who are you?" he asked numbly.

"I'm with the show!" Molly snapped. "Now get her out of here!" She pointed at the woman on the floor.

"Nasturtiums," the woman was sobbing as she swayed from side to side. "Van Briggle . . . lost . . . my beautiful nasturtiums . . ."

Paolo tenderly removed the glass from the woman's lap and placed it in the overturned cardboard box near her feet. The woman watched Paolo as he moved each piece of pottery as if he were transferring a baby bird to a new nest. She seemed immensely comforted by his delicacy. Finally, she allowed him to help her stand. She gathered the box in her arms and let herself be steered away from the exhibit.

"I'll make sure no one else gets in," Molly assured Paolo as she marveled at her own nerve. Who was she to be giving orders to the security guard? Still, she thought, he wasn't exactly a man of action.

Molly made a full circle of the room, but could see no traces of evidence that would indicate how Alexandra ended up being hung from Lee's statue. Aside from the presence of a dead body and Alexandra's discarded shoes and Gucci purse, which was lodged between Lee's marble boots, nothing seemed out of place around the exhibit. There were simply no signs of the violent act that had been committed in this space.

As Molly double-checked the display case of coins, documents, and daguerreotypes, Jessica and Borris entered the exhibit area.

Jessica immediately screamed and covered her eyes with her hands. Borris turned toward Molly with a completely dumbfounded expression before enfolding Jessica in his arms. The other appraisers came running into the room en masse. Yelps and shouts of surprise and dismay filled the air, but everyone remained a careful distance from the corpse.

Time moved into a slow-motion crawl as Molly stared at the other appraisers. A shiver ran down her spine as she realized that there was no possibility that Randy had killed Alexandra. Was someone else in this group a murderer? She scanned the faces of Lindsey, Alicia, Tony, Victoria, Patrice, Garrett, Jessica, and Borris, but they all registered only horror mixed with pity at their latest coworker's gruesome ending.

Everyone seemed to be waiting for someone to break the trance. As the minutes ticked by, a heavy feeling of unspoken accusations and nervousness descended on the silent group.

Finally, Tony cleared his throat and said, "Guess she talked shit about the wrong general last night." He tried to laugh, but the sound came out as a strangled squeak and as the others glared at him in disgust, he squatted down on the floor and put his head down in his arms. "What is happening in this goddamn museum?" he asked in a muffled plea. Alicia softly touched his mop of brown hair and he leaned against her leg like a small child.

"Who could have done this to her?" Lindsey asked, pulling a tissue out of her cavernous needlepoint handbag. "I wish we could get her down. She looks awful up there."

"I'm going to be sick!" Jessica clamped her hand over her mouth and ran off in the direction of the Ladies' Room.

Borris turned to follow, hesitated, and then looked in silent appeal at Molly. She simply nodded and headed after Jessica, relieved to be in motion and heading away from Alexandra's corpse.

As she headed for the restroom, a team of policemen jogged down the hallway. Molly recognized the burly, red-headed figure of Officer Combs.

"You again?" he asked, none too kindly. "I don't like how bodies seem to pop up when you're around. What's your rush?"

"Look." Molly's eyes narrowed. "*I* didn't find this one

and I'm going to the bathroom to check on a friend of mine. I think she's sick."

"Well, get her and go straight to the cafeteria. We'll be questioning all of you antique freaks from there." Combs signaled at one of his officers. "Make sure they go straight downstairs." He uttered a tired sigh as he continued down the hallway. "Robeson's not going to like this mess."

Molly threw Combs a look of malice, but he was already on his way toward the Civil War exhibit and the group of startled appraisers.

Molly quietly opened the bathroom door to find Jessica leaning over one of the sinks, splashing cold water on her face and into her mouth. Tracks of black mascara ran down her cheeks and her face was covered with red blotches. She glanced at Molly in the mirror but didn't speak.

"You okay?" Molly asked in a whisper. She felt that there was something extremely fragile about Jessica in this moment.

The petite woman mechanically patted her face dry with a paper towel and then pressed her hands against her temples. "No," she replied so softly, that if Molly had not seen her lips move in the mirror, she would not have know that Jessica had spoken at all.

"The police are here. . . ." Molly faltered. She was never good at comforting people. She could never find the right words to say. "They'll make this right. There's a really good guy in charge of this . . . tragedy."

Jessica turned away from the mirror and looked at Molly. Her eyes were filled with despair. "You don't understand. I . . . I may have had something to do with . . . with Alexandra's death."

Molly froze. "What do you mean?"

Jessica reached for another paper towel and blew her nose into it. "I can't say. Not yet." She gazed at her disheveled reflection in the mirror. "What will Borris think? Oh God . . ."

Molly moved closer to her friend until she stood beside her. In the mirror, Molly's own reflection looked wide-eyed

and pale. "Jessica, the police are here. If you know anything, anything at all, you'd better tell them. This Detective
Robeson isn't one to screw around with. If you've got
something to hide, he's going to find out."

Jessica shook her head from side to side. "I know, I
know. Damn it!" she shouted, her voice banging off the
tiles like a cannon shot. "He'll never forgive me . . . he'll
never understand!"

"Who? Borris?" Molly asked. Then she grabbed Jessica
by the shoulders until the older woman looked up and
faced herself again in the mirror. "Listen, Borris loves you.
If you love him, then tell the truth."

"I will, I will!" Jessica promised. "But to him first, before the police."

Molly hesitated. She dropped her hands from her friend's
shoulders and moved off to the side. "Do you want to try it
out on me first?" she asked as gently as she knew how.

Jessica threw her wad of paper towels in the trash and
ran her hands through her cropped white hair. "No, thanks.
I *will* tell Borris, though, as soon as we go. I promise you."

That would have to be enough, Molly thought. She noticed that half of Jessica's damp paper towels had missed the
trash bin. She automatically reached down to gather them up
when she spied a small square of white paper laying on the
ground.

Picking it up, she unfolded it and saw a note that could
only have been scrawled to Alexandra.

A—

Meet me at the Civil War exhibit just after midnight.
I must see you.
I've wanted you, but I had to wait.
All will be made clear tonight.

Jessica sucked in a sharp breath as she looked at the
note. "I got one of those, too. Same handwriting."

"Did yours say to come here last night?" Molly asked.

Jessica stared at the note, her dark eyes opened wide in disbelief. "No. I got mine weeks ago. It's from the same person, though. I recognize that writing."

"Who is it, Jessica? *Who is it?*" Molly asked more harshly than she had intended.

"I don't know exactly!" Jessica yelled frantically. "I don't! Mine wasn't signed either!"

"What did it say?"

"Borris first." Jessica abruptly turned toward the door. "After that, it doesn't matter who knows." And she went out.

Molly put the note inside a paper towel and folded the towel in half. She nodded at the policeman waiting outside the restroom for her as she watched Jessica's small figure moving down the hall.

"This was in the bathroom." She handed him the paper towel. "There's a note in there. I think it might be evidence."

"Did you touch it?" the officer asked.

"Yes. I picked it up and read it. I didn't know what it was."

"Okay," the officer said. "I'll give this to Detective Robeson. Let's get you to the cafeteria now. And you'd better get some coffee," he suggested kindly. "It's going to be a long day."

FREDERICKSBURG, VIRGINIA 1778

"They call themselves the 'Hazard Club' after the dice game, but it seems clear that their name has a more dire meaning," Elspeth said and she stood up, leaning heavily against the slant-front desk for support. *"I will burn this letter, and then no one will know of the club's wicked assignment or of my shame."*

"No!" Thomas grabbed Elspeth's hand as she reached out to release the parchment into the blazing hearth.

Elspeth's blue eyes grew round with surprise as she watched Thomas's dirt-smudged hand close upon her own white-laced sleeve. "Pardon me, miss, but if you burn that letter, the others in the Hazard Club will not be revealed. We must let them believe their secret place is yet undiscovered and then catch them in the act of . . . um, what is it they have planned?"

"They plan to destroy the munitions factory," Elspeth said, folding the parchment neatly into a small square once again. *"In two nights, on the full moon."* Elspeth handed

Thomas the document and he replaced it within the hollow niche in the slide support and then pulled the writing lid back down. His hand lingered on the smooth, simple finish of the black walnut and he was instantly comforted by its reliable strength and durability.

"My father is just like this piece you made, Mr. Fleming—full of secrets. And my own brother, my dear Charles! He has marched north to join with General Washington and my father betrays him even now, as he faces battle for the first time. Why he's barely more than a child, but he ran off and enlisted before my father had a chance to talk sense into him. Now I know why Father was so upset when he found out." She spit his moniker out as if it tasted foul to her tongue. "He wasn't concerned for his son's welfare, but that his child had chosen the wrong side!"

"I'm sorry, miss." Thomas searched for something to say. "You can help your brother by protecting our weapons. I know a few men who can be trusted through thick and thin. We shall stop the plans of the Hazard Club, never fear."

"And what shall I do?" Elspeth asked angrily. "Serve my father tea and cakes as if nothing has happened?"

"He must not know you have discovered his secret. Your life could be in danger, miss—"

"—Elspeth, please. You and I are in this together now . . ." Elspeth managed an almost indiscernible wry smile.

"Thomas, at your service," he said with an awkward bow. His bent leg had long since robbed him of any hope of grandiose gestures, but Elspeth was moved by his composure and felt assured that he was the type of man who was exactly as he appeared: simple, loyal, and honorable.

"We shall form our own society, Thomas. You and I will bring down the Hazard Club with a single blow. If there are any complications, then I shall come to your shop and warn you. Now I will give you all the details of the planned attack against the munitions factory so that you can share

them with our fellow patriots. In return, I want to see my father arrested, but not harmed. Agreed?"

Thomas nodded his assent, feeling a growing respect for this young woman's pluck.

Elspeth related the details of the short letter. Once she had finished, she began removing a ribbon the shade of cornflowers from her hair. "Give me your hair tie," she demanded. "We shall trade to show our allegiance to one another."

"It matches your eyes," Thomas stated shyly, holding the delicate piece of silk in his large palm.

Elspeth smiled a bittersweet smile, taking the piece of leather Thomas held out to her. "At least I have made a friend today. It eases the pain a trifle."

"Aye, that you have. If any trouble should arise for you, miss . . . I mean, Elspeth, seek me out and I shall protect you."

"My thanks, but you had better go now. My maid is half-witted, but not so half-witted that she would believe it would take this long for you to measure our dining room. Good luck and go with care."

"You as well. I shall see you again once all the traitors are under lock and key." Thomas moved to the front door. "You are a brave young lady. The patriots are fortunate to have you on their side."

"You as well, Thomas Fleming. I shall see you in three days," Elspeth said as she shut the door.

Outside, Thomas glanced down at the blue ribbon in his hand. He brought it to his face and smelled a hint of jasmine. Clutching the ribbon gently in his fist, Thomas rushed back to the workshop, where he began to plan the fall of the Hazard Club.

Chapter 11

Pray, for what do we move ever but to get rid of our furniture, our exuviæ; at last to go from this world to another newly furnished, and leave this to be burned?

—*The Writings of Henry David Thoreau*

The cafeteria was filled with anxious appraisers and *Hidden Treasures* crew members in their black T-shirts. The subdued whispering coupled with all of the black clothing created a funereal atmosphere. Molly's eyes darted about in search of Jessica, but at that moment Detective Robeson and a host of other giant policemen entered the room.

"Holy Christ," mumbled Patrice. "The Titans have arrived."

"Who?" Alicia asked nervously.

"You know. Greek Mythology. The Titans were enormous beings who once ruled the earth. They were taller than the mountains and could shake the ground when they walked. This group looks just as alarming."

"That's their intimidation factor," Alicia replied, twisting a clump of her shiny black hair into a knot. "And it's working."

"All right, people!" Officer Combs called for quiet. The

room was instantaneously still. "We're calling you in for questioning one at a time. You will follow me to the staff lounge, be fingerprinted, questioned, and then taken to another room. No one leaves this building until we say so. Do not talk about this case. Get food or drink as you need and if you must use the facilities, ask an officer for permission and you will be escorted to the restrooms. Only one person at a time in the restroom. Is this clear?"

Several heads nodded. "Now, we've got about forty people to question so we have decided to proceed alphabetically. We will begin with Adams, Christopher Adams."

Most the women in the room couldn't help but follow Chris's progress to the front of the room with appreciative stares. Molly was again struck by the surreal color of his aquamarine eyes as he turned to smile at someone who had whispered "good luck." His tight, black T-shirt stretched across his muscular back as he quickly approached Officer Combs.

"To the lion's den I go." He tried to sound nonchalant, but his clenched fists and white knuckles revealed his nervousness.

"It'll be over in no time," Molly offered, feeling sorry for the handsome young man. She was rewarded with a shy grin before Combs grabbed Chris by the arm and led him away as if he were already deemed guilty.

Ten minutes later, Combs returned, list in hand. "Appleby, Molly!" he yelled even though Molly was seated front and center. She felt as though she were heading for the electric chair as all eyes in the room fastened on her. Garrett, who was seated beside her, patted her hand and gave her a ridiculously comic wink. She hoped her rear end didn't look big in her stretch khaki pants as she trotted off next to Combs.

Molly was fingerprinted in less than a minute and then given a moist towelette to attempt the futile removal of black ink from her fingers. Scrubbing at her right thumb, she was led before Detective Robeson and asked to sit in a rock-hard wooden chair in front of him. Only a spartan metal table separated them. Robeson turned his legal pad to a fresh page and began talking.

"So let's start with last night, Miss Appleby," he said in a no-nonsense tone. Not a single trace of yesterday's gentleness lingered. "Tell me about what you did since I saw you yesterday. What did you do for dinner, for example? Leave no detail out, please. You never know what could turn out to be important."

Molly stared at Robeson's massive hand as he gripped his pencil like a vise. She gulped and began to recite every nuance of last night's meal at Elmo's, from the seating arrangement, to what everyone ate, to Victoria's dramatic entrance. When she reached the part about Alexandra declaring the Dahlonega coins a fake, Robeson's eyes finally left his paper and came to rest on Molly's face.

"Hold on, hold on. Tell me more about these coins."

Molly repeated what she had learned from the gentleman curator in the seersucker suit. She explained what he had told her about the rarity of the coins and their incredible monetary value.

"So this local curator quoted you a value of close to five hundred thousand dollars?" Robeson asked, a spark of interest appearing in his molasses-brown eyes.

"Yes, sir," Molly said, relaxing. Once again, she felt that she could be of help to the taciturn detective. She could already envision the headline of the next issue of *Collector's Weekly*. It would read, "Reporter Aids Richmond Police in Solving Two Homicides."

"Now there's a motive," Combs mumbled and Robeson shot him an aggravated glance.

"Please continue." Robeson raised his pencil and held it poised over the legal pad.

"A motive *and* a means," Molly added smugly to what Combs suggested.

"What *means*? Explain." Robeson lifted one eyebrow like an expectant schoolteacher.

"There was a blackout on Tuesday. It only lasted about

five minutes, but that would have been long enough to steal the Dahlonega coins and replace them with fakes." Molly remembered the pinprick of light she had seen near the display cabinet containing the coins. "I didn't think anything of it at the time," she continued excitedly, "but someone *could* have been back there, swapping the coins! I saw a light, you know, like one of those penlight things." Again Molly drifted away into colorful visions of bold newspaper headlines. Surely all of the South's major papers would want to run such a sensational story.

"Hmmm." Robeson took a few notes. "Let's get back to the dinner, now."

Disappointed in Robeson's lack of fervor over her testimony thus far, Molly went on to describe Jessica knocking over the wineglass and Alexandra's denouncement of General Lee. She finished by repeating who went home in which car.

"So you, Borris, Jessica, and your mother returned to the Traveller just before ten o'clock. Is that right?"

Molly nodded. "The others are staying at the hotel a few miles west of here. I don't remember the name, but it's a chain hotel. Garrett took Victoria to the hotel in his car, because the minivan was full, but he's staying with us at the Traveller. I don't know when he got back. I'm a pretty heavy sleeper."

"And what about this morning? What did you do?" Robeson scribbled on his pad.

"Not too much to tell there. I got up at about seven, had breakfast, came here, forgot my ID badge, went back to my hotel for it, came here again, and saw the body." Molly examined her stained fingers unhappily. "Will I be able to wash after this?"

"Yes," Robeson said distractedly. "Did you see anyone else at your hotel before coming here?"

Molly remembered returning to the Traveller in order to retrieve her ID badge. She hesitated, but then described the short conversation she had overheard between Jessica and Borris. Robeson was bound to find out anyway.

"What do you think *that* was about?" Combs demanded.

"I have no idea." Molly shrugged innocently. "I just met these people a few days ago."

"Combs"—Robeson pointed at the door without looking up—"go get the next person for questioning."

Combs sulked but did as he was told. Now that she was alone with Robeson, Molly's hands began to grow clammy. Robeson stared at his pad, unblinking and silent, while Molly wondered what he was thinking.

"I don't think they're the ones," Molly offered quietly. "Borris and Jessica, I mean. That note . . ." She struggled to put her thoughts into words. "It implies some kind of intimate meeting. At least that's the way I read it. Borris and Jessica are in love with one another, even though she won't admit it, so neither of them would be involved with Alexandra."

"So." Robeson cupped his large chin with his hand and rubbed his stubble. "Who do you like for it, then?"

Molly hesitated, not comprehending this "cop talk" phrase, but then she translated the question: "Who is the killer?"

"Randy's in the clear for this murder. He's still in jail, right?" Molly asked.

Robeson nodded in agreement.

"Someone didn't want Alexandra talking to that local curator this morning. She had to be killed before she spoke to him. No one else knows coins, except for Garrett, so unless he or the curator examined them and raised the alarm, no one would believe for certain they were fakes. If no one examined them, then whoever stole the original coins could get away with robbery. Today is the show's last day. Tomorrow the crew packs up. He or she would have been scot-free within twenty-four hours."

Robeson said nothing. The clock on the wall circulated

its red second hand forward with a persistent hum. "Any holes to this theory?" Robeson finally asked.

Molly sighed. "Yeah, plenty. Why kill Alexandra when her death only draws attention to the fake coins? And why kill her in the museum? It's like the killer wanted to make a big statement, but now the whole world will be looking for him."

Robeson stood. "I'll take your statement into serious consideration. If you think of anything else, let me know." He strode past her and opened the door. "And Ms. Appleby," he said as he looked down at her benevolently, "good work finding that note."

Molly smiled. "Thanks." She paused in the doorway. "Um, will you want to talk to my mother?"

Robeson shook his head. "Not at the moment. You're free to go as well. Just don't return to the cafeteria."

"Yes, sir." Molly avoided eye contact with Combs as he led a terrified crew member toward the fingerprinting station.

"Do I need a lawyer?" the man asked, his hands violently trembling over the inkpads.

"Not unless you've got something to hide," Combs stated wickedly. "And where do you think you're going?" he asked Molly sharply.

"Detective Robeson said I could leave," she retorted. "So I'm leaving!" And then unable to think of some caustic remark to sting him with, Molly stuck her tongue out at the stunned policeman.

The first thing Molly did upon arriving at the Traveller was to take off her pointy shoes, which had been mashing her toes together until they formed a warped triangle. After kicking them aside, she resolved to trade in style for comfort where her feet were concerned, and then flopped onto the comfortable bed with a sigh of relief. She wanted to spend a few minutes trying to digest all that had happened in the last few days. Randy killed Frank and now Alexandra had been murdered. Was there a connection between the two murders or was someone else simply inspired by Randy's act of violence?

Molly could only assume that Randy had killed Frank out of pent-up rage. So Frank's was a murder ignited by hatred mixed with a little insanity. Someone must have killed Alexandra to prevent her from meeting with the curator and firmly establishing that the valuable Dahlonega coins were actually fakes. That crime was motivated by fear, but also by hatred as well. Stringing Alexandra up so that she would hang from Lee's marble neck was a deliberate and almost vengeful act. But who would do such a thing?

As Molly began thinking back on all the conversations from last night's dinner, she began to grow sleepy. I'll just close my eyes for a second, she thought. Within minutes, she was fast asleep.

Two hours later, Molly awoke with a throbbing bladder. The four cups of coffee she had consumed that morning had filled her close to the bursting point. She was hungry, too. After taking care of her more immediate needs, Molly pulled out a large bag of fat-free pretzels, a spiral notebook, and a pen from her bag. Sitting at the mahogany writing desk, she tore open the bag of pretzels and began to create a list of all those present at last night's dinner. It was time to figure out who the killer was.

Molly knew that she could eliminate Lex, Clara, and herself as possible murderers. That left Garrett, Victoria, Jessica, Borris, Tony, Patrice, Lindsey, and Alicia. Unless two of them were working together, Molly did not think any of the women had the strength to pull Alexandra's body into the air and secure the woman's dead weight to Lee's statue. Even though Alexandra probably weighed a mere 130 pounds, that still was a formidable weight for another woman to lift.

Molly was just beginning to create a column named "motive" next to the name of each appraiser when the phone rang, scattering her thoughts completely.

"Hello?" she answered crossly, not bothering to mask her annoyance at being interrupted. How could she become a famous heroine if she had no time to think?

"Molly?" a familiar voice asked.

Molly's heart skipped two beats. "Mark? Is that you?"

"God, Molly. I've been trying to reach you for days! Didn't you get my number in Ohio?"

"No. That new receptionist, Britanni, said you didn't leave it for me," Molly said, disliking the whiny, defensive tone that had crept into her voice.

Mark groaned. "Of course I did. And the number *she* gave me for *you* is completely wrong. I've been waking up this poor old man night after night. He's ready to kill me."

Molly laughed, relief flooding through her that Mark had not forgotten about her. "It is *so* good to hear your voice, Mark. Things are really crazy up here."

"So I've heard," Mark said seriously. "I talked to Clayton yesterday about the death of Frank Sterling. Are you okay?"

"Yes, I'm fine." Molly reassured him. "In fact, there was another murder last night." She went on to describe the group dinner, how Alexandra had been strangled, and how she, Molly, had been of invaluable assistance to the Richmond police force. This last bit was slightly exaggerated, but Molly could never resist an opportunity to make herself look good in front of Mark.

Mark was worried. "So there have been no arrests?"

"Not yet."

"Molly, I don't like this. Don't stick your nose into this one. Let the police find the murderer. Why don't you come home? The show's over now anyway, right?"

Molly squeezed the receiver affectionately. She loved it that Mark was fretting over her. Just the way he said "home" seemed like he was really saying she should return to *him*.

Maybe their relationship could really become official once she was back in North Carolina. Shaking away rosy visions of Mark sweeping her feather-light body into his arms and swinging her around like a top, Molly replied, "It's sweet of you to worry about me, Mark, but everything's fine. And the police need all the help they can get. Now, tell me what's going on with you. What happened with your brother?"

"Don't try to change the subject. Johnny got into a car accident and his leg was broken. I went to Ohio to help him home from the hospital and to stock his fridge and stuff. His girlfriend's taking next week off of work, so I'm coming home tomorrow."

"Maybe we'll *finally* get to spend some time together," Molly said hopefully.

"Only if you promise to stay out of this mess, Molly. What's the name of this bed-and-breakfast you're in?"

"The Traveller, after Lee's famous horse. Why?"

"I just want to set that Britanni straight when I get back to the office on Monday," Mark replied sternly.

"I think she saw your picture on the staff wall and developed a crush on you," Molly teased. "Can't say that I blame her."

Mark's tone softened. "Look Molly. Come home tomorrow. I'll take you out wherever you want to go."

Molly was highly tempted by the tender pleading in Mark's voice. "We'll see. This is a huge story, Mark. Swanson would string me up like a set of Christmas lights if I left now."

Mark uttered a defeated sigh. "You're probably right. Just be careful, please. I'm going to call you tomorrow night as soon as I get in." He paused. "I miss you, Molly."

Molly felt warmth flow through her face. "I miss you, too," she whispered, smiling. After she hung up, she practically bounced off the bed and grabbed her pad listing the names of the appraisers. It was time to do some sleuthing, but first, she needed to discover the secret Jessica had been keeping. She looked at her watch. It was time for tea. Hopefully, Borris and Jessica were back from being questioned and Clara would be available as well. Her mother would help Molly straighten out her theories by playing devil's advocate to everything she said.

Barreling down the stairs most ungracefully, Molly arrived in the dining room to the welcome sight of her mother's crown of thick brown hair, her head bent over an antique furniture reference guide. She also recognized the tantalizing aroma of warm bread pudding.

Clara looked up from her book. "You sounded like a herd of elephants just now. Where's the fire?"

"No fire, but if that's bread pudding with vanilla custard sauce then my day has just improved significantly," Molly said, pouring herself a cup of tea.

"What's going on around here, anyway?" Clara demanded. "Jessica and Borris came straight in the front door and then locked themselves in the parlor. They've been in there almost an hour and I can't hear a word they're saying." She frowned in annoyance. "I can't stand it! Would you put down that spoon and go do some snooping."

Molly grinned at her mother. "And people wonder where I get my nosiness from? Look, Ma," she said spooning a generous portion of bread pudding loaded with plump raisins on her plate, "I haven't had any lunch today, so don't be shocked at how much of this I eat. Plus, I need the energy. You and I have a murder to solve."

"I thought Randy was already in jail." Clara remained nonplussed.

"Not *that* murder. There's been another one. Now be quiet so I can fill you in on all the details."

"Oh boy," Clara closed her book and took a swallow of tea. "I can see that cocktail time is going to start a little early today."

Chapter 12

I have gone through almost trackless forest, over rugged roads, or crumbling doorways; I have gone on the spur of a moment of notice of a sale or of any division of an estate, the breaking up of a home, or the division of property.

—PAUL BURROUGHS, *SOUTHERN ANTIQUES*

Strong afternoon sunlight slanted into the front parlor of the quiet bed-and-breakfast. The bookshelves flanking the fireplace were loaded with antique reference guides, mostly about porcelain collecting, and a dozen binders filled with pristine back issues of *Southern Living*. A pair of sterling Tiffany candlesticks holding cranberry-colored beeswax candles stood proudly on the mantel and an array of glass paperweights lined the space between the candlesticks. Occasionally, a shard of sunlight would catch a splinter of cobalt or emerald green within one of the paperweights and the color would soar outside of its casement, like a ghost rising from a coffin.

Seated in a wingback chair, Jessica sat staring down at her folded hands. Across the room in a matching chair, Borris gazed emptily at the intricate patterns of the crimson and navy blue wool Caucasian rug. He traced the ochre border of diamonds with his left foot as if deep in thought. Finally, he stood, glancing briefly toward the bay windows and out onto the street beyond, before wordlessly leaving the room.

As the French doors dividing the parlor from the hall opened, Molly and Clara watched Borris expectantly. He glanced at them briefly, sorrowfully, his stately face mottled with red patches where he had dragged his hands roughly across the skin. With an expression of anger mixed with confusion, Borris opened his mouth as if to speak, then abruptly turned and burst through the front door. He slammed it so hard behind him that the glass panes rattled.

Mrs. Hewell scurried into the hall from the kitchen. "Hello?" she called as she approached. "Here for tea?" She stopped as she noticed Molly and Clara already seated in the dining room. "Oh good! I was worried the bread pudding would go cold."

"It's absolutely delicious," Molly quickly assured her.

"And where is the charming Englishman and that delightful couple who usually join you? Busy at work?" Mrs. Hewell looked around.

Trying to distract Mrs. Hewell before she spotted Jessica sitting forlornly in the parlor, Clara jumped up and said, "Oh, I would just love to know more about your collection of sterling tea strainers. I snooped around your kitchen yesterday and saw them hanging above the sink. Where on earth did you find them all?"

Mrs. Hewell beamed. "Each one has its own story. I'd love to tell you about them, my dear. Come along with me."

Confident that Mrs. Hewell would be tied up for longer than Clara might like, Molly made her way quietly into the parlor.

"How did it go?" she asked Jessica softly.

"Well, now he thinks I'm a total schmuck, but what else could he think?" Jessica looked up. Tears swam in her eyes but she refused to let them fall. "I didn't tell the detective the whole truth this morning, so I'll have to go back in now."

"Would you like me to come along?" Molly asked, gazing at her friend anxiously.

Jessica's shoulders sagged in resignation. "Thanks. I could use the company."

"I'd better let them know we're coming," Molly said. "Let me go upstairs and get my keys. I'll call Robeson and then take you down to the station."

"I'll be here." Jessica leaned back in her chair and closed her eyes. "It's time to face the music."

"You believe you've been an unintentional accessory in Ms. Lincoln's death?" Robeson asked calmly. From his chair set back in the corner of the room, Combs stared at Jessica like a hungry wolf that has suddenly happened upon a wounded sheep.

"Yes, Detective," Jessica said, taking a swig of water from the plastic bottle she always seemed to have with her. "But I need to start from the beginning in order to explain all of this. And it's a long story."

"We've got all the time in the world," Robeson replied casually. "You just tell us what you came here to tell us. However you need to do it is up to you."

"Thank you," Jessica nodded in gratitude.

"It all started with me and Saul, my ex-husband. We met back in college. He was studying business and I was trying out all different branches of the arts, but I found my real passion when I took a class in metallurgy. Seems I had a natural, God-given gift for jewelry-making. In fact, I sold so much of it during the last two years of college, that I was able to save enough money to pay for graduate school.

"The summer after our college graduation, Saul and I got married. Boy, I thought our future was so neatly mapped out. Saul got an MBA and I began to make a name for myself as a jeweler by creating copies of famous pieces of historical jewelry, mostly antiquities. I could copy anything from an Egyptian necklace to a pair of Byzantine earrings. Of course, my jewelry was much more affordable. Saul worked as an investment banker, but it wasn't long before he quit and we opened a jewelry store featuring my work and all of the other regular stuff, like watches and engagement rings. We also carried antique furniture and some old art.

"We were living in Atlanta then. Everything was going great. I gave birth to beautiful twin boys named Jacob and James. Over the next two or three years, our store, Rosen Jewelry & Antiques, made so much money that we opened a second store, and then a third. It was this success that was to spell the end of my marriage. You see, Saul hired a retired jewelry appraiser to run our third store, but this man didn't want to work weekends, so Saul also hired a ditzy blonde named Barbara to cover those hours. She seemed honest, reliable, and even had some retail experience, but she knew nothing about jewelry. Saul said he had a good feeling about her, so he hired her anyway.

"Good feeling? Ha! He *felt* her all right. Apparently, they had an affair through the entire second half of our marriage—that would be eight years. When I began to grow increasingly suspicious, Saul began to seriously plan his escape. He transferred all kinds of funds to secret accounts and put everything he could in his own name, from our new house, to cars, to the third store—you name it. I was too busy designing jewelry and raising our sons to bother too much about the financial side. Oovay! Would I come to regret that!

"The day after the twins graduated from junior high, we threw them a huge party. It was the last time they would ever see their father. The next day, Sunday, Saul got up before everyone else, put a suitcase in the car, and disappeared. Every dime in our accounts, including the trust set up for the boys' college fund, was gone. Even the money in the store tills was taken, along with the entire inventory of three shops. Of course, Barbara was gone, too.

"To make a longer story a little less long, let me say that I hired a private investigator who eventually found Saul sunning himself at a mansion in Coconut Grove, Florida. My P.I. served Saul with a lawsuit and divorce papers at the same time. Little good either one did me. Saul died two days later from a heart attack. Personally, I think God struck Saul down with some invisible lightning, but believe it or not, his death left me even worse off than before. He left everything to Barbara, who gave birth to a little girl shortly after they moved to Florida. I am *still* contesting Saul's will."

Jessica took a big breath, and then exhaled slowly as if releasing some of the anger she had gathered in the telling of her tale. "My boys are hard workers. They helped me stay afloat with one store until I was invited to join *Hidden Treasures*. We moved to a duplex in Charlotte and my mother moved in with us. Jacob and James, they took part-time jobs instead of playing sports or dating or doing all the things high school boys should be able to do. Both of them are going to apply to N.C. State this spring, but even with financial aid, I'm not making enough to send them both. The damned lawyers . . . they've been sucking me dry for years . . ."

Here Jessica had to pause. Talking about her dutiful sons and her husband's betrayal was something she had never done, not with anyone. Emotions were welling up in her chest and making it difficult to breathe.

"Give yourself a minute," Robeson said kindly. "Can I get you anything? Coffee?"

Jessica shook her head. "No. Let's just get this over with. This is the second time I've told this story today and I'm not getting any better at it."

Combs shifted impatiently in his chair.

"Three months ago, a man called me at home, before I started taping this season's show, and asked me if I could make him six gold coins. He said he had seen my work replicating Roman coins, and wondered if I could do the same with some old American coins. He was going to use them to make a 'special gift' for his wife. He wanted six, three dollar Dahlonega coins because his wife was from that part of Georgia. He said his name was David Smith and that he would pay me eight thousand dollars in cash to make the coins. He said he didn't care what the coins were really made of, just that they looked like gold and were as authentic-looking as possible. He mailed me several excellent photographs of the three dollar Dahlonega coin he wanted replicated, detailed dimensions, and a money order for two thousand dollars.

"Now, I know I should have questioned Mr. Smith a little further on *why* he wanted these coin fakes, but I didn't. I knew the story about a gift to his wife was garbage, but I needed the money. He gave me three weeks to get them ready. I made the coins and sent them to a P.O. Box in D.C. and he mailed me a money order for another six thousand dollars.

"I thought this was the end of my dealings with Mr. Smith, but a few days after I banked the money order, and just before I left to start this season's taping in Tampa, I found a small, handwritten note placed under my windshield wiper. I don't remember it verbatim, but it said something like, 'Tell no one about the coins. You will be given more opportunities to work for us.'"

Robeson lifted his eyes from his legal pad. "Are you sure that it said *us* and not *me*?" he asked.

"Pretty sure." Jessica frowned in thought.

"Do you still have that note?" Combs demanded.

Jessica looked at him as if seeing him for the first time, but she answered the question by focusing her attention on Robeson's face. "It's back home in Charlotte. I don't know why I didn't throw it out. Of course, I knew then that the coins were likely made for some illicit purpose, but what could I do? I had taken the money. What was done was done."

Robeson tapped his pencil against his chin. "How did you make the coins?"

"It wasn't that hard." Jessica shrugged. "I had all of the raw materials from my days in the jewelry business. Saul took the entire inventory of jewelry, but I kept all of the tools. First, I created a model of the original coin out of

Plaster of Paris—that took the longest because I had to do a ton of detailed carving for that step—then I used silicone rubber to produce a negative mold of the plaster. I made seven of those. One for each coin Mr. Smith requested and an extra in case I screwed up."

"Do you still have the molds?" Combs asked curiously.

"The extra one? No, I tossed them after I banked the money order. After that, I melted down a bunch of nickels and filled the silicone molds. Once the coins were out, I dipped them in gold plate and checked over the fine details. Everything looked good except that they were way too shiny."

"But you were able to fix that," Robeson stated.

"Yes. I used a tool like the dentist uses to polish your teeth. With a soft pad, I buffed the finish and removed the shine. I don't remember making a tail on the letter *D*, but the smallest slip of the wrist and any mark could have gotten on the original mold. Alexandra must have really had a good eye to spot that mistake, but anyone who really knew coins only had to hold one of my fakes to know both the weight and color was off."

"What did *you* think about the Dahlonega coins you saw in the Civil War display?" Robeson asked. "Didn't you recognize them?"

Jessica leaned forward. "That's the thing! I never checked that exhibit out. I've been pretty busy and frankly, wars just aren't my thing. I'm tired of battles, Detective." She fixed her eyes straight at Robeson and said earnestly, "The first I heard of the Dahlonega coins were at dinner last night. That's why I spilled the wine. I knew that those fakes were mine. This morning, I was heading for the exhibit to check them when I heard about Alexandra . . . about her death. I *still* haven't seen the coins, real or fake."

Robeson set his eyes on the small woman sitting before him and issued the fiercest, most daunting stare in his arsenal of deadly looks. After a few seconds, which seemed to last forever to Molly and Jessica, he obviously decided that

Jessica was telling the truth. His rigid body relaxed and his dark eyes returned to his pad. "Are there any other details you can think of that might tie into this investigation?" he asked.

"Just that the handwriting on my note was the same on the note Alexandra received. Whoever she met that night, it was the man I knew as David Smith."

"We need your note, I'm afraid." Robeson turned to Combs. "Find a man to go to Charlotte. He'll need to leave today."

"Does that mean I'm going home?" Jessica's voice rose hopefully.

"It does. If we need anything more from you, you'll have to return to Richmond." Robeson stood. "I appreciate your coming forward with this information. I cannot say that there will not be repercussions concerning the forgery of the coins, but I will do my best to exonerate you in exchange for your help with this investigation." Combs spluttered until his shock at what he considered his superior officer's leniency became a spasmodic coughing fit. "However, I must advice you not to leave North Carolina and to leave us with all of your contact information. Regardless of your coming forward, you are still very much involved with an ongoing murder investigation."

Jessica bowed her head meekly. "I understand. I just want to spend some time with my boys."

"Officer Combs will be by your hotel with a statement for you to sign. Please read it over carefully. He will also be bringing with him an officer who will accompany you to Charlotte. Please give this officer the note and any materials you used in making those coins."

Molly put her arm around her weary friend and ushered her from the room. "You did the right thing, Jess. It'll work out, you'll see." But Molly didn't know whether she believed her own words, and she turned away so that Jessica wouldn't see the doubt and anxiety flashing through Molly's gray eyes.

Outside, Jessica paused before getting in Molly's Jeep. She looked out into the oncoming twilight and allowed one tear to escape down her smooth cheek. "I've loved Borris for three years, Molly. I didn't want to, but I do. I swore I'd never be with another man, that I'd never let anyone threaten the peace I have with my sons, so I've been fighting him off. He kept trying to show me that I could trust again and I kept driving him away." She wiped at her face as another tear slipped out and then examined her wet palm, as if wondering where the moisture had come from. "Today it looks like I've finally succeeded."

Jessica was gone by sundown. The Traveller was oddly still. Borris had not returned and Garrett was nowhere to be seen. Clara waited for her daughter's return in the parlor. A Welsh mystery set in a remote mountainous village lay open on her lap and a highball glass filled with Crown Royal and soda perched on a stand within easy reach.

"How did it go?" she asked, her gray eyes soft in the lamplight. "I saw Jessica leave with a policeman. She's not being arrested, is she?"

Molly flopped down in the other wing chair. "No. She made a mistake, but she's no murderer. She could have been, though, with what her husband did to her."

"Why don't you tell me over dinner?" Clara asked, taking a sip of her cocktail. "Mrs. Hewell said there's a neat little restaurant called the Olde Tobacco Warehouse within walking distance. They are supposed to have a four-story atrium that takes your breath away. Doesn't a plate of chicken cooked in sherry sauce sound good about now? And she also highly recommended the roasted garlic mashed potatoes."

"Yum, let's go!" Molly jumped up hungrily. "Boy, I'd never survive on one of those no-carb diets."

"Well, there are no carbs in this drink and I'm going to finish it, so you may as well fill me in on what happened at the station while you're waiting."

Molly sank back down into her chair and gave a condensed version of Jessica's sad tale.

"That poor woman!" Clara exclaimed. "At least your father took off right after you were born. Her sons must not know what to think—their father just up and leaving them like that. What scum!"

Molly didn't want her mother to launch into some bad-father tirade, so she quickly said, "So let's assume that Mr. Smith is really one of the *Hidden Treasures* appraisers. He commissioned the fake coins, arranged the blackout, switched the coins, and killed Alexandra."

"Which men do we have to choose from again?" Clara asked, draining her glass.

Molly stood and beckoned for her mother to follow her outside. Arm in arm, they strolled down the sidewalk towards the Olde Tobacco Warehouse.

"Patrice, Borris, Tony, and Garrett. Those are our suspects."

"Hrmph," Clara snorted. "Patrice couldn't pull a body up twenty feet into the air any more than *I* could. It could only be Borris if he was just pretending to be in love with Jessica while, in fact, the whole time he was manipulating her into unknowingly help him commit several crimes."

Molly shook her head. "I don't believe that. Anyone can see Borris sincerely loves Jessica, unless he is an incredible actor."

Clara frowned. "No. He's the genuine article. And it simply can't be that charming Englishman, though *he'd* make an excellent actor. And I don't know anything about this Tony fellow."

"Tony is a big teddy bear. That overgrown kid doesn't have a malicious bone in his body," Molly said firmly.

"Since we don't know these men from Adam, we can't really deduce what would drive any of them to murder. That's why there's a police force, Molly," Clara nagged. "You don't have the slightest idea what secrets were divulged during today's questioning."

"That's true, but I *do* know that the motive is obviously money. There was a robbery before there ever was a murder," Molly replied defensively and then abruptly stopped in her tracks in the middle of one of Shockoe Slip's cobblestone side streets. The sudden lack of movement caused Clara's linked arm to jerk backward roughly.

"What are you doing, Molly?" Clara snapped. "I think my arm just came out of its socket!"

Molly stood paralyzed, her eyes wide with the shock of comprehension. "What would you do with six stolen coins, Ma?" she finally asked.

Clara shrugged impatiently. "I don't know. Hide them in the litter box?"

"You can't just put them on eBay." Molly's words flowed so quickly that she began tripping over them. "You'd have to have a buyer or know of a black market."

"Which one of those men would know of a market for stolen coins?" Clara asked, her interest in the case returning.

"A coin collector!" Molly screeched excitedly, and then realized exactly what this conclusion meant. She covered her face with both of her hands and wailed in despair, "Oh my God, and I *kissed* him! Ma, I kissed the killer!"

Chapter 13

*Knowing what to look for when buying old or antique furniture is
a skill that may take years—and several mistakes. There are even
some who feel that recognizing a really fine old piece of furniture
is an instinct which cannot be taught.*

—*The Illustrated Guide to Furniture Repair and*
Restoration

"Who did you kiss?" Clara asked excitedly as
they began walking again. She was already imagin-
ing herself surrounded by cherubic grandchildren, all dying to hear the history behind every antique in her historic
North Carolina shotgun house.

Molly tucked a strand of dark hair behind her ear and
then realized that she and her mother had come to a stop directly in front of Olde Tobacco Warehouse. The restaurant
looked exactly like its name: an old tobacco warehouse. It
was a large, brick building with oversized windows framed
in aged timber. Inside, Molly and Clara were amazed by the
unique layout. As Mrs. Hewell said, the restaurant was four
stories high, with an open atrium in the center. Large plants
and tall potted trees peppered the floor and an enormous
chandelier hung down from the distant ceiling. A hostess in
skin-tight black pants led them to a table on the first floor,
called the Garden Atrium. The strains of a jazz band playing

on the second floor hung in the air above and mingled with the hum of clinking silverware and conversation. Dozens of waiters and waitresses moved among the floors, carrying trays laden with delicious-smelling food.

Their waiter, a rotund, gray-haired man wearing a black button-down shirt and a long, off-white apron greeted them with a friendly smile and introduced himself as Peter.

"Would you care to peruse the wine list?" he asked.

Clara waved it away and ordered a bourbon and soda. "With your best, *non-watered* bourbon," she added firmly. "Do you want something, dear? A piña colada, perhaps?" Clara prompted her unusually taciturn daughter.

"We make a terrific mango colada," the waiter offered.

"Just a Diet Coke, please." Molly waited for Peter to leave and then whispered fiercely, "I kissed Garrett, Ma. He did something really sweet, or at least I assumed he did, and so I kissed him."

Clara flicked her wrist in a dismissive gesture. "Oh, that doesn't count. I've kissed dozens of people in the heat of the moment at auction. You know, when you've slipped in a bid right before the gavel falls and that piece of rare pottery or gorgeous cherry stand becomes yours for a song." The waiter arrived with their drinks. Clara ordered an appetizer and then leaned in toward Molly. "You can't seriously believe that Garrett is the killer!"

"But I do." Molly took a deep sip of her soda. "You see, the note Alexandra received implied some kind of intimate meeting, like a romantic rendezvous. The only person I've ever seen Alexandra thaw out around is Garrett. Even Borris mentioned how she had a crush on him for ages. They worked on the same show back in England."

"Well, Garrett *is* a charmer, but just because she liked him doesn't mean he wrote the note. And didn't you tell me that she was sent here for sleeping with someone *else* involved with that show?"

"It's not just my suspicions about the romantic nature of

the note. Garrett's a coin collector as well. He could have planned the whole coin robbery! Alexandra discovered the fakes and he was forced to stop her."

A large plate containing a wheel of melted Brie covered in raspberry sauce arrived at their table. Clara scooped a piece of homemade bread into the cheese and popped it into her mouth, even though the cheese was still so hot it was bubbling.

"Delicious! Try some, madam. It's not like you to lose your appetite when baked cheese and fresh bread are concerned." She waited while Molly mechanically bit into a forkful of steaming cheese. "Do you have any proof that would incriminate Garrett?"

Molly shook her head. "Ow, this is hot!" She took a hasty drink of soda. "No, of course I have no proof."

"You don't really know this man and you don't have a single shred of proof. This doesn't look very conclusive, cupcake. Any member of the crew could have been wooing Alexandra for all *you* know." Clara looked around and their attentive waiter instantly appeared at their table. Clara ordered the chicken cooked in a creamy sherry sauce and shitake mushrooms for herself and tournedos of beef smothered in béarnaise sauce for Molly. "Oh, well, we can't eat Mrs. Hewell's free food the whole time," she added under her breath as she noticed the prices for the first time.

Molly was fully lost in thought. Suddenly, she brightened and sat up in her chair. "Ma. Garrett knows a coin dealer in town. If I want to find out more about his true character, I could find out from the dealer. He has a shop around here, in Shockoe Bottom. Garrett mentioned the location to me at the museum the other day."

"I guess it's worth a try." Clara shrugged. "But he'll never be open tomorrow. It's Sunday."

"Excuse me, Peter," Molly asked their waiter as he paused to refill their water glasses. "Do you know if there's a store around here that sells old coins?"

The man held the water pitcher in midair and frowned in

thought. "Hmm, I'm not sure. There are a couple shops that sell vintage stuff and second-hand books near the flea market on Seventeenth Street. I don't live in this part of town, but that would be your best bet. Your entrees will be right out."

"We'll check out the Seventeenth Street area. Thanks."

Clara dabbed at her mouth with her white starched napkin. "Let me guess. We're going to walk home in that direction so that you can find the coin dealer's store."

Molly smiled. "You're so clever, Ma. Yes. And then I will call him tomorrow morning and tell him I simply *must* interview him for *Collector's Weekly* before I leave town. If I butter him up enough, I might learn something about Garrett and how good an actor he actually is."

"Well, *I'm* going to go on that Canal Walk Mrs. Hewell told me about. I need to get some exercise after all of this wonderful food." She patted her flat stomach as Molly enviously eyed her mother's trim waistline. Her own pants were feeling especially snug about the middle. "Lex is leaving in the morning," Clara continued, "but I'll stick around until you go. That means you'll have to drive me home, but I refuse to leave you up here alone. You're bound to get in some enormous muddle before the police have a chance to tidy up this case."

Sunday morning dawned with the irrefutable suggestion of autumn. A crisp, light breeze blew across the weighty heads of saffron-colored chrysanthemums planted in terracotta pots outside the Traveller's front door. As Molly parted her gauzy lace curtains and looked out the window, the morning sun already seemed weaker than it had the day before.

Molly flipped open her notebook to the page where she had scribbled the name of the one coin shop she and her mother had located after last night's dinner. The number for "To Coin A Phrase," was listed under "Coins and Collectibles" in the phone book. Checking her watch, she picked up the phone, punched in the numbers, and received a voice mail recording providing the shop's location, hours, and the owner's pager number. The owner gave his name as Jared Freeman. Molly paged him and waited, enjoying her coffee and the birdsong outside her window.

The phone rang moments, later. "Mr. Freeman?" Molly answered hopefully.

"Yes. To whom am I speaking?" the dealer spoke with a slow, upper-class Southern lilt.

"My name is Molly Appleby. I'm a writer for *Collector's Weekly*. A friend of mine, Garrett Huntington, mentioned that you were the area's most reputable coin dealer and I thought I would try to get an interview with you before I leave town."

"Of course, Ms. Appleby." Mr. Freeman could scarcely hide his pleasure. "Mr. Huntington is an old friend. I'd be delighted to accommodate you. When would you like to schedule this interview?"

Molly pressed ahead. "Actually, I was hoping to meet you at your shop sometime today."

Mr. Freeman hesitated. "Well, I normally attend church service at ten, but I could meet you around noon. Would that suit you?"

"Absolutely. I'll see you then." Molly hung up, feeling elated at the thought of discovering the true nature of the enigmatic Englishman.

Downstairs, Garrett and Clara were discussing the merits of genuine butter over margarine when making Yorkshire pudding. Molly was relieved to witness her mother's casual manner. She didn't want Garrett to realize that she was on to him. Clara handed Molly a plate piled with scrambled eggs and French toast while Garrett produced a winning smile for her behalf.

"I feel like I haven't seen you for days," he said flirtatiously.

Molly glanced at him only briefly. "With two murders, I'm sure none of us will be allowed to leave town anytime soon." Then she forced herself to soften her tone. "I guess the D.C. show will be postponed now."

"It does seem that way, indeed. And what will you two lovely ladies spend the day doing?" he asked, passing Molly a pitcher filled with warm maple syrup.

"Thanks." Molly drizzled a zigzag of syrup over her toast. "We're going to go on that Canal Walk. Mrs. Hewell recommended it as an entertaining source of exercise."

"That sounds brilliant. Mind if I tag along?"

As Molly struggled to come up with a polite excuse why he couldn't accompany them, Clara spoke up. "You don't want to come with us, trust me. I need some fall clothes and we are going to hit every store in Carytown until I find some decent sweater sets and a pair of black cotton pants."

Molly wondered if Garrett would realize that it was highly unlikely for such specialty boutiques to be open on a Sunday morning, especially in Virginia. Most people would be at church, and then go out for their large, midday supper, and only then would the shopkeepers open their doors. It was more likely that the majority of the shops in Carytown would remain closed all day. Molly's forehead began to grow clammy as she nervously studied Garrett to see whether he would catch Clara's fib.

Luckily, Garrett grimaced playfully and gave off a shudder of distaste instead. "Right. I think I'll pass. Perhaps we'll meet for dinner, then." He stood and took his empty plate into the kitchen.

At that moment, Borris entered the dining room. His eyes were red rimmed from lack of sleep and his salt-and-pepper hair remained uncombed. His shirt was disheveled and the laces on his left sneaker were completely untied. Saying nothing, he sank down in a chair and stared into the empty coffee cup set before him.

Clara immediately filled his cup and began fixing him a plate. "You might as well eat," she nagged gently.

Borris robotically sipped some coffee and gazed down at his food as if he didn't know what to do with it. "Has *she* already eaten?" he asked angrily.

Molly glanced sideways at her mother. "Jessica's gone." She replied very softly.

Twirling a forkful of eggs, Borris met Molly's eyes. "Gone?"

"She had to go back to Charlotte," Molly whispered. "She has to show the police the copy of her note—the one telling her to keep quiet." From the kitchen, Molly could hear the sound of riotous laughter. At least Garrett was too busy humoring Mrs. Hewell to overhear this conversation, Molly thought in relief.

Borris instantly grew alarmed. "Is she alone? Who knows about this? She could be in danger." He flung his napkin on the ground, stood, and then collapsed back into his chair again. "Of course, it's none of my business is it?" He threw his arms up in anguish. "She wants nothing to do with me, obviously!"

Clara leaned forward and said sternly, "First of all, Jessica is in the company of a police officer, so she's perfectly safe. Second, she is in love with you, you silly man. She thinks you won't accept her knowing about . . . her mistake, so she deliberately tried to push you away."

Borris sat in stunned silence. "I don't care about those damned coins! She loves me?" He straightened in his seat and his eyes became lively. "Did she say that?"

"Yes." Molly jumped in encouragingly. "And she doesn't have to come back to Richmond immediately, so—"

"—I'm going to Charlotte!" Borris leaped up again.

"But you're not allowed to leave town, are you?" Molly asked worriedly.

Borris paused in the doorway. "No, but *I* didn't kill anyone, so I'm going." He fished around in his pants pocket and shyly withdrew a small jewelry box. "I bought this ring a year ago, when we were taping a show in Baltimore.

Jessica appraised it for an older lady and kept talking about what a wonderful piece of estate jewelry it was. A dark blue sapphire surrounded by a small circle of diamonds. See?" Molly and Clara admired the beautiful ring. "I followed the lady outside and bought it from her. I know that Jess and I have only been friends since we've met, but I've always wanted something more. After yesterday, I thought I'd throw the damned thing in Richmond's James River, because she said she would never commit to another relationship again. She said the first time was the man's fault, but this time *she* was the bad seed. That I should wait for someone with a better character. Imagine that? All she did was make some fake coins! I told her I could easily forgive her, but she said she couldn't forgive herself." Borris paused for air. "But if Jessica said she loves me, even if she said it to *you* and not to *me*, then she's going to be wearing this ring by the end of the day, so help me God."

"You'd better at least let me tell the police where you've gone," Molly warned.

"Fine," Borris agreed. "But give me a head start." Color flowed through his cheeks and a boyish smile appeared on his face, lighting it with the expectation of bliss. "Wish me luck," he said, taking the stairs up three at a time.

"Good luck!" Clara called after him. "I hope they invite us to the wedding," she told Molly. "There's nothing like eating a good piece of wedding cake while sipping a glass of champagne and criticizing what everyone else is wearing. Come on, madam, let's get moving ourselves."

"What is the Canal Walk?" Garrett asked Mrs. Hewell as she loaded plates into the dishwasher.

"Oh, it's a splendid little walking tour along the James River. There's a tour group you can join for free. The tour takes about ninety minutes and you'll hear all about the history of the two canals as well as walk off some of my *healthy* breakfasts."

Garrett nodded with interest. "And where would a chap pick up this tour?"

Mrs. Hewell puckered her lips in thought. "Let's see. I believe they leave from Cary Street and Twelfth. But the Valentine Museum also offers a Canal Walk, but that focuses more on the historic Shockoe area."

"Indeed?" Garrett remarked quietly. "I know a fellow who deals in coins down in that area. Perhaps I'll pay *him* a visit before I take that tour. I wonder if his shop is one of the stops on the Appleby women's tour . . ."

"Well, have fun, dear," Mrs. Hewell said as she straightened up from bending over the dishwasher. She was surprised to catch something dark move across Garrett's face, momentarily clouding his handsome looks, but just as suddenly as the shadow appeared, it was gone. She hurried by him into the dining room to clear up the breakfast service. "I wonder who just walked on *his* grave," she muttered to herself as she nosily stacked china and gathered silverware.

A few minutes later, Garrett had returned to his room and Borris appeared in her kitchen. By the time Borris explained that he was checking out, proudly showing her the ring he meant to give Jessica that very day, Mrs. Hewell had forgotten all about Garrett's sinister look. She insisted on packing a bag lunch for a very fidgety Borris as she plied him with heaps of outdated but well-meaning romantic advice. Finally, Borris was allowed to make it out the door after planting a friendly kiss on his hostess's plump cheek. Mrs. Hewell whistled off to her home behind the bed-and-breakfast to share the exciting news with her completely disinterested husband.

Chapter 14

It is not always that I have gone to some white-columned mansion of other days . . . where within its guarded confines rare pieces were well-preserved. The doorways at which entrance had often been sought, have been largely neglected doors, along the river country where old settlements remain to tell the story of grandeur now departed.

—PAUL BURROUGHS, *SOUTHERN ANTIQUES*

"To Coin A Phrase" was located above a small coffee shop that doubled as a bookstore. A crimson and gold wooden plaque with a carved coin hung above a narrow doorway and gave one the impression of standing at the entrance to an English pub rather than a door opening to a steep flight of stairs. The brightly lit staircase led to another simple wooden door upon which two signs were posted. The first was a warning against shoplifting and the second announced the presence of surveillance cameras. When Molly rapped on the solid door, a hazel eye appeared through the peephole and she could hear a series of deadbolts being unfastened.

Jared Freeman, a tall man in his early sixties with graying brown hair, opened the door wearing a friendly grin. "Welcome, welcome. Please come in." He shook Molly's hand. "Sorry about all the locks, but this isn't exactly an upscale neighborhood and I can be a bit paranoid about my inventory."

As Molly introduced her mother, Jared bent gallantly over Clara's hand with a gentlemanly bow. "I believe I've seen you before, Mrs. Appleby. Is that possible?"

Clara's eyes sparkled as she noted the expensive cut of Jared's sand-colored suit and the winkling of his gold Rolex. "Of course. I've seen you at several of Tilman's estate auctions before, right? And call me Clara. We're all antique people here—that makes us practically family."

"I'm honored that you've chosen to interview me," Jared said to Molly, then turned back to Clara and added modestly, "As you can see, my shop is rather small. I conduct most of my business via the Internet these days."

"At least that frees you up from keeping endless store hours." Clara walked over to a waist-high display case and began examining the coins.

Molly took out her notebook and began to ask Jared the usual litany of interview questions. How long had he been in business? What inspired him to choose to become a dealer? What was the finest or most memorable coin he had ever bought or sold?

Jared perched comfortably on a three-legged stool next to his vintage manual cash register during the short interview. He spoke in a soft, pleasant voice and answered all of Molly's questions succinctly, but also provided her with several humorous anecdotes certain to charm all of the readers of *Collector's Weekly*. Molly was enjoying her interview so much that she almost forgot her primary reason for tracking down Jared Freeman in the first place.

"That's great, Mr. Freeman. This is going to make a terrific piece. I'm going to photograph you by your fabulous antique cash register, and then perhaps you can show me some of your better coins and I'll snap a few pictures of them as well."

As Molly took photos, Clara flipped through a reference book on coin collecting and remained uncommonly unobtrusive.

"So how long have you known Mr. Huntington?" Jared asked after Molly had taken his picture.

"I just met him a week ago. I'm in town covering the taping of *Hidden Treasures*," Molly said, relieved that Jared had brought up the subject. "Garrett's quite a guy. How long have you two known one another?"

"Oh, I've been buying rare coins from him for almost ten years now." Jared left his stool and moved toward a tall display case. "I only buy near mint to mint coins and Garrett has an excellent eye. I have never failed to make a profit on a coin I've purchased from him."

"Any idea where he finds such good coins?" Molly asked cautiously.

Jared laughed heartily. "Now you know dealers won't kiss-and-tell about their sources. I only hope Garrett continues to get ahold of the same quality coins he's always sold me. I only buy a few per year from him, mind you, and I always have to pay him in cash, but I'll never discover *where* he's getting his coins."

"Did Garrett sell you something wonderful this time?" Clara batted her eyes at Jared. "Can we see it? I know absolutely nothing about coins, but I bet *you* could educate me a bit."

Jared flushed with pleasure, but then his face quickly fell. "Actually, I sold *him* a coin at the show, which is a rare treat, believe me. Then Garrett stopped by unexpectedly yesterday to sell me a real beauty. I turned around and sold it over the phone to one of my regular customers within minutes. Unfortunately, I've already shipped that coin by FedEx, so I'm afraid I can't show it to you." He looked wildly around the store, desperate not to lose Clara's favor. "However, I could show you a picture of one just like it." He scrambled over next to Clara and leafed through one of the many reference guides displayed neatly in a book rack. "Ah, here it is."

"This one?" Clara queried as she pulled her reading glasses from her deep purse. Jared watched her every move with adoration. "Yes," he cooed. "This is an early half dollar, called a Capped Bust Half Dollar because Lady Liberty is wearing a cap and is posing in such a way that she reminds one of the busts from classical Greece or Rome."

"What year was the coin you bought?" Molly wondered.

"The one I acquired from Garrett was a Capped Bust 1836 Half Dollar in mint condition. A gorgeous thing." Jared puffed out his chest as if he were personally responsible for the creation of the fine collectible.

"Is that valuable?" Clara leaned in toward the smitten coin dealer.

"I should say so. In today's market it lists at around eleven thousand dollars. I give my best customers a discount, of course, but you get the idea."

Clara watched her daughter's face contort with a combination of shock and anger, so she steered Jared to another display case and began asking him questions about the gold coins locked inside while Molly tried to gain control over her raging emotions.

Finally, Molly thanked Jared for his helpfulness and promised to let him know when the article was to be published. Clara handed him one of her business cards and invited him to attend one of Lex's upcoming auctions.

"I'd love to!" his hazel eyes gleamed as he thanked Clara. "Please let me know if Lex gets any estates with any coins."

"I will," Clara promised and stepped outside to the full blast of her daughter's wrath.

"That bastard!" Molly shouted. "He told me that coin was a fake! He gypped some needy widow! I'll kill that piece of sh——!"

"Molly!" Clara shouted. "Calm down! *Mr. Freeman* sold the coin at that price. Who knows what he had to pay Garrett for it?"

"Look, I saw Garrett count some bills into that woman's hand, Ma. We're not talking thousands of dollars. She'd be lucky if he gave her three hundred dollars! He knew *exactly* what that coin was worth! He took advantage of a widow who's a hard-working single mom to boot! I'd say we just learned something about his character, wouldn't you?" Molly stormed up the street.

"Where are you going?" Clara demanded. "What about our Canal Walk?"

"Screw the Canal Walk!" Molly shouted back over her shoulder as she turned east in the direction of the Traveller. "I have a bigger fish to fry!"

As Molly and Clara were climbing the steps up to Jared Freeman's coin shop, Detective Paul Robeson was standing at his office window, watching one of his officers hold open the door of a patrol car for one Randy Merrill.

"That's one less redneck hanging out in our jail," Combs said upon entering Robeson's office. "D.A. said our evidence was too circumstantial, so we had to let him go."

Robeson watched Randy spit a glob of mucus on the sidewalk outside the police station before raising his middle finger to anyone unlucky enough to be in the immediate vicinity.

"Guess he doesn't want a ride back to his hotel," Combs smirked. "And he says he's going to sue us, too."

Robeson sighed. "Don't they all. Did you warn him about staying away from Molly Appleby?"

"Sure did, boss." Combs watched as Randy stalked down the street, his lips moving rapidly in what was no doubt a string of obscenities. "He's going to be pissed that he's out on a Sunday. All the liquor stores are closed."

Robeson sighed. "We've got another round of questioning to go through today. Before we get all wrapped up in that, you'd better get ahold of that producer and bring him in. His cast and crew are going to be staying in our beautiful city a little while longer."

"I'll call him right now," Combs answered with barely disguised irritation. He was no secretary.

"And Combs"—Robeson turned back to the window—"call the owners of that antique desk we've got sitting in the evidence room. They should be informed that it cannot be returned to them until these cases are solved. I wouldn't go into too much detail if I were you. Just tell them their desk is now officially evidence in a criminal case and we will return it as soon as possible."

Combs nodded, and knowing full well that Robeson could see his reflection in the glass, he fought back the grimace struggling to appear on his face. Back at the wobbly desk in the stuffy room he shared with three other officers, Combs picked up the phone and barked at Guy to drive himself to the station immediately.

"And I need you to provide me with the name and phone number of the person who owns that desk, the one that had the mold put all over it."

"That would be with Frank's files," Guy protested. "They're all in his briefcase. I'm sure his wife would—"

"—Just stop by her room and get it for me, why don't you? We'll be expecting you within the next half an hour." Combs hung up on the spluttering producer with a smirk of satisfaction. "Those TV people. Think they're above everyone else."

By the time Combs had polished off a bag of cheese puffs and two Dr Peppers and had read all of the comic strips in *The Richmond Times Dispatch*, an officer was leading Guy to the interview room. Combs hustled into Robeson's office just as the detective was sorting through the papers in Frank's weathered brown briefcase.

"Here we go." Robeson scanned over a pink receipt. "Eleanor Calloway. Here's her number." Robeson slid the piece of paper over to Combs. "Go ahead and use this phone."

Combs shot his superior a dirty look but picked up the phone and dialed.

"Mrs. Calloway?" he asked as the scratchy voice of an elderly woman came on the line. "My name is Officer Combs from the Richmond police department . . ." Combs began. "No, ma'am, I'm not selling anything. Actually, I'm calling about your old . . . um . . . antique desk, the one you lent Frank Sterling. Yes, the appraiser for *Hidden Treasures*." Combs rolled his eyes in irritation as Robeson watched impassively. Suddenly, Combs perked up and gestured for a pen and paper. Robeson slid both items across the desk toward the burly officer. "You say you sold it? To the man who picked it up? Ma'am, this is very important. Do you happen to remember his name? Yes?" Combs scribbled excitedly on the pad. "That *does* sound familiar. Thank you, Mrs. Calloway."

"So she sold the desk right before Frank got it, huh?" Robeson rubbed his chin. "To whom?"

"I don't get it," said the befuddled Combs as he slid the pad of paper back across the desk.

Robeson's dark eyes grew round with astonishment as he read the name written on the pad. He stood up and put his gun in his pocket holster, his massive arm muscles rippling in anticipation. "Let's go, Combs."

"Where?" Combs asked in surprise. "What about the producer?"

"Leave him. We've got ourselves a *real* suspect to interview."

At the same moment Randy Merrill was being released from jail, Garrett was watching Molly and Clara from the cover of his rental car. The two women walked west on Grace Street and then turned south onto seventeenth. If they are really going on the Canal Walk, Garrett thought, which was likely as both women wore casual slacks, plain cotton T-shirts, and tennis shoes, they should continue heading south until they reached the water. When they paused to enter a shop located across from the city market area, Garrett swore under his breath and circled around the block where he was able to park the car out of sight.

Heading in the direction of "To Coin a Phrase," Garrett passed a produce seller. The woman, a blonde in her early thirties whose skin was overly tanned from too many hours spent tending her crops in the sun, openly stared at Garrett. She gave him a coquettish smile and bent over her rows of peaches and apples to reveal an ample bosom. Garrett avoided her eyes and then the sudden vibration of his cell phone, which he had tucked into his pants pocket, made him jump. The woman giggled.

"Hello?" Garrett said impatiently. Then he grew quiet, listening to the caller intently for several long seconds. "You wouldn't dare," he finally replied, hissing into the phone. He then slammed it shut and shoved it into his pocket with a violent thrust. Casting a brief, malevolent glance at the upper windows belonging to the coin shop, Garrett's golden eyes narrowed into tigerlike slits as he turned and hastily strode back towards his car.

"What's the rush, hon?" the disappointed produce vendor called after him.

"Piss off!" he snarled without the slightest trace of the usual gallantry he practiced upon all women.

Chapter 15

One of the more important things to look for, then, is that the wood grain of any components which are either adjacent or at right angles to each other, runs in one direction, otherwise the stresses created by shrinkage or expansion would cause the wood to split.

—THE ILLUSTRATED GUIDE TO FURNITURE
REPAIR AND RESTORATION

When Molly and Clara stepped through the Traveller's front door, the roar of a vacuum cleaner greeted them loudly. Mrs. Hewell wore a white apron patterned with bright cherries over her Sunday best, a lilac-colored floral dress, sheer pantyhose, and tennis shoes. The rosy-cheeked proprietor looked up as her two guests entered the dining room and quickly switched off the noisy machine. Molly noticed that a crease of worry had formed on Mrs. Hewell's forehead and her eyes lacked their customary merry sparkle.

"Hello, ladies," Mrs. Hewell greeted mother and daughter. "Sorry to be cleaning at the moment, and especially on a Sunday, but . . ." She broke off and gestured at her shoes. "Mr. Hewell and I always walk to our church service and when we returned, Mr. Huntington was receiving a guest in his room." She paused, not wishing to gossip about one of her guests.

"Is something wrong, Mrs. Hewell? You look a bit

upset." Molly put a hand on the older woman's round shoulder.

"They're having an awful fight, Mr. Huntington and his friend," Mrs. Hewell confessed, her cheeks flushed pink. "The doors to our guest rooms are thick, but those big keyholes . . . I heard some *ugly* words, ladies. When words like that come on the television, I switch the channel." Mrs. Hewell's cheeks grew even redder as she became more flustered. "Even down here I could hear them clear as a bell. I would have asked Mr. Hewell to speak to Mr. Huntington, but he's gone out to visit a shut-in we know. Does it every Sunday."

Clara scowled. "We'll speak with him. There's no need for such childish demonstrations. I would have expected better manners from an Englishman."

Molly grabbed her mother by the elbow. "Ma, wait a minute. Mrs. Hewell, did you get a look at Mr. Huntington's guest?"

Mrs. Hewell shook her head. "No, I sure didn't. I don't want to either. I wish he'd just leave. I'd like to set the table for tea, but perhaps you two would prefer to take your tea on the back porch, where it's quiet . . ."

"Nonsense!" Clara headed for the stairs. "Those *gentlemen* can move their *discussion* to the back porch."

Molly hustled up the stairs behind her mother. The slightly muffled shouts of two male voices could be heard coming from inside of the Wedgwood room, but she didn't think Mrs. Hewell could hear specific words unless she had been listening very carefully. Pressing her own inquiring ear to the keyhole, Molly was able to pick up Garrett's conversation with his mystery guest quite clearly.

"—*You're* the pillock that screwed up!" Garrett was shouting. "Damned, bloody ass! I told you to use the blanket chest, not the desk! Now the whole thing is off. *I'm* getting the hell out of here!"

"What about me?" the other man demanded angrily. "I'm getting *nothing* out of this deal! And I can't just jet off to

England while the shit hits the fan. You *owe* me, Garrett. After all these years . . ." His tone became quietly menacing.

Molly could hear drawers being opened and roughly slammed shut. "This could have been our last score, but you screwed it up! I don't owe you a bloody thing!" Garrett laughed wickedly. "You'd still be polishing furniture in that discount store if it weren't for me, you ungrateful wanker."

"So you've just been using me?" the other man growled. "I thought you cared, but you've only ever cared about the money."

"I admit that I found you attractive once," Garrett answered coldly. "But I'm not in love with you, if that's what you're wondering. Now, stand aside. I'm getting out of here and I suggest you do the same. Perhaps we can try again next year, but for now, it's all off."

Now that the shouting had stopped, Molly was having a difficult time hearing every word. The tension within the room was so palpable, however, that it seemed to seep between the doorjambs and flood into the hall.

Clara plucked at her daughter's sleeve. "What are they saying?"

"Shh!" Molly swatted at her mother's hand. Who was the other man? Something about his voice was familiar.

"This isn't over, Garrett," the man threatened. "You're taking me with you or *you're* not going at all."

Garrett laughed raucously. "That's a good one. What are you going to do, kill me, too? First Frank, then Alexandra, and now me? That would be bloody foolish of you. Now get out! I'm tired of talking rubbish. I've got a plane to catch."

Molly inhaled sharply. Garrett had accused his friend of murder! Right behind the door she leaned on was Frank and Alexandra's murderer! And Garrett was his accomplice!

"Ma," she whispered fiercely. "Go call the police! Use the kitchen phone." Molly handed Clara Detective Robeson's card. "The killer's in there. He just confessed. Hurry!"

Clara hesitated. "Don't do *anything* while I'm gone,"

she whispered and pinched her daughter's arm roughly to reinforce her point.

Molly nodded in wide-eyed agreement and put her ear back to the keyhole. All she caught was Garrett saying "Toodles, luv," as his footsteps approached the door. Scurrying backwards away from the keyhole, Molly stood and prepared to flee for the cover of her room, when she heard a blood-curdling shout, followed by a loud crash. She froze in her tracks and held her breath. A second later, the unmistakable thud of a body hitting the ground assaulted her ears.

Paralyzed by shock and fear, Molly stood outside the door to her room, her mouth agape. She couldn't even whisper a warning to Mrs. Hewell, who came bustling up the stairs with a heavily laden silver tea tray. Mrs. Hewell put her fingers on her lips in a conspiratorial gesture and began to whistle as she approached the door to the Wedgwood room.

Shaken from her trance, Molly quickly blocked Mrs. Hewell with her body. "Don't go in there!" she uttered desperately. "Come into my room."

Mrs. Hewell looked at her in surprise. "Your mother sent me up," she said meaningfully, jerking her head in the direction of Garrett's door. "She's already invited *your* guests to come right over. I don't want Mr. Huntington missing his tea. He's got an awfully strong sweet tooth, you know."

What was her crazy mother up to? Molly's mind raced. Was Mrs. Hewell sent up here to stall Garrett and hold the killer until the police arrived? Molly dashed into her room in search of an object to use as a weapon as she listened in horror to Mrs. Hewell rapping on Garrett's door.

"Mr. Huntington?" she called out sweetly. "I've brought you and your friend some tea."

To Molly's dismay, she heard the door open and a man's voice calmly say, "How nice, thank you. Garrett's just . . . he's in the bathroom at the moment. Can I take that from you, it looks quite heavy?"

"Oh no, I'll just put it down over on the desk," Mrs. Hewell said breezily. "I've carried heavier trays than this in my time."

Without pausing to think her plan through, Molly grabbed her purse, switched on the mini tape recorder tucked inside, and shoved the letter opener from her own desk inside her pants pocket. She dashed into the room on what she hoped were Mrs. Hewell's heels, but the plucky proprietress was already unloading two tea settings onto the desk.

A man stood watching her carefully, his body held unnaturally erect, with every muscle tightly tensed. Molly instantly recognized his attractive physique, and when he turned a pair of aquamarine eyes upon her, she forced herself to smile, despite that fact that she was returning the gaze of a murderer.

"Hello, Chris," Molly said, amazed that her voice sounded relatively even. "Coming to join us for tea? Mrs. Hewell makes the most wonderful cinnamon scones."

"Not today," Mrs. Hewell corrected as she lifted the empty tray. "We're having my special sweet potato bread instead. That's my regular Sunday special. All right then, tell Mr. Huntington to enjoy his tea."

Molly watched in mortification as Mrs. Hewell exited the room. As Molly moved to follow, Chris leapt in front of her and slammed the door shut.

"Oh, no, you don't." Chris narrowed his brilliant eyes and pointed a finger at her. "Garrett said you've been nosing around all week. I bet you've been sitting out there with your ear pressed to the keyhole, mmmm?"

Molly backed up, stepping onto a bathroom towel that crunched gratingly under her feet. She looked down in surprise at a shard of moss green Wedgwood. Mrs. Hewell would not be pleased, she thought illogically. That must have been the crash I heard. Did Chris bash Garrett over the head with the Wedgwood urn?

Refocusing her attention on Chris, Molly considered her chances of escape. Chris was about her height, but his wrestler's body was thick with powerful muscles and he was amazingly light on his feet. Plus, he had already killed two, possibly even three people.

"I could scream." Molly locked eyes with Chris, hoping that if she challenged him, he'd reveal his plan for her.

Chris made his point very clear by withdrawing a small revolver from his pants pocket. "If you make a sound, you die." He snarled and aimed the revolver at Molly's chest.

Molly stared at the small black gun as if it were a black tarantula waiting to leap from Chris's hands onto her body. She quickly decided that her best bet was to play meek and stall Chris until the police arrived.

"Okay." She raised her hands in nervous submission and backed across the room toward a stiff, ladder-back chair. She sank down onto the creaking woven seat and dropped her purse to the ground, hoping her recorder would pick up every sound.

Molly's hasty surrender seemed to allow Chris to relax. His eyes were shining over brightly with anger and what Molly was certain was a touch of insanity as well.

"What have you done with Garrett?" she asked softly.

Chris smiled crookedly. "Like I told the landlady, he's in the bathroom. That traitor is quite"—he struggled for the right word—"indisposed."

"I can see why you'd be angry at Garrett," Molly said soothingly. "But why did you put that mold on the desk? What did you have against Frank?" Molly prayed that Chris would be distracted by her questions. Luckily, the hand with the gun dropped to his side and Chris sat down on the edge of the bed.

"All of this was Garrett's master plan. Frank was just supposed to get sick. Sick enough to be off the show for the week. Who knew the mold could actually kill him? You can't be too sensitive in today's world. As you can see, only the fittest survive. Poor Frank, what a loser." Chris shook his head with no trace of genuine sympathy. In fact, the crooked smile had reappeared on his face.

"You needed to get rid of him so you could hide the real

Dahlonega coins in the desk's secret compartment, right?" Chris nodded his head in agreement. "But when Frank died, you planted the rag in Randy's truck to throw suspicion on him."

"Aren't you just the little detective?" Chris sneered mockingly.

"And Alexandra had to die because she discovered the fake coins Garrett had Jessica make. Garrett wrote the note and gave it to Alexandra, probably when he drove Victoria back to her hotel after our dinner together." Molly thought furiously. "Except that Garrett didn't meet her at the museum. You were waiting there for her."

"Yes, I was." Chris nodded triumphantly. "And I heard how she had talked shit about General Lee. He got the last word on that bitch, now didn't he?" The bright light in his eyes gave Chris a feverish appearance. His left foot bounced up and down on the carpet in a frenzy of jitters. His body language made it clear that he was quickly reaching the end of his patience.

"Look, you're so attractive, Chris," Molly hastily lied. At this moment, he was no longer the show's handsome furniture assistant; he was a killer, an unbalanced puppet without a puppeteer. To Molly, the figure standing over her with the gun in his hand was the most grotesque person in the world. What was taking the police so long? "Even if things didn't work out between you and Garrett, you could have anyone you want." She spoke rapidly, sensing that Chris was now bored with their conversation. "Why don't you get out of here and start over? *I* won't say anything. You can even take my car."

Chris jumped up from the end of the bed, his face contorted with fury. "Don't tell me what to do!" he shouted, holding the gun up to Molly's chest again. "I'm not stupid!" His voice lowered to a dangerous whisper. "As soon as I take care of you, I *will* get lost. Don't you worry about me, sweetheart."

"But what about the coins?" Molly squeaked desperately. "You're going to leave empty-handed? I could get them for you. I can get into the police station—"

"I *said* I'm not stupid, now—" A sudden knocking on the door interrupted Chris's imminent threat.

"Yoohoo!" Mrs. Hewell cheerfully banged. "Mr. Huntington? Are you all done with your tea? I've come to collect the cups."

"Goddamn all women," Chris growled. He pulled Molly to her feet and jammed the butt of the gun viciously into the small of her back. "Move!" he whispered in her ear. "Get into the bathroom. You make one sound, I kill the landlady, and then I'll come back for you. I've got nothing to lose now, understand?" his aquamarine eyes glittered feverishly.

Inside the bathroom, Molly stifled a scream. For there was Garrett's body, dumped unceremoniously in the claw foot tub. Blood ran down the side of his sandy blond hair and stained the white porcelain. Molly stared at him and gasped.

As she watched Chris shut the bathroom door, Molly caught a momentary glimpse of silver before Chris suddenly dropped like a stone on the other side of the door. Instantly, Mrs. Hewell's kind face appeared, peering around the doorframe.

"Are you all right, dearie?" she asked, her pink face framed by loose wisps of gray hair.

Molly exhaled in relief. "Yes . . . I'm okay."

Mrs. Hewell caught sight of Garrett's body. "Heaven save us!" she shouted. "Is he . . . ?"

Molly quickly bent over Garrett and felt for a pulse on his neck. It took her a few seconds to find it. She had often wondered how people in films could always locate the pulse on their first try. "He's alive," she pronounced, noting that there was still a small trickle of blood flowing from his head wound.

"He doesn't look alive," Mrs. Hewell fretted.

"Dead men don't bleed," Molly said, sinking down against the tub. She nervously eyed the pair of inert feet in leather loafers on the other side of the cracked bathroom door. Mrs. Hewell followed Molly's gaze.

"Don't you worry about him, dearie. Those Victorians knew how to make one solid sterling tea tray. He's out like a light."

At that moment, Clara stepped into Garrett's room and called Molly's name. Detective Robeson was right on her heels, followed by Combs and two other officers.

"Here, Ma!" Molly replied to her mother's call, feeling like a shaken baby bird fallen from the nest. Clara took one look at her ashen-faced daughter and enfolded her child tightly in her arms. "Mama's here," she whispered.

Molly nestled in her mother's arms for a moment, breathing in Clara's familiar scents of gardenia perfume and sweet pea hand lotion. After a few minutes, Molly finally stopped shaking and was able to drink some of the hot, sweet tea Mrs. Hewell offered her.

Detective Robeson stared back and forth between the three women in the bathroom, the dented silver tray laying on the rug, and the two, prone bodies belonging to Chris Adams and Garrett Huntington.

"What the hell is going on?" Combs voiced the question Robeson was just thinking to himself.

Molly pointed at Chris. "He's the killer, Detective." Then she pointed at Garrett. "And he's the mastermind behind it all." Mrs. Hewell moved away from the tub so that Robeson could examine Garrett. Robeson took out his cell phone, dialed, and began to provide details for the paramedics.

As his boss called the paramedics, Combs put his hands on his hips, his pale skin flushed beneath the freckles. "And just how do you know all of this with such certainty?"

"I'm hoping I've got it all on tape," Molly said, recovering some of her nerve. "Check in my purse, over there by the ladder-back chair."

Combs ran a hand through his red hair. "Ladder-back?"

"Oh, *I'll* get it," Clara snapped and dug Molly's minirecorder out of the purse. She pressed the rewind button and Molly listened contentedly as her purposefully timid voice, followed by Chris's angry one, rang out clearly from the tiny speaker.

"Good girl!" Clara said proudly as she handed the recorder to Combs. The other police officers looked impressed.

"Nice going." One of them praised Molly.

"Won't stand up in court," Combs sulked, jealous of the attention Molly was receiving. "Miss Appleby's interference may just cost us this case."

Clara refused to have her daughter's display of courage and quick thinking diminished. "Well, *this* will certainly make your questioning easier, now won't it? Without my daughter's help, you might *still* be barking up the wrong tree." Molly stood and walked over to her mother's side.

"Actually, we were on our way to pick up Mr. Adams. We found out he bought that old desk before the show even began so we knew—"

"Officer Combs!" Robeson snapped his phone shut and raised a pointer finger at Combs. "Get Adams out of here and go downstairs to meet the paramedics."

A chastised Combs, along with two other officers, carried the unconscious form of Chris Adams out of the room. Within minutes, the paramedics arrived with a gurney and loaded Garrett onto its thin white mattress. Robeson asked a fidgety Mrs. Hewell to leave the room in its present condition so that he could go visualize Molly's story as she told it. Fortified with more tea, Molly quickly relived the eventful afternoon.

"And what's that in your pocket?" Robeson asked after she was done, eyeing the point stretching the fabric of her pants pocket.

The letter opener! Molly had forgotten all about it. "Lot of good that did me," she laughed weakly as she ran her finger along the dull blade.

"Miss Appleby, you could have gotten yourself killed," Robeson sternly reprimanded her. "As Officer Combs said, we were on our way here after another *Hidden Treasures* crew member told us Chris Adams was on his way to visit a *friend* at the Traveller. If I had arrived to find another dead body, I would have been most . . . aggrieved."

Molly opened her mouth to defend herself when Robeson's phone rang. He excused himself and went out into the hall to take the call.

Frustrated by Robeson's scolding, Molly looked appealingly at her mother. "He *does* have a point, cupcake. You could have been hurt! What would I do without you? You're all I have in the world." Clara's eyes welled up with tears.

Suddenly, a thought struck Molly. "Ma," she said jumping out of her seat. "Keep an eye on the door, will you?"

"Why?" Clara was instantly suspicious.

"There's another mother I met whose whole life is her child. We've got to make things right by her."

Molly grabbed Garrett's suitcase and popped it open. Rifling through the case, she checked zippered pockets and dug furiously through the toiletries bag. Hands shaking with agitation, Molly found what she was searching for. Rolled up inside one of Garrett's dress shoes was a wad of money held together with a rubber band. Molly shoved the roll of bills into her own purse and closed the suitcase. Just as she returned to an upright position, Robeson came back into the room.

"Chris Adams is coming to and though he's got a splitting headache, I need to question him immediately. I'll be taking your recorder for the moment, Miss Appleby. You'll both have to come down to the station to give statements," Robeson told them. "Please tell Mrs. Hewell to come as well."

"Can we have some time to gather our wits?" Clara demanded belligerently. "My daughter and I haven't even eaten lunch today."

"Of course," Robeson conceded graciously, recognizing

a formidable adversary when he saw one. "Take as long as you need."

Molly was just digging into her second bite of warm sweet potato bread when Mrs. Hewell arrived from the kitchen carrying a small bowl of whipped cream. Without asking, she dumped a hefty dollop onto the top of Molly's slice and shook one loose from the serving spoon onto Clara's as well.

"You are a wonder!" Molly exclaimed. "First you save my life and then you serve me homemade whipped cream."

"Well, did you think I'd make you eat the canned kind?"

"Reddi-wip?" Clara laughed. "My cats love that stuff. As soon as they hear the sound of me spraying some on my bowl of ice cream, they come running."

The women laughed companionably as Mrs. Hewell sank into one of the dining room chairs. "We've never had such excitement here. I must say it's quite tiring."

"How did you know to come into Garrett's room at just the right moment?" Molly asked.

Mrs. Hewell smiled wearily. "I listened as your mama called the police. They asked her so many questions that I decided I had better put my ear up to the keyhole until the police arrived. Good thing, too. When I heard that nasty man tell you to get in the bathroom, I knew I only had a few seconds when his back would be turned to close the bathroom door. That's when I came in and clobbered him." Her eyes glittered brightly. "It felt good, too."

"Well, we both appreciate your bravery," Clara said.

"I'm sorry about your Wedgwood urn." Molly frowned in sympathy. "Was it very valuable? And now your tea tray is dented, too."

"Don't worry, dear. Everything's insured. And it's always nice to have an excuse to go to every auction in town.

My husband won't be happy, but as long as I leave him supper in the oven, he'll survive."

"Boy, will I miss your cooking when I'm back in Durham." Molly cut another, thinner slice of sweet potato bread off the loaf.

"Back in Durham?" a male's voice questioned teasingly from the hallway. Molly's head whipped around in disbelief. "You can't leave yet. After all, I just got here," complained a grinning Mark Harrison.

Chapter 16

It was unquestionably that nostalgia which imprinted upon American furniture much of its English or Dutch aspect, for the desire to have around one objects that bring back memories of home is hard to eradicate from the hearts of men.

—ARTHUR DE BLES, *GENUINE ANTIQUE FURNITURE*

Clara watched with interest as her daughter flung herself into the open arms of the tall, wide-shouldered young man standing shyly in Mrs. Hewell's hall. Holding her forgotten teacup aloft, Clara was able to catch a clear glimpse of light blue eyes, ruddy cheeks, and sun-streaked brown hair before the man's gentle face was buried in Molly's neck.

"Well, that's a hero's welcome!" he exclaimed softly, pulling away from Molly's embrace. "And all I did was show up with the intention of protecting my best girl. I flew in from Ohio this morning and drove straight here."

"I'd better be your *only* girl." Molly playfully elbowed Mark in the side. "And I don't need protection any longer. The case, as they say, is closed. But I'm glad you came, nonetheless."

"Hrrrrrmph," Clara cleared her throat, eager to be introduced to the man her daughter was obviously interested in.

"Ma, this is Mark Harrison. He and I . . . work

together . . ." Molly fumbled for an explanation. As she and Mark couldn't seem to get in the swing of full-time dating, she could hardly introduce him as her boyfriend.

"I can't believe Molly hasn't told me more about you," Clara began as Molly made frantic signals for her to keep quiet.

"Mrs. Appleby." Mark smiled sincerely. "It's a pleasure to meet you. Molly talks about you all the time."

"Well, I'd *love* to hear what she says." Clara arched her dark eyebrows at her flustered offspring, finally taking a sip of tepid tea.

"But right *now*, we have to go down to the station and give our statements." Molly tugged at her mother's sleeve.

Clara wasn't quite finished appraising Mark. She looked him up and down like a horse buyer examining a prize thoroughbred up for sale.

Mark's ruddy cheeks flared bright red as he noticed Clara's scrutiny. He turned to Molly. "I'd better come with you. If you're giving a statement, then that means you haven't kept your nose out of this mess like you promised to."

Clara stood and clapped Mark on the back. "You and I are going to get along just fine," she beamed. "Molly gets rather stubborn at times and she won't listen to *my* advice. I'm glad someone else is in the picture when it comes to cautioning her to be more sensible. Ha! Just wait until you hear what nonsense she pulled this afternoon. She probably won't tell you but"—Clara paused for dramatic flare—"she was held at gunpoint today!"

"Don't do that!" Clara shrieked at a young police officer bent over the interior of the slant-front desk. The man, who was as smooth-cheeked as a boy, was so startled that the screwdriver he held in one hand crashed on the floor while the small flashlight he held in his other hand rolled off the surface of the desk and broke into three pieces near his black-booted feet.

"Don't force that panel, for heaven's sake," Clara said more quietly, but with the same level of firmness that she'd used when eight-year-old Molly would plead for dessert before dinner. "That glue hasn't been tampered with since this desk was made," she explained to the stunned officer. "There may be a secret panel in there, but it wasn't used recently."

"Listen ma' am . . ." the officer began.

"Are you looking for the Dahlonega coins?" Molly asked him excitedly, squeezing in next to her mother and completely blocking the remainder of the overhead light.

"Do you mind?" the officer snapped, overwhelmed.

"I'm an antiques expert," Clara said authoritatively. "And I refuse to watch you pry apart this incredible piece of antique furniture, bumbling about until you've ruined it, when I can offer you my expertise. Now . . ." She inhaled swiftly, allowing the bewildered officer no opportunity to retort. "Molly, show me the secret panel Frank showed you."

Molly pointed and the officer carefully pulled out the vertical pillar to the right of the cupboard door and handed it to Clara.

"That's a common place to put a secret panel." Clara nodded without surprise as she examined the vertical drawer. "But if the coins aren't here, there may be another hiding spot. Sometimes these pigeonhole desks had two or three secret spots." She turned to her daughter. "Why are you so sure the coins made it back inside this desk anyway?"

"Because Garrett was yelling at Chris for putting the mold on this piece and not the blanket chest. By covering the desk with mold, Chris forced the police to seize the one piece of furniture Garrett wanted to keep tabs on at all times. He even bought the desk using Chris's name so that it could be shipped out of the country with the coins still inside. If there were any trouble, the desk would be linked to Chris, not Garrett. If everything went smoothly, Chris would never know that Garrett was pretending to be him when he bought the desk."

"Both men claim to know nothing of the whereabouts of the missing coins," the young officer chimed in.

"Have you tried a metal detector?" Clara asked.

"Yes, ma'am. But all the metal around the keyholes kept setting it off."

"How did you get choosen for this task?" Clara asked, not unkindly.

"I'm sort of famous around the station for solving puzzles," the young man said, embarrassed. "Crosswords, jigsaws, word scrambles, that sort of thing. I'm real good with my hands, too," he added.

"I'm certain you are." Clara smiled. "Can you reassemble your flashlight for me?"

"Sure, I can do that."

A minute later, Clara was aiming the thin beam of the flashlight into the cavity created by the missing panel. She shook her head. "I don't see anything."

"Put your hand in and feel around, just in case." Molly directed. "Here, hand me the flashlight while you're doing that."

Molly opened the central cupboard door and peered inside, shining the flashlight into the corners of the tiny, dark space. Blinking, she thought she saw a sliver of white, no larger than a splinter, sticking down from the top right seam of the cupboard. At the same moment, Clara gasped.

"There's a teeny hole back here. It's a release button, my God! I need a bobby pin or a paper clip to push it in with. My fingernail is too big. Quick!"

The officer dug around in his toolbox until he found a metal thumbtack.

"Perfect. Thank you." Clara complimented the young man and he smiled from ear to ear.

Clara stuck the tack's point into the minuscule hole. The tack came into contact with a piece of wood that resisted for a moment but then gave way with a click. The small archway above the cupboard popped out a few centimeters. Clara had discovered a secret drawer.

"A secret within a secret." Clara breathed as her daughter gently pulled the drawer away from the desk's frame. "The man who made this piece was a master craftsman."

Molly pulled out a small envelope from inside the drawer. Inside, wrapped in layers of tissue, were the six Dahlonega coins.

"Gotcha!" the officer yelled with a boyish whoop. He scooped up the envelope from Molly's hands and dashed off towards Robeson's office.

As Clara stood lost in admiration over the desk, Combs appeared and jerked his meaty thumb at Molly. "You first. Statement time."

"I'll come with you," Mark said, putting a possessive arm around Molly's shoulders as he stared down at Combs.

It was difficult for Molly to get through her statement. Between the disparaging comments uttered behind her by the irascible Combs and Mark's startled exclamations of horror, she was finally able to complete her narrative and bid farewell to Detective Robeson and the city of Richmond's police department.

"Try to stay out of trouble, Miss Appleby," Robeson said, shaking her hand. Molly thought she detected a twinkle in the corner of Robeson's dark eyes, but before she could take a second look, Mark was ushering her out of the office. They sat on a bench outside the front door to wait for Clara.

"He should be thanking me!" Molly sulked. "I helped catch the bad guys and Mom found the hidden coins. Damned chauvinists."

"I don't think that's the case," Mark said soothingly, picking up Molly's hand. "I'm sure they appreciate your help, but the police just don't want to encourage . . . ah . . . citizens getting too involved with taking law enforcement in their own hands."

Molly wasn't listening. She was busy thinking about

how she could spin at least one of her articles on *Hidden Treasures* so that her role in capturing the villains was subtly revealed.

As Clara finished giving her statement, she stood and returned Robeson's firm handshake. "Now, I know you warned my daughter about sticking her nose into hazardous entanglements and I'm grateful for that. I'd like to see her focus on *other* activities." Combs gave Robeson a smug wink. "But . . ." Clara lowered her voice dangerously. "Since Molly and I both facilitated in the capture of your murderer and his accomplice, perhaps you'd like to do us a good turn . . . ?"

Robeson stared impatiently at Clara. She blinked innocently and plowed on. "What will happen to the antique desk once this case is closed?"

"It will go up for public auction, along with anything else in our evidence room that needs to be cleaned out at the time," Robeson stated flatly.

Clara handed Robeson her card. "I want you to call me the second you find out about that auction. My daughter is turning thirty this year and that desk would make the perfect gift. Will you do that for me?"

Robeson took the card, hesitated, and then nodded. He was ready to be done with the two Appleby women. At least Mrs. Hewell was waiting outside with a basket of her finest cinnamon scones. He could smell the cinnamon seeping under the crack of his door. He hoped to have a moment alone with her as she was reputed to be an excellent cook. Perhaps she had a secret to the timing of soufflés.

"Thank you," Clara said, interrupting his thoughts. She swept out of the room like a queen leaving a group of admiring courtiers. Combs gazed at Robeson with a self-satisfied grin.

"You got something to say, Officer Combs?" Robeson's eyes bored holes into the burly, red-haired officer. Combs blanched.

"No, sir."

"Then send in Mrs. Hewell." Robeson let his enormous

bulk settle into his creaky chair. "And get us some coffee to go with those scones."

That night, Mrs. Hewell made a pot roast with glazed carrots and potatoes followed by a blackberry pie. She invited Molly, Clara, and Mark to join her for dinner as her husband was still out visiting his friend from church.

"I don't usually do dinners for my guests, but we've been through so much together that I feel we're more like family now." Mrs. Hewell bustled about the table, seemingly unfazed by the day's events and pleased to have company for dinner.

"I'm ready to go back home and kiss my seven cats," Clara said, digging into the deep bowl of mashed potatoes. "But I will miss you, Mrs. Hewell. You must come visit me in Hillsborough some time."

"I'd love to!" the older woman flushed. "And that way, I could visit the newlyweds, too."

Clara looked hopefully at her daughter's ring finger. "Oh?" she squeaked breathlessly.

Mrs. Hewell beamed at her guests. "Borris called this afternoon. He and Jessica are eloping tomorrow. Vegas-bound! Isn't that wonderful?"

"It is indeed," Clara agreed. "I hope Jessica doesn't get in too much trouble over this coin business."

"Me, too." Molly turned to Mark. "Isn't it romantic how Borris rushed down to Charlotte and wouldn't take *no* for an answer?"

Mark squirmed in his seat, painfully aware that the eyes of three women were watching him with the utmost intensity. "Uh . . . sure. Could you pass the rolls?"

Later, when Mark and Molly were clearing the table, Clara pulled Mrs. Hewell aside. "Is Mr. Harrison staying in his own room?"

Mrs. Hewell's eyes flew open wide. "Of course! Where

else would he be staying? I've given him the Limoge, the one Jessica was in."

"Can't you tell him all the rooms are full?" Clara whispered rather maniacally. "Then he'd *have* to stay with my daughter."

"Oh, no, I couldn't lie, Mrs. Appleby." Mrs. Hewell looked simultaneously insulted and horrified. Then her expression softened and she put a warm hand on Clara's cheek. "Don't worry, my dear. They'll find their way to one another. You'll see."

Clara's shoulders drooped. "I suppose, but I never even knew Molly was interested in this man."

"They're sweet on each other, that's clear enough to anyone. Good night, my dear. I'll see you in the morning."

"Good night." Clara smiled and then headed up to her room humming. Pausing on the stairs, she heard her daughter's laughter and Mark's placid voice from within the kitchen. "Maybe I'll be buying that desk as an engagement present instead," she told herself gleefully.

The next morning, Clara left for home in Molly's car while Mark and Molly were still having breakfast. Afterwards, Molly, ignoring the serious penalty of impersonating a police officer, called human resources at Richmond Doctor's Hospital to discover if Jasmine Jones was one of their employees. She was told that Mrs. Jones worked the day shift in the hospital cafeteria.

Unfolding the roll of bills she found in Garrett's shoe, Molly placed them inside a padded manila envelope and asked Mark to drive her to the hospital on their way home.

"What for?" he asked in sudden concern.

Molly filled him in on how Jasmine had brought her coin to be appraised and was tricked out of a large sum of money by the wily Garrett. Mark's face flashed through a variety of emotions as he listened to the injustice inflicted upon the single mother. When Molly was done with her story, she impulsively leaned over and kissed Mark at the next red light. She loved the way he wore his heart on his sleeve. He was nothing like Garrett, she thought. Some shallow, handsome stranger would never attract her again. She was ready to work on her commitment to Mark, and she had an idea of how to get to the next level of their relationship. She was more than ready to claim this fine man as her own.

"How much money is in there?" Mark glanced at the envelope as he merged onto the highway.

"About ten grand, all told. This should help Jasmine with her bills."

"Wow! Ten grand! So you're leaving her all that money in an envelope? Why don't you just go in and give it to her?" Mark asked, pulling in front of the hospital.

Molly held the envelope tightly in her hand. "I don't want to embarrass her or anything. It's better if she gets to open it after work, when no one's staring at her. It's going to be a pretty big shock, after all. I think she'll need some privacy."

Mark hopped out of the car and opened Molly's door. "You're an angel, Molly Appleby."

Molly looked up at him with a mischievous glint to her gray eyes. "I'm going to drop this off. And then you get me home, Mark Harrison," she whispered huskily, brushing her lips against his cheek, "and I'll show you that I'm not."

RICHMOND, VIRGINIA 2006

The desk was put up for auction on a blustery March afternoon. The auction was unusually well attended for a seized and unclaimed property sale. The items ranged from an assortment of jewelry, used cars, bicycles, electronics, and a scattering of small household items. Unfortunately for Clara Appleby, a photograph of the desk had been included in the newspaper advertisement announcing the sale. Eager buyers representing the Smithsonian, Colonial Williamsburg Foundation, The Metropolitan Museum of Art, and both the Fredericksburg and Richmond Historical Societies had already looked the desk over with black lights and magnifying glasses weeks ago. Each society sought to purchase such an exquisite piece of American furniture history.

Clara groaned as she took her seat, recognizing some of the power buyers immediately. Five minutes later, she still sat in shock, hands quivering, her bidding card unused on her lap. The final bid came in at $175,000 with all proceeds to benefit the Fallen Officers of Virginia Fund. With one gavel strike, the benefit fund would be able to send a dozen young men and women to college and the high bidders from the Colonial Williamsburg Foundation would add another piece to its already stellar collection of federal furniture.

Propped up on a carpeted dais, the desk sat at a safe distance from the public behind a crimson velvet rope. Thousands of visitors walked through the museum that spring, each one pausing to glance at the reproduction of the Declaration of Independence that rested on the desk's writing surface. Little did they know that a real historical document lay hidden scant inches beneath that reproduction. Undiscovered by a lifetime of owners, appraisers, and finally, the team of Colonial Williamsburg furniture experts, the desk held onto its greatest treasure. For inside a hollow within its left slide support, a faded and yellowed paper was folded into a tiny square. This letter read:

Radford, Virginia 1810
To Elspeth,
    I know not where to write you, so I shall write this letter and place it in the secret place in your father's desk, which belongs to me now. I purchased it from your aunt when she came to occupy your family's house after you and your father disappeared. Each time I look upon it I remember standing in your house and boasting of my clever craftsmanship by showing you the third secret compartment. What a young fool I was. How strong and beautiful you were! As you can see, I have learned to write. My wife Mary, who has departed this life, was a schoolteacher. She taught me my letters. It is a great joy to be able to read, now that I am old and my joints are too sore to allow me to craft furniture. I find much solace in the words I once could not comprehend.
    I searched for you, Elspeth. I searched for years. You haunted my thoughts like a ghost. I heard many

rumors about where you were taken. Your father escaped arrest the night at the munitions factory. A dockworker from Portsmouth claimed that by the light of the full moon, Captain Tarling, with his struggling daughter bound and gagged, boarded one of his ships and returned to England. A trader from Norfolk told tale of that same ship veering south, where your father established himself in the West Indies. This trader also said that your father's fortune grew enormous through the slave trade and that you perished from an illness within a fortnight of arriving there.

I could never confirm either story, as your father changed his name several times. We caught every other member of the Hazard Club that night, Elspeth, except for your father. Believing that my failure to capture him has cost you happiness or worse, your very life, has brought me much anguish. Not knowing your fate has been the greatest regret of my lifetime. I swore to protect you and I did not. But it is time to let the past lie now, so I place this letter along with your token, where I shall not look upon it again.

My sight grows weak now. The daylight is fading above the great hills. When twilight comes I shall think of your blue eyes again, as I do each night, and as I shall do every night until I see you once more. On that great day, I can finally ask for your forgiveness.

Your Own,
Thomas

The fragile sheaf was carefully bound with an old silk ribbon. The ribbon is faded and tattered at the edges, but if it were ever rescued from its dark nook and again held beneath the light, it would reveal a soft and delicate shade of cornflower blue.

A Brief Note on Secret Hiding Places in Antique Furniture

People learn at an early age to squirrel their treasures away in creative hiding places. Even young children follow a deep-seated instinct to tuck their favorite belongings into a shoebox and hide it under the bed or in the back of the closet. This urge to hide a sparkly hair bow or a Matchbox car can carry over into adulthood. The existence of secret hiding places comes as no surprise, as architects, furniture makers, and jewelers have created secret niches within houses, furniture, and even the smallest pieces of jewelry for centuries.

Medieval castles contained secret passageways meant for escape, an old house can have secret doors, rooms, or panels meant for hiding people or objects within, then why not construct a piece of furniture with a secret compartment as well? The human race has always kept secrets; whether political secrets of global significance or a clandestine token, such as a love poem from an unacceptable suitor, there is no shortage of things that need to be hidden.

The most common pieces of antique furniture in which to search for hidden compartments would include a variety of desks, chests of drawers, blanket or storage chests, and portable boxes. Occasionally, you might run across a wardrobe with a secret drawer across the bottom, a sideboard with a secret panel hidden beneath a piece of carving, or even an eighteenth-century headboard containing a hollow area in which the master of the house could conceal a weapon—many pieces have the potential for secret hiding places, but the trick is to discover them!

An antique desk created with the purpose of storing documents is a hopeful place to begin. In fact, a desk containing pigeonholes, such as fall or slant-front desks, secretaries, kneehole desks, plantation desks, and ladies writing desks, might have been built with at least one hidden compartment. If your antique desk has a central cupboard in the pigeonhole area, check the panels of wood called pilasters flanking the cupboard. As in *A Fatal Appraisal*, one or both of these pieces might slide out to reveal a vertical hiding spot. Put your fingers inside the cupboard and search for a button or a pin. Either press the button or pull the pin to release these "document drawers." Sometimes the secret space is located behind the cupboard. Again, see if your forefinger can discover a depression in which some kind of release latch is built. Press with one hand and pull out the entire center section with the other. If your desk has no cupboard or central section, check any horizontal facing panels near the pigeonholes for a false drawer. Sometimes the hidden area is actually located beneath the writing surface. This area might resemble a small, shallow well in which documents can be tucked away.

In the case of a chest of drawers, sometimes one of the strips of wood separating the drawers is actually a secret drawer itself. Created without pulls or handles, this hidden drawer is meant to fool anyone but the knowledgeable owner as to its existence. Sometimes the skirt of a chest of drawers is a false drawer and can be pulled out by grabbing it underneath and pulling forward. This is called a "slipper drawer." Always check for a release mechanism before pulling out the false drawer.

My mother owns a case piece with an unusual secret space; it is a North Carolina tall chest or a "High Daddy" as it is called locally, dating to circa 1800. When my mother was examining the piece, she noticed the top back board was attached with screws made much later than 1800, yet the other horizontal back boards were attached to the case with old cut nails. She then carefully removed the board with the "newer" screws to discover two small drawers tucked into the open cavity behind the crown molding. In one of the drawers was a yellowed piece of paper dated 1911 detailing the family history of the High Daddy. What a find! My mother speculates that the drawers were added at the time of the Civil War in order to keep valuables safe from marauding soldiers.

Boxes of all shapes and sizes are a great place to look for secret hiding places. The best way to check a box for a secret compartment is to look at its overall shape. Now open the lid and see if the compartment inside looks as deep as the overall height of the box. If not, you might find that the box has a false bottom. That false bottom can be pried upwards using a thin blade or even a long fingernail to reveal a space below. Sometimes the hidden space is actually in the lid and is covered by a thin piece of wood or a fabric lining.

Some hidden places in boxes can be revealed by pressing a button or moving a lever. For example, my father owns a mahogany box in which a tiny button is cleverly placed near one of the hinges on the back. You can only see this button if the box is open. Once the button is pressed, a thin, secret drawer pops out on the front of the box, towards the bottom. I won't mention how my father learned to regret his decision of proudly showing his three children where he hid the "emergency money." He found himself short a twenty or two more than once afterward.

A good rule of thumb when seeking out hidden panels is not to force anything. If glue cracks or wood starts groaning as you are prying at what you hope to be a secret panel in your grandmother's eighteenth-century secretary, you might be completely ruining the value of your antique by tearing it apart. Slashing the silk lining of your two-hundred-year-old document box in the hopes of discovering gold coins or letters written by Benjamin Franklin might only result in a damaged box with an empty secret compartment.

Keep in mind that like a child's treasured purple crayon or hoard of stale Halloween candy, some of the valuables placed in a secret hiding place may not be valuable to you at all. We'd all like to pull out a false drawer only to discover the signature of the piece's maker (along with the date of course), or a jeweled ring used to poison a villainous character ages past (ideally with a cyanide tablet still intact). These instances are unlikely, however. So as you examine the hollow legs of your antique dining room table with a flashlight or insist upon watching over the upholsterer's shoulder as he replaces the fabric on your federal side chairs, I hope that your antique does yield an undiscovered, untouched secret compartment. If it does, I hope that you find something that sparks your imagination—a baby's bootie, a simple bracelet engraved with two sets of initials, a wrinkled photograph of a beautiful and haunting young face. Whatever you find, I hope your discovery brings a bit of excitement and mystery into your life. After all, that's what a good secret is all about.

Examples of Hidden Compartments

Late nineteenth century Tantalus with storage area.

Inside view of storage area, where a gentleman might store items to accompany an evening of gaming, smoking, or sharing a splash of scotch with friends. The black arrow points out the well-concealed release button.

Once the release button is pressed, a shallow drawer pops out. Here, a gentleman could store coins, private letters, or even a bit of snuff.

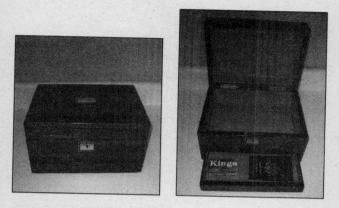

My father's mahogany "treasure" box. The release button is located between the two hinges. It wasn't hidden well enough to keep three kids from peering inside.

A Piedmont North Carolina black walnut blanket chest, c. 1830.

LEFT: An interior view of an unusually deep till (a till being a small box with a hinged lid attached to one side of a blanket chest for convenient storage of smaller items). When the till lid is open, the front panel may be raised to reveal a secret drawer with a tiny nail for a knob.

ABOUT THE AUTHOR

A former middle school English teacher, **J. B. Stanley** has dabbled in the antiques and collectibles world by trading on eBay, working part-time at auction houses, and contributing articles for *Antiqueweek*. Having lived in central North Carolina for eight years, J. B. Stanley now resides in Richmond with her husband, two young children, and three cats. For more information, please visit www.jbstanley.com.